SWEET VENOM

TERA LYNN CHILDS

templar

A TEMPLAR BOOK

First published in 2011 by Katherine Tegen Books,
an imprint of HarperCollins Children's Books, a division of
HarperCollins Publishers, New York, New York USA.

First published in the UK in 2012 by Templar Publishing,
an imprint of The Templar Company Limited,
Deepdene Lodge, Deepdene Avenue, Dorking, Surrey, RH5 4AT, UK
www.templarco.co.uk

Cover design by James Fraser
Cover photograph © 2012 by Aleksandar Nakic

First UK edition

ISBN 978-1-84877-932-7

Printed by Nørhaven, Denmark.

For Shane, mentor… inspiration… friend

CHAPTER 1

Gretchen

Hydras have a distinctive odour. It's somewhere between the acid tang of burning hair and a boat full of rotting fish. You can smell them from miles away.

Well, you can't. But I can.

Some beasties smell mildly unpleasant; others could peel paint. Hydras definitely fall into the latter category.

As I steer my car – Moira, named for the fickle fates as a constant reminder to take charge of mine – into a spot across from a dilapidated seafood shack, the stench is practically overwhelming. Moira's upholstery is going to stink for a week. I pencil in taking her to the car wash on my mental to-do list, right after replacing my favourite cargo trousers, which got shredded in my last fight, but before polishing the bladed weapons in the armoury.

I twist the key out of the ignition and do a quick gear check: Kevlar wrist cuffs in place, smoke bombs in left cargo pocket, zip ties in the right, and my handy-dandy, military-grade, metal detector-defying, twin APS daggers snug in their sheaths and hidden inside my steel-toe Doc Martens. Nothing like a well-stocked pair of black cargoes to make me feel girlie.

The hydra shouldn't be much trouble – balancing nine heads on a massive serpent body throws off their centre of gravity so they're not exactly graceful – but it never hurts to be prepared.

Even if I ever get caught off guard, I've got a backup monster-fighting kit stowed under Moira's driver's seat and another in my backpack.

Though the gear makes things easier, all I really need to take a beastie out is the pair of retracted canines that will fang down at the first sign of trouble. They're my built-in secret weapon. A defence legacy passed down from my ancient ancestor.

"Seriously," I mutter as I climb out onto the sidewalk. "Can't they give it a rest for a while? Maybe take an extended vacation somewhere cold and icy."

This is the fourth time in the last week that the aroma of dark and nasty has pulled me out for the hunt.

One more visitor from the abyss this week and I'll leave the gear at home and work out my annoyance with my fists. Hand-to-hand combat won't send a monster back to its prison-realm home, but it'll make me feel a hell of a lot better. Who says keeping the human world monster-free can't be good therapy at the same time?

I palm the remote for Moira's keyless entry and am about to lock her sleek, black doors when I realise I've forgotten one element of my monster-fighting gear that is critical, at least when I'm hunting in human-heavy territory.

"Slick, Gretchen," I tell myself. "Real slick."

You'd think after four years – a quarter of my life – this would be second nature.

Moments later, I'm crossing the street, my sporty mirrored sunglasses shielding my eyes. Not from the sun, of course. It's not like hydras yearn for daylight. No, they'd rather drag me out in the middle of the night, when dives like this are the only thing open.

Darn inconsiderate when school starts tomorrow.

I walk up to the weathered wooden shack, peer through the dirt- and grime-crusted window, and scan the late-night diners. All distinctly human.

If my eyes weren't practically tearing at the stench, I'd think the hydra wasn't here.

Then I catch sight of the narrow staircase off to the right of the bar, leading to an upstairs dining room. Well, at least that will make cornering it easier.

As I push open the door, the combination of putrid eau de hydra and decades of fried-fish-fillet residue is enough to make me nearly lose my heat-and-eat lasagna all over the sandy floor.

But I don't have time for nausea. There's a bloodthirsty monster prowling for a meal, and if I don't stop it, no one will. I'm the only one who can see it.

"Anyone see a slithering nine-headed serpent pass this way?"

I snicker. I would love to see the reaction if I actually asked the question loud enough for anyone to hear.

Then again, this is San Francisco. They might not react at all.

Bypassing the drowsy bartender, I head for the staircase. Monsters generally prefer dark corners and back alleys – and, apparently, second-floor dining areas – which makes them occasionally harder to find but easier to attack. They'll take any less-populated area that's available, though, which is fine by me. The fewer witnesses to our fights, the better. The safer. The human world doesn't need to know monsters walk among them. As long as I do my job right, they never will.

I'm up the stairs, three at a time, in five seconds flat. The instant I step out onto the second floor, I see it, cosying up to a trampy redhead doing her best impersonation of a low-class prostitute. Monsters have the worst taste in women.

I scan the room, checking for potential threats and exits. Besides the stairs behind me, there's an emergency exit at the back. If I position myself behind the redhead, I'll be able to intercept on either path.

As for threats, there's a pair of mounted swordfish displayed on the wall and some framed pictures of deep-sea fishing boats that might hurt if used as projectiles. Nothing really to worry about.

Thankfully, the dining area is sparsely populated.

Other than the hydra and its prey there is only a trio of drunken businessmen at the far end. Judging from their raucous volume and the dishevelled state of their ties, odds are they're probably pretty much oblivious to anything but the next round. If I do this right, they won't notice a thing.

Straightening my back, I march over to the unlucky couple and tap the girl on the shoulder, making sure I'm centred between the stairs and the door.

"Can I help you?" Red snaps in a very non-solicitous tone.

"Yes," I reply. "You can leave."

"Excuse me?" She crosses her arms defiantly under her chest, like I'm going to be frightened away by her aggressive boobage. "I don't know who you think you are, but—"

With a quick flick of my wrist, I pop my sunglasses up and lean down to look her directly in the eye.

"You were just leaving," I say, keeping my tone even.

Her eyes widen as her brain disengages. "I was just leaving," she repeats.

Then, as if pulled by some unseen rope, she stands and crosses to the stairs, disappearing out of view. When the hypno wears off, she'll wonder how she got wherever she's going. But serpent-beastie will be long gone by then.

With the girl safely out of the way, I evaluate the now standing hydra. From the necks down it looks like an overgrown lizard who's been hitting the gym. Too muscular for my taste – I don't go for the bulging reptilian type – but I can see how some girls might want to hit that. From the necks up… well, whoever said two heads are better than one never met a hydra.

Too bad humans can't see its real form.

All monsters can affect a sort of false appearance – in faerie circles known as a glamour – so their hideous, grotesque features are hidden from unsuspecting human eyes. Unfortunately for the monsters, I'm not an unsuspecting human. I'm a descendant of the gorgon Medusa, and I suspect a whole heck of a lot. My eyes see their true nature, and this beastie's true nature is a slimy, scaly, nine-headed snake. Not exactly the perfect specimen Red thought she was getting.

The hydra's eyes lock on mine before I drop my sunglasses back into place. Too bad my freaky hypnosis power only works on humans. Then again, that would make my job way too easy. Where's the fun in that?

"Huntress," it snarls.

"I prefer Gretchen. But, you know." I flash it a bored look. "Whatever."

The freak show moves awkwardly, its undulating tail taking out a couple of chairs.

I check over my shoulder to make sure the drunken trio hasn't noticed – they haven't – then turn back to face my foe. It might look big and scary, but this isn't my first hydra rodeo. I know just how to take it down.

As the freak show reaches for me, I spin right, dodging the grab and sending the monster lurching forward. With the creature off-balance, I take a well-aimed leap onto its back. It writhes, trying to throw me off. I wrap my legs around the scaly body and my arms around one of the necks and squeeze. The table goes flying. I need to hurry, before someone decides to notice all the noise.

Inching my way down its back, I lean off to one side, searching for the spot where its thick, armour-like scales give way to a softer underbelly. My fangs drop. I dive forward, sink my fangs into the tender flesh, and sigh as my snake-girl venom pours into its bloodstream.

There is no better feeling than this sweet surge of victory.

In a flash, it's gone and I'm thudding to my knees on the floor.

Bye-bye beastie.

CHAPTER 2

Grace

Things are going to be different in San Francisco. I mean, obviously things *are* different – like the mega-tall buildings, the millions of people and the predominance of concrete over grass. This town is pretty much the complete opposite of Orangevale in every way.

But I want Grace Whitfield – *me* – to be different too.

Frozen like a statue on the sidewalk, I stare up at the imposing facade of Alpha Academy, the private prep school whose full-scholarship offer is half the reason we've moved to the city. It's a giant cube of glass and steel, a monument to modernity that makes the simple single-storey stucco and Spanish tile of Orangevale High look like something from California's prehistoric past. This building gleams shiny and new in the morning sun. The perfect place to start over. I know this is the opportunity I've been waiting for all my life. After sixteen years in the same small 'burb, going to the same schools with the same students, I finally get to be someone new. Someone not me.

Before I can smile at the thought, a person knocks into my shoulder, sending me and my backpack tumbling.

"Excuse you much?" The girl gives me a disgusted look, dusts off her shoulder like I might have given her a virus, and stomps off towards the sparkling glass double doors.

Everything about her screams *confident*. Rich brown hair with auburn highlights that swings as she walks, dark-wash skinny jeans and a magenta V-neck sweater that cling to every single curve, and (most of all) the superior-to-absolutely-everyone attitude. Just as different from me as San Francisco is from Orangevale.

The new me should say something to her retreating back. I *want* to say something like *No, excuse* you *much*, since she, you know, crashed into me. But I don't. I stand there, watching her disappear into my new school, a huge lump of dread in my stomach at the realisation that nothing has changed. I'm still the same old Grace, the quiet, passive pushover who can't stand up for herself.

So much for different.

"Grace Whitfield?"

I look up from my spot on the bench across from the guidance counsellor's office. The counsellor, the woman who just called my name, gives me an encouraging smile.

She looks nothing like the balding, middle-aged, tweed coat-wearing counsellor in Orangevale. The one who'd rubber-stamped all my advising sessions and handed me the appropriate papers about SAT prep classes before ticking off my name and moving on to the next kid on the list. Not that I needed his help – I know what I have to do to get into a good school and earn a scholarship – but it might have been nice if he'd looked up from his computer for two seconds.

My new counsellor has all of her attention focused on me, and commands my attention in return. I can't help but study her immaculate appearance. She's tall and graceful, like a ballerina, and wears a sharply tailored skirt suit in a soft, warm grey that matches her high heels. A petal-pink blouse ruffles out around her lapels. Although her image says poised and elegant, I get the feeling that beneath the surface she is a woman of extraordinary strength.

She seems like she could run a billion-dollar company in her spare time. She would never let anyone plough over her and march off without a word. I'm an eco-geek who can't even walk into my new school without getting trampled by another student.

I stand, feeling awkward and underdressed in my recycled jeans, organic green T-shirt, and hot-pink Converse. Not only because of the counsellor, but also because of confident girl and the few students who've trickled in through the office while I've been waiting. They look like they walked out of a department-store window display.

Too late to change now. Besides, it's not like I have high levels of fashion hiding in my closet. Mostly more of the same.

"I'm Grace," I say, extending my hand.

I expect her to shake it, formal and business-like, but instead she holds it gently and presses her other palm over mine. Her smile positively sparkles. She gives me a squeeze as she says, "I'm Ms West. I recommended you for the scholarship here at Alpha. You shone above all the other applicants. Your computer skills were especially impressive."

"I—" I swallow over the strange feeling of tightness – of pride, maybe – in my throat. A good feeling. "Thank you."

"After reviewing your entrance exam and your previous school records, I have prepared a preliminary class schedule for you," she explains as she motions me into her office.

I rub my hands against my jeans as I follow her inside.

Other than the small acrylic sign on her desk that says STEPHANIE WEST, GUIDANCE COUNSELLOR, the sleek grey surface is virtually empty. In fact, the office is pretty much empty. Only the desk, chairs, a pair of tall file cabinets, and, on the wall behind her desk, a massive framed photo of a beautiful white sand beach and a turquoise sea. No clutter, no colour other than the water in the picture. It's very calming. Which is, I suppose, a good quality in a counsellor's office.

Ms West lowers herself gracefully into the big black leather office chair, indicating that I should take a seat in one of the armchairs facing her desk. I choose the one on the right, swinging my backpack to the floor as I sit.

"Considering your plans to attend a top-tier college,"

she says, handing me a sheet of paper, "I thought you might be interested in adding a second foreign language."

"Do you think that's necessary?" I ask. "Will it help my admissions chances?"

"It certainly doesn't hurt." She looks me in the eye as she speaks. "But I think your transcript is strong already."

"Then I think I'll stick with Spanish." I appreciate her honest answer.

"All right," she says. "What about a physical education class? We offer a broad selection, including virtually all sports, as well as kickboxing and tae kwon do."

My records must not have been too enlightening, because she clearly doesn't get me at all. Give me a laptop or a smartphone, and I'm an all-star, but athletics is a bit beyond my skill set. I'm not a superklutz or anything, I'm merely lacking in the finer points of hand-eye coordination beyond basic keyboard functions.

When I shake my head again, she pulls out a folder from her desk drawer and opens it, turning to a sheet of green paper near the back.

"Alpha is dedicated to providing our students with a well rounded education in a variety of disciplines, not focused exclusively on rigorous academics." She smiles as she scans the paper. "The elective opportunities are truly astounding. I'm sure you will find something to your liking."

The green sheet she hands me must have almost fifty classes listed.

The choices are a little overwhelming. At Orangevale High we had your standard Maths, English, Sciences, History, Languages (Spanish or French) and one elective. Our elective choices were limited to art, choir, band or study hall. It's hard to wrap my public-school brain around the array of private-school electives. "I don't know. I guess, maybe—"

"You don't have to decide right now," she interrupts. "Orientation and assembly will take up most of today. Why don't you take the list home and decide tonight? You can come by before school and let me know what courses you've chosen."

"Great," I say as I slip the paper into my backpack.

We spend the next few minutes going over the schedule for today, my core class schedule for tomorrow, graduation and extracurricular requirements, and things like dress code and attendance policies. Mom, Dad and I already filled out a mountain of paperwork over the summer – hasn't this school heard of electronic forms? – but there are still a few for me to sign.

I wonder if my brother, Thane, is going through the same thing at his school.

"Are you ready for your first day at Alpha?" Ms West asks with an enthusiastic smile.

I take a deep breath. *Am* I ready? New home, new city, new school, new friends. Hopefully. New life. New me.

I feel equal parts fear and anticipation. But one look

in Ms West's sharp eyes and I feel a jolt of confidence. I feel strong and invincible. How can I let myself be afraid of change, when it's what I want? The chance to become the strong, confident young woman I've always dreamed of being.

This is the first step.

"Yes," I say, gathering my courage. "Ready."

"Do you have any questions or concerns before I send you to class?"

I square my shoulders and shake my head. I'm ready for this.

"If you need anything," she says, "my office door is always open."

I nod, trying to mimic the same air of self-assurance she exudes, as if I appreciate her offer but will never need the help because everything will work out in no time. The facade makes me feel a little more sure of myself, of my future at Alpha and in San Francisco.

The power of positive thinking.

She leans out into the hall. "Miranda, would you come here please?"

When Miranda shows up at Ms West's door, my false confidence quivers and that sense of dread plops into my stomach again.

"Yes, Ms West?" asks the girl who ploughed through me in front of the school.

"This is Grace Whitfield," she explains, gesturing

to me. "She's new at Alpha. Since you two have the same homeroom, I thought you might give her a quick tour and then show her to class."

"Of course," Miranda says with a blinding fake smile. "It'd be my pleasure."

Think positive, I tell myself. Maybe I misinterpreted her earlier comment. Maybe she's a really nice person. Maybe she'll be friendly, now that she knows we share a class. Hitching my backpack up on my shoulder, I smile and hold out my hand. "Nice to meet you, Miranda."

She smiles and shakes my hand. For a second I believe this positive thinking thing really works. Then, as soon as Ms West turns back to her desk, Miranda drops my hand like it's a plague-ridden rat, rolls her eyes and stalks out of the office.

My shoulders sink.

"Have a wonderful first day," Ms West says.

"Thanks," I say, turning to give her a quick wave before following after Miranda's retreating back.

As I stand outside the girls' bathroom, waiting for Miranda to emerge, I'm pretty certain this isn't what Ms West had in mind for a school tour. After throwing me a look that said she'd rather eat glass than lead around a loser like me, Miranda stalked off into the corridor outside the main office and made a beeline for the bathroom.

She's been in there for over five minutes.

I glance at my schedule. Every day at Alpha begins with homeroom, an hour-long period for finishing up homework, going to the library or seeking help from other teachers. Nothing like the twenty-minute roll call and stay-in-your-seats-for-announcements madness that passed for homeroom at Orangevale. Homeroom here sounds useful.

Around me, the corridor is starting to fill with students. The typical first-day-of-school insanity. Girls are shrieking, diving into group hugs with friends they haven't seen all summer. A few couples are taking advantage of the chaos to engage in some pretty inappropriate kissing and groping. Some kids, probably freshmen, are wandering around looking slightly lost and terribly frightened. That won't be me – I won't let it. I'm a junior now, an upperclassman, and I'm not going to let the unfamiliar environment make me feel like a lowly freshman again. No thank you.

I've never been a Girl Scout, I don't even know their motto, but I still believe in being prepared. I swing my backpack round and dig through the pile of papers Ms West gave me until I find the school map printed on the back of the "Welcome to Alpha!" letter. According to my schedule, I have Mrs Deckler for homeroom in room 117.

After tracing my finger over most of the ground floor, I find room 117 in a back corner. I squint at the map – it's no 3D-rendered interactive virtual environment, but it'll do – and then scan the corridor, deciding that if I go to the end of the main corridor and turn left, I'll find my classroom.

Miranda's still in the bathroom though. And, as much as I think she'd be overjoyed to find me gone, I don't want to pull a disappearing flake act on the first day.

I continue studying my map, trying to get a feel for the layout of the school, mentally extruding the walls and creating an image of the building in my mind. There are four floors, with the upper levels reserved for grades five to eight. All of my classes will be on the first two floors, so I focus on those maps. It's when I'm scanning over my current location that I see what – after waiting ten minutes – I should have already guessed. The girls' bathroom has two entrances.

With a groan, I zip my backpack shut and head down the corridor towards room 117, clutching my map and schedule. I don't need to pop into the bathroom to know that Miranda's long gone.

I follow the gleaming white corridor past open classrooms and walls of lockers. At the end, I make a left, proud of my map-reading skills. Four doors later I find Mrs Deckler's class.

And I'm not at all surprised to find Miranda already at her desk when I walk into the room.

Pausing for a second in the doorway, I give myself a little pep talk.

This is it, I tell myself. *This is the moment to leave doormat Grace behind and become… fearless Grace.* Confident *Grace.* If I take the offensive, I can turn this moment around. I can make sure that my time at Alpha isn't spent feeling powerless. I take a deep breath, form the words of a biting, witty comment in my mind, and open my mouth.

"Did you get lost?" Miranda asks before I can utter a sound. "I waited outside the bathroom for like ten minutes."

"I…" How do I respond to that? A complete and total lie. "What?"

She leans forward, as if to say something confidential, but her whisper is anything but quiet. "Are you constipated? Nurse Callahan probably has some laxatives or something."

Most of the dozen or so kids in the half-full classroom erupt in barely concealed snorts and giggles. Whatever reputation-establishing comment I'd been about to make completely evaporates into abject humiliation. My cheeks burn to the point of combustion. My ears quickly follow. Every life-changing hope I had bursts like a bubble hitting concrete. There is no recovering from a comment like that. Ever.

Tales of my digestive distress will probably circulate throughout the school by lunchtime. Even freshmen will feel sorry for me, while being thankful it's not them being thrown under the social bus.

I do the only thing I can do; I duck my head and hurry

to the back of the classroom. Slipping into an empty desk, I make myself as small and invisible as humanly possible.

"Miranda is a vortex of evil."

I look up from being preoccupied with my backpack – aka pretending to be too busy to notice the stares and snickers – to find the girl at the next desk studiously doodling in her notebook.

"I'm sorry?" I ask, not sure she actually said something.

She jerks her head, sending a wave of black hair with white tips in Miranda's general direction at the front of the room. "Never apologise for Miranda-bashing. It's my favourite pastime."

"Oh." Looks like I'm not the only person on the receiving end of Miranda's bad attitude.

"I see we're trying out a new hairstyle to start the school year, Vail." The teacher behind the big wooden desk smiles at the girl next to me. "Shall we expect new colours weekly?"

Vail shrugs and goes back to her drawings.

As Mrs Deckler enlists Miranda's help to hand out some paperwork, I lean slightly to my left and say, "I'm Grace Whitfield."

The only indication that she hears me is a momentary pause in the motion of her pencil. A hesitation over the next eye socket in a sea of skulls and crossbones. Then, as Miranda passes between us and *accidentally* drops my paper onto the floor, my neighbour mutters,

"Suck a lemon, Sanders."

"Couldn't afford to dye all your hair, Vail?" Miranda pretends to carefully set a paper on Vail's desk before sending it sailing into the aisle. "Next time I'll lend you the fifty cents."

"Save it for your implants fund."

Vail flashes a sympathetic look at Miranda's less-than-overflowing chest. A giggle escapes before I can help it. I smack a hand over my mouth when Miranda spears me with a death look. Then, apparently deciding to pretend to take the high road, she stalks off. Vail goes back to her doodling. I swallow my laughter.

"I wish I could do that." I sigh.

"What?"

"Tell off girls like that," I explain, leaning down to grab both our papers off the floor. "My mind always freezes."

For several long moments I think she's not going to respond. Her attention is fully focused on filling in the spaces between her skulls and crossbones with smiley faces. As I set her paper on the edge of her desk, I notice that the smiley faces have fangs.

I shrug and start reading over my paper, a pretty standard set of classroom rules.

Mrs Deckler gets up and clears her throat like she's going to start reading the rules or something, and Vail finally says, "Standing up to Miranda is easy." She pulls the rules sheet on top of her notebook and turns her doodling attention to the pink handout. "You just have to stop caring what she thinks."

As Mrs Deckler starts droning on about attendance policies and how to ask for a library or study pass, I sink further into my desk. That's my problem. I can't *stop* caring what the Mirandas of the world think of me.

Unless something dramatic happens, San Francisco Grace is going to have pretty much the same experience as Orangevale Grace. Guess I'll have to get used to doormat status.

CHAPTER 3

Grace

My head bounces against the window as the city bus hits a pothole. At this point, accidentally getting knocked unconscious would give me a welcome excuse for forgetting my first day at Alpha. Is a little amnesia too much to ask for?

Except for the mild welcome from Vail in homeroom, the rest of the day has gone pretty much according to Miranda's evil plan. Why didn't I stand up to her when I had the chance? Too bad real life doesn't have Pause and Rewind. My first day would have gone infinitely better if I could have stopped time long enough to think up a comeback to Miranda's snide comment.

Instead, I spent all day replaying the moment in my mind.

The bus driver announces my stop. Slinging my backpack over my shoulder, I stand and move to the back doors. I'm about to step down into the stairwell when the bus pulls away from the kerb. I hold on to a pole to keep from flying into a little old Chinese lady's lap.

The bag in her arms squirms, and I'm half afraid there's a live chicken in there.

"Excuse me," I say, trying to get the driver's attention.

He ignores me, continuing through the intersection and to the next stop, where another passenger pushes past me out the door. I hurry down the steps and leap to the sidewalk before the bus can take off again. Guess I'm too used to school bus drivers, who are required to make sure you get off at your stop. City bus drivers don't seem to care.

As I trudge the extra two uphill blocks back to our street, I make a mental list of anything good that happened today. I know Mom is going to ask, and I want her to think everything's great.

Let's see, there was Vail in homeroom. She didn't exactly go out of her way to be friendly, but she wasn't horribly rude, either. Which is more than I can say about the rest of Alpha. That's something.

There was the counsellor, Ms West, who seemed pretty cool. Mrs Deckler was nice too, and already knew I'd have English with her in addition to homeroom. Counsellors and teachers in Orangevale never cared that much.

And I have a whole world of electives to choose from. I browsed them at lunch – having no one to eat with, I slipped away to the library to eat my avocado-and-beansprouts sandwich alone – and narrowed down my selection to about five choices. With no first-day-of-school homework, picking my electives is my main task for the night.

I reach our block, and while I dig out my key ring, I try to focus on the positive. Mom worries, and I don't want her to think I'm unhappy at the new school. Even if I am.

No, I have to give it more than a day. Tomorrow could be infinitely better. It can hardly be worse. I can't act *less* confident.

In Orangevale I never had to use house keys. Mom was always home, the door unlocked, ready with an after-school snack. Our building in San Francisco is a multi-storey U-shaped thing with a locked front gate leading into the courtyard and a locked main entrance. The only ways inside are using a key, getting buzzed in by a tenant or sneaking in after someone else. I tried that last one the first day in town and got a dirty look from one of our neighbours, so I don't think I'll be using the sneaking-in technique again.

The key turns easily in the lock and the gate swings open with a high-pitched squeak. I make sure it closes and locks behind me before heading towards the door. I love the courtyard. It's full of shady trees and brightly coloured tropical flowers that smell like I've always imagined Hawaii would. A little piece of paradise in the big city.

At the lime-green front door I flip to another key on my ring. Everything – the door, the trees, the flowers –

is a stark contrast of colour against the bright white of the building rising up on three sides. Too bad the interior isn't as vibrant and cheerful.

I head into the gloomy hallway, with its dark wood floor and insufficient lighting. It creeps me out a little. Too many shadows and hidden corners.

I hurry to the stairwell and run to the second floor. After one near-death experience in the classic – aka creaky and ancient – elevator, I've decided I could use the exercise of taking the stairs.

At our apartment door, I select the third and final key on my ring and burst inside. My rotten day forgotten, I set my backpack on the dining table and follow the smell of brownies to the kitchen.

"Mom, I'm home!" I shout, grabbing a still-warm treat from the piled-high plate on the counter.

She emerges from the back hall wearing paint-splattered jeans and a matching smock. Since we've been in the apartment only a little over a week, she's still finishing up the decorating and unpacking. Judging from the shade of soft taupe dominating her clothes, I'd guess she's tackling the master bedroom today.

"So…" she prods with a huge smile on her round face, "how was your first day? Tell me everything."

As a rule, I don't lie to my parents. I don't even usually keep things from them. We're very close, and I want it to stay that way. But this move has been difficult in so many ways – the long family talks after I got the scholarship, the concerns about uprooting me and Thane in the middle of our high school careers, the last-minute decision that meant a last-minute move. If Dad hadn't got that promotion to the San Francisco office, we'd still be in Orangevale.

Now Dad's working crazy hours, and I know Mom is still stressed about everything. I don't want her worrying that we've made the wrong decision, which is why I smile and say, "It was great. I think Alpha is going to be really good for me."

"Thank goodness," she says, ignoring her freshly painted state and rushing forward to wrap me in a tight Mom hug. "I was so worried."

"And all for nothing," I tease. Mission accomplished. Mom is relieved, which means the smile on my face isn't as forced as it was a minute ago. "You've got brownie in your hair."

She runs her fingers through her black-brown waves. "Did I get it?"

"I'm not sure," I say, leaning in to inspect. "I can't tell under all that paint."

"Ha ha." She teasingly smacks me on the shoulder. "Not funny."

I shrug. "I thought it was."

She steps around me into the kitchen and heads for the sink.

"And you found the bus and everything easily enough?" she asks over her shoulder.

"Mmm-hmmm," I say around my mouthful of brownie. Mom doesn't need to know about the bad bus driver any more than she needs to know about Miranda or my solo lunch in the library.

Mom busies herself with washing the few dishes in the sink while I finish my brownie. Moist, chocolatey goodness. The perfect cure for my disappointing day.

I pour myself a glass of pineapple Fanta to wash down the last crumbs.

"Where's Thane?" I ask after a big gulp. "Isn't he home yet?"

"The public schools have a later schedule. He gets out twenty minutes after you," she answers, drying her hands on a kitchen towel. "He should be home soon. Do you need anything?"

"Nope, I'm good."

"Okay, then I'll get back to my painting." Her smile is thrilled but weary. She's excited to be doing up the apartment, but also exhausted. "Shout if you need anything."

"Want some help?" I offer. With no homework to do, I need something to distract me from the mental replay of today's lowlights.

"That's sweet," she says, "but I'm almost done." At my skeptical look, she adds, "Really."

"You're sure?" When she nods, I say, "Okay." I refill my Fanta and head for the dining table.

I pull out the packet of Alpha Academy papers the counsellor gave me this morning and dig for the electives lists. I have to choose two, in addition to Spanish, and the first one is easy. I don't boast about it much, but I'm a bit of a computer geek. Okay, I'm a serious computer geek. Ever since I got my first laptop in third grade, I've been fascinated by computers and technology. It's my dream to work for one of the big software companies some day.

I circle Computer Science on the list.

The other elective, however, is a harder choice.

At lunch I marked stars next to Journalism and Yearbook. I've always been intrigued by the media. I don't have any experience, but I'm sure I could learn the necessary programmes easily enough. But then this afternoon I overheard someone say that Miranda is social editor on the school paper, and I don't need that conflict. I erase the star next to Journalism.

For some reason I also starred Ancient Greek and Tae Kwon Do. When Ms West suggested languages and athletics this morning, they didn't sound appealing at all. But as I read over the list, they started to look kind of interesting. Now, in the quiet of our apartment, they seem weird again. When would I ever use Greek? And my trying martial arts would probably only lead to injury – mine or someone else's. I erase both stars.

The last star is on Pottery and Sculpture. When I was in elementary school, I always loved art classes when we got to be hands-on with clay. I was never any good at it, but it was fun. It might be a nice reprieve from the rigorous academics at Alpha. It wouldn't do anything for my college applications, though.

I'm about to erase the remaining stars and circle Yearbook when the lock on the front door clicks open. There is no other sound, just the whisper of a breeze against my back as the door soundlessly swings open. I know it's Thane. No one moves as quietly as my brother. He's like a ninja cat burglar.

If we paired his stealth with my computer skills, we could be an epic spy team.

"Hey, Thane," I say without turning around. I draw a dark circle around my elective choice. "How was school?"

"Fine."

Did I mention that Thane isn't big on talking either? Some days I think he's a recovering mime. But I know he's just really thoughtful. He spends a lot of time in his head. He also has some emotional baggage – protective walls that none of us have been able to fully crack. We chip pieces away from time to time, but mostly his life before he came to live with us is a well-guarded mystery.

"You must be Grace," another, brighter, boy voice says. "Thane told me all about you."

Jerking back from the table and nearly knocking my

chair over, I turn to see who Thane has brought home.

My breath catches in my throat.

The boy standing at my brother's side is, in a word, adorable. I'm completely dumbstruck. He's taller than Thane by a couple of inches, making him about six foot. His dark hair falls in haphazard curls over his brow, his ears and the collar of his rugby shirt. His eyes are a pale mint-green with a light-brown ring around the pupil. And his mouth is spread in a wide, curving smile, showing bright teeth and a charming set of dimples.

Maybe *adorable* doesn't cover it.

"H-h-hi," I manage, looking away from his beautiful eyes.

I know I haven't got much of a backbone in general, but I don't usually lose the ability to speak complete words. There's something about him, about the whole package, that makes my skin tingle all over.

I've never reacted like this to a boy before. Sure, I've had my share of crushes and loves from afar, and even a quasi sort-of-boyfriend in my freshman year. None of them caused this whole-body reaction.

"This is Milo," Thane says, seemingly oblivious to my transformation into girl drool, thankfully. "He's a goalie."

Holy goalie.

Well, soccer explains Milo's presence. Thane may be quiet and shy and reserved in real life, but he comes alive on the soccer field. He's a completely different person when he's chasing down a ball or taking aim at the goal. Soccer is practically his life.

He says he doesn't want to play professionally. I don't know why not. I'm pretty sure he could if he wanted to.

"We have Physics together," Milo says, dropping into the chair at the head of the table. "Homework on the first day." He shakes his head. "What kind of teacher does that? Pure evil, I'm telling you."

Thane slips through the kitchen to tell Mom he's home, and I'm still struck silent by Milo's presence when my brother gets back. Thane takes the chair across the table from me and pulls out his textbook. He grumbles, "Homework."

"Uh, yeah," I say, my brain suddenly demanding that I figure out a way to stay here at this table. No matter what. "Me too."

Wait. Why did I say that? I don't have any homework. I don't even have any textbooks. I'm losing my mind.

"We were going to do our homework and then, after dinner, go on a tour of the neighbourhood. I'm kind of an expert." Milo sets his homework out on the table. "You interested?"

Uh, yeah!

No, keep it cool, Grace. Don't act like a total freakazoid.

"Sure," I say, forcing myself to sound casual and not insta-stalker scary. "Sounds fun."

Milo smiles and then flips open his Physics book and

starts on his homework. I glance up to find Thane staring at me, his dark-grey eyes unreadable. I raise my brows. He shifts his attention to his textbook.

After living in the same house for so long, I'm pretty much used to Thane's odd, silent behaviour. If he has something to say, he'll say it. He just doesn't have much to say very often. I shrug it off and instead focus on trying to find something in my backpack that can pass for homework.

Finding nothing, I dart to my room and grab my laptop off the desk. I can always find something to do with a computer.

Back at the table, I wake up my laptop and click open the word processor. In a new document, I start composing a list of things I want to change about my life. Starting with finding the ability to talk to cute boys.

I'm a little amazed that Mom approved this evening field trip. Thrilled, but amazed. She's always been a little more on the overprotective-of-her-chicks side, and letting us both out into the big bad city after dark is uncharacteristic.

But then again, I'm sure she and Dad could use a night alone. They haven't had a moment of peace since we started packing up the old house.

Plus we both have cell phones, bus passes and – I steal a glance at Milo – a native guide. Of course, Mom didn't know that, instead of walking around our neighbourhood, we'd catch the bus heading to Fisherman's Wharf to join the sea of tourists.

"Coach Guerrera likes to run the forwards into the ground for the first week," Milo tells Thane as the bus bounces down the street. "But after that he lets up. I think he just wants to weed out the quitters."

Thane nods.

Apparently that is enough of an answer for Milo, because he keeps on talking soccer. "He used to play professionally in Argentina, so he's got the legs to back up his demands."

I kind of tune out the words. Other than to watch Thane play, soccer is not really of interest to me.

Milo, on the other hand, is definitely of interest. And talkative – especially when Mom was peppering him with questions over dinner. Already I know he is a Bay Area native, is a senior like Thane, has three older sisters and hates mushroom pizza and avocado. Oh well, he can't be one-hundred-percent perfect.

With each bump in the road, Milo's dark-brown curls bounce as if gravity has no control over them. It makes me smile every time.

"This is our stop," Milo says as the bus pulls up in front of a hotel.

I jump up to follow him and Thane to the door, not wanting to get stuck on a bus for a second time today.

The street we're on is practically deserted, but one block north we step into a churning ocean of people, all ages and sizes and nationalities.

Distracted from my Milo watching, I gawk at the bustle of activity. There are street performers dressed as break-dancing robots or playing unrecognisable exotic instruments beneath giant crab sculptures. A woman in a long, exotic print dress with a shawl over her head tries to give me something, but Milo waves her off. He doesn't stop the man who hands me a brochure for a Bay cruise. It's utter chaos, but somehow everything flows perfectly together, like some kind of crazy, hectic ballet.

I'm surrounded by energy and I try to absorb as much as I can.

I follow the boys onto the pier, sticking close so we don't get separated. I'm pretty sure I'd never find them again. As we push through the Thursday-night crowd, I marvel at all the shops: seashells and pearls, souvenirs, socks, bath salts, candy and crystals, restaurants serving seafood and ice cream and a hundred kinds of crêpes.

No wonder this is such a popular tourist attraction.

"Watch out," Milo says, tugging me against his side as a tourist with a camera the size of my head nearly knocks me over. "You okay?" he asks.

I nod, dazzled by the feel of Milo against me. "Yeah, thanks."

"No problem." He beams, and for a second it feels

like we're completely alone in the crowd.

"I'm hungry," Thane says, killing our moment.

"We just ate," I complain, mostly because Milo's attention – and his hand – is now off me.

"Me too." Milo agrees with Thane. "Everything here is overpriced for the tourists. Have you guys ever had dim sum?"

Had it? I've never even heard of it. Still, even though I know it's a bonehead answer, I'm on the verge of saying, *All the time,* because I don't want Milo to think I'm an uncultured hick. "Sure—"

Before I can finish, Thane says, "No."

"Excellent!" Milo's eyes light up brighter than before, and I'm really glad I didn't get the chance to fib.

"I haven't," I finish quietly.

The look Thane throws me suggests he knew what I'd actually been about to say.

"Then I'll get to introduce you to it." Milo starts walking back in the direction we've come from and then off to the west. "The best all-night dim sum in town is only a cable car ride away."

I have to practically jog to keep up with his long strides. We cross to a dead-end street where a line of people stand waiting. They're all looking expectantly up the hill. I turn and see an ancient-looking cable car gliding down towards the dead end.

When I knew for sure we'd be moving to San Francisco,

I researched the city online. I read a lot about the cable cars and their history and construction. I know the ropes and brakes are supposed to be safe, but I'm not entirely convinced. As I watch the people climb off and the car execute a complicated, man-powered turnaround, I'm getting a little apprehensive.

"Don't worry," Milo says quietly in my ear. "It's fun."

A warm, melty feeling spreads from my ear to the rest of my body. I smile and let him lead me to a seat while he and Thane stand, hanging out over the street. I look around and see that other riders are hanging out over the street too, but it doesn't make me any less nervous.

My eyes stay squeezed tightly shut for most of the ride, so I don't remember much. There are a lot of jerks and stutters, and one time, when the car stops for a couple of minutes, I hear a lot of shouting. I force one eye open and find Thane and Milo gone. Panicked, I lean out to search for them, only to find them – and a bunch of other passengers – actually *pushing* the car up the track. I keep my eyes open long enough for Thane and Milo to return to their spots, and then clamp them shut again.

Two stops later, as the car slowly climbs up a hill, I feel a warmth on my cheek just before Milo whispers, "You're going to miss the best part."

Despite my fear, I force my eyes open. For a second, Milo fills my vision. Then he leans back and reveals the view. We're at an intersection at the high point of a hill.

Straight in front of me is a narrow street leading steeply down to a wider one, full of light and lanterns and activity. It's beautiful.

I smile at Milo for making me open my eyes.

I smile even bigger when he smiles back.

At the next stop, Milo's hand wraps around mine and tugs me to my feet. We've survived. Next time, I'll keep my eyes open the whole way.

"This is the world-famous Chinatown," he says, still holding my hand as he leads me down a very steep street.

My heart is racing, and not just because of the harrowing ride.

"And this," he says, pulling up in front of a glass storefront full of hanging meats and birds and unidentifiable things, "is the world's best dim sum parlour."

Although I can sort of see through the windows, they have layers of dirt caked at the corners, as if every so often someone grabs a rag to wipe only the centres. It doesn't exactly scream Great Place to Eat. Or even No Health Code Violations.

Milo throws the door open wide, flashes me a brilliant grin and says, "Wait until you taste it."

Shoving my hesitations about the sanitary conditions aside, I follow Thane through the door and to a once-white Formica table with chipped edges. I take the seat opposite Thane, which means that – deep breath – Milo is sitting next to me. My blood is pounding in my ears, and I have to make the hostess repeat her request three times before I finally hear her ask, "Hot tea?"

"Yes, please," I say, ducking to hide my blush.

"No menus?" Thane asks.

"Not with dim sum," Milo explains. "The waiters will bring around trays of dishes, and if we see any we like, we get them." He spins a small piece of paper beneath his finger. "They stamp this order sheet to keep track of what we eat."

"Sounds complicated," I manage.

"It's great," Milo promises with a wink.

I'm not so sure. But when the first trayful of goodies comes by, my mouth waters at the wonderful smells. It's like I never even ate dinner.

"Barbecue pork buns are the best," Milo says, pointing to a metal tin containing three puffy white balls of dough. "Just don't eat the paper stuck to the bottom."

The waiter places the tin on our table, pulls a stamp from his apron, and marks a symbol onto our order ticket.

"Oh," I say, eyeing the pork buns. "I, um—"

"Grace is vegetarian," Thane explains, so I don't have to.

Milo gives me a serious look. Great, now he thinks I'm some kind of hippie-granola weirdo. No, I'm just eco-conscious and doing my part to lighten my footprint. I wave a mental goodbye to my very slim chance with him.

But then he says, "Why didn't you say something?"

He calls the waiter back over, and soon there is a tin

of doughy buns – these filled with barbecued veggies – sitting next to the pork.

"Thanks," I say, and then drop my gaze to the food. Cute and considerate. As if Milo weren't already my dream guy.

It takes only a quick tutorial from Milo for me to manage the chopsticks well enough to pick up my bun and lift it to my mouth.

"Uh-oh," he says, as I'm about to take a bite. He reaches towards me and, for a heartbeat, I think he's going to touch my cheek. Instead, he peels a thin piece of waxed paper off the bottom of my veggie bun. "Trust me, this does not add to the experience."

I laugh at his teasing comment, but inside, my heart is doing cartwheels. *Play it cool, Grace.* Don't want him to think I'm totally boy-illiterate.

As if I'm totally together, I lift the bun the rest of the way to my mouth and am about to bite in when a repulsive smell washes over me.

Instant nausea.

I clap my free hand over my mouth as the bun drops and rolls, forgotten, to the floor.

Milo asks, "What's wrong?"

"Grace?" Thane's jaw clenches into a block of stone. "What is it?"

If I weren't on the verge of heaving the remains of Mom's veggie stew, I'd appreciate Thane's protectiveness.

He's always been that way, ready to throw himself into anything if he thinks I'm in danger. But then I guess that's what big brothers are for.

At this moment, though, it's all I can do to keep my stomach contents where they belong. I close my eyes and shake my head.

"We should go," Thane says.

Milo nods. "You get her outside and I'll pay the bill."

"No," I whisper, swallowing down the nausea as best I can. I don't want to ruin this night. "I'm – I'll be fine. Just give me a—"

The front door to the restaurant opens with a whine and the stench hits me tenfold. I feel my eyes roll back as my body tries to reject the smell. Or to protect me from whatever's causing it. I've never had such a violent reaction to an odour before.

"Maybe we should…" I force my eyes open, but instead of Milo's adorable face or my brother's strong one, my gaze focuses on the *thing* that has just walked in the front door. The creature.

The body looks like a normal man, with arms and legs and everything in between. The head, though… It's the head of a bull.

I'm not joking. A man with the head of a bull has just walked into an all-night dim sum restaurant as if it were normal.

I look at Thane for reassurance, hoping the panic I'm

feeling shows in my eyes, telling him everything he needs to know. He turns to look at the door then back at me, jaw clenched and eyes wide. "Let's go."

I nod.

"What's going on?" Milo turns and looks too. "Do you two know that guy?"

"Guy?" I choke. Is he blind? Can't he see?

For that matter, can't everyone see? Why isn't anyone screaming or running away? Slowly, I scan the rest of the tables. No one else seems to have taken notice of the man-bull, who is now crossing the main floor and heading for the back room.

I look at Thane, certain he must have seen it.

But no, the look in his eyes now is simply concern for me. Did I just imagine the look of recognition I saw a moment ago? Milo doesn't see it, and neither does Thane. No one does. I'm the only person who saw a slobbering beast instead of a man.

Which can only mean one thing.

"I'm just..." I shake my head. "I don't feel great."

Both boys nod, as if it's totally normal and logical and not at all out of the ordinary, when it's anything but. There's only one possible explanation for this hallucination. I must be going crazy.

CHAPTER 4

Gretchen

Even twenty minutes in a scalding shower can't completely wash the stink of minotaur off my body. I lather-rinse-repeat five times, hoping to purge the lingering residue from my hair. Getting up close and personal with a monster is never pretty, but sometimes it's worse than others.

By the time this one popped back to wherever he came from, my pores were plugged with his toxic odour. Dis. Gust. Ing. I might have nightmares.

With one white fluffy towel wrapped around my chest and another cocooning my hair, I cross to the library and drop down into the desk chair in front of the computer. I glide the mouse over the sleek black surface and click open my email.

"Nothing from Ursula," I think out loud.

This is getting weird. She usually sends me some kind of message if she's going to be gone overnight. I've been living with the woman for four years, and I still have no idea where she goes or what she does when she disappears for days at a time. At first I was too nervous to ask.

42

The woman saved me from the streets and gave me a purpose. I wasn't about to piss her off by questioning her movements. Now I accept her random hours as normal and keep up my half of the don't ask, don't tell policy.

How many other sixteen-year-olds have free range of an awesome loft and a Mustang and no curfew? I know how lucky I am. Fighting beasties and keeping my questions about her whereabouts to myself are prices I'm more than willing to pay.

But when I last saw her a few days ago – has it been a week already? – she promised it was finally time to answer some of the lingering questions about my Medusa heritage and my huntress legacy. I would finally find out the full deal about being the latest descendant of the mortal gorgon, instead of just knowing the piecemeal story she's fed me over the years.

Ursula has been scarce ever since.

Four years' worth of patience is running out, and she goes and vanishes. I'd say it wasn't fair, but whoever said life was supposed to be? I didn't ask for awful selfish parents who liked to hit me when the drink and drugs ran out any more than I asked to be responsible for keeping the human world safe from monsters. You can't change destiny.

Composing a new message to Ursula, I type up my report as fast as possible. I still have school in the morning and about an hour of homework left to do.

To: roamingursie@magicmail.com
From: grrretchen@wazoo.com
Subject: Hunt Report #0427
Target: Minotaur, male
Discovery: Scent of ~~wretched puke~~ sour hay and bile while sniff-testing the air from the balcony window.
Location: Chinatown, all-night dim sum restaurant, back room
Result: Discovered the subject on the verge of attacking human couple on ~~sappy~~ romantic date. Used eye hypnosis to keep human couple focused on ~~sappy~~ romantic date. Had little trouble engaging and neutralising minotaur given his massive head and lack of coordination. Entire incident over in less than five minutes.
Sightings: None
Unit: Gretchen Sharpe

I'm not sure why Ursula makes me fill out my name in the report. It's not like there are other descendants of Medusa to do this dirty work. I'm not even sure why she makes me write up the reports at all. Who cares about how I took down a Cabeirian horse in the frozen foods aisle or a cyon chryseus at the base of Coit Tower?

From what little Ursula has told me, San Francisco is the only vortex for monster activity. She and I are pretty much the front, back and only line of defence.

And although she can see them, she can't fight them like she used to. She's cagey about her age, but she has to be sixty at least. Not spry enough to wrestle a siren on a rampage. That's partly why she's training me.

That's not the only reason though. One day, a few months ago, I overheard part of a hushed phone conversation. I wouldn't normally eavesdrop, but I heard my name and was curious. But the only other words I could make out were "Zeus must be behind this, cousin" and something about not trusting Athena.

Clearly, something bigger than me is going on.

That's when I started asking questions again. Ursula kept putting me off, telling me it wasn't time yet. And now that it's time, she's nowhere to be found.

I take a frustrated breath and force it out. There's nothing I can do about it right now. I'll keep on with business as usual until Ursula gets back. Then I'll pin her down for the promised answers.

The only other messages in my inbox are spam. I trash it all, shut down the computer and head for bed. School time will be here too soon, and I can't exactly be late for the second day. That would draw way more attention than I need. A girl's got to stay below the radar if she wants to keep slaying monsters in her free time.

In the dream, I'm asleep at my desk in biology. The sheep of Euclid High School – pretty much the entire student body – are the actual, wool-covered, bleating variety. And the teacher lecturing at the front of the class has a forked tongue. Well, three actually. One for each head.

"Misssss Ssssarpe," she says, first with one mouth, then echoing with the other two, trying to rouse me. "Misssss Ssssarpe!"

I try to ignore the three-headed, serpent-tongued teacher, burying my head in the crook of my arm to block out the fluorescent light.

"Miss Sharpe!"

I jerk up at the sound of Mrs Knightly's shout. "Yes?"

She frowns at me from the front of the classroom. The sheep – back to their regular, trend-obsessed, mindless human selves – all stare and snicker at me. I casually swipe my hand across my mouth, in case I'm having a drool moment. All clear.

"First warning," Mrs Knightly says before turning back to her notes about photosynthesis on the board.

It's just bad luck that I have biology first thing in the morning. I actually like the subject – and Mrs Knightly too, not that I'd ever admit it to the ball-buster – but with my nocturnal schedule, I'm usually barely awake for first period. It's still early enough in the semester that she's giving me warnings. She's even given me a slide on the homework I forgot to do last night. If past experience is anything to go by, though, her leniency will last about two weeks. After that, it'll be straight to the office for every little offence, which is the last thing I need.

Keeping my record clear and uninteresting to school counsellors, administrators and welfare officers is mission critical. The last thing Ursula and I need is someone with a government badge and a sudden interest in my guardianship. It's not like our situation is easy to explain.

When Ursula found me, I was on the short path to nowhere, living in a warehouse, stealing candy bars and energy drinks to survive. I can still picture the moment she appeared, seemingly out of nowhere, inside my makeshift home. The scent of lemongrass hit me first, sweet and tangy against the dust- and rotting garbage-filled environment. Then she was there.

I scrambled to my feet, grabbing the broken bottle that was my only defence against intruders.

"You have no need of that weapon with me," she said, stepping forward. Her long, shimmery grey dress rippled around her. "I am here to help you."

"Don't need no help," I snapped.

Her soft eyes smiled. "I am sure you do not." Another step forward. "But I hope you will accept it all the same."

"No thanks." I flung the bottle at her, skewing my aim so it missed by a mile. I turned to run.

Before I took a step she was in front of me, blocking my path.

"How'd you do that?"

"Don't you want to know about your destiny?" she

asked, ignoring my question. "The one the oracle told you about."

I jerked back. How could this stranger know about the fortune-teller I'd visited a few weeks ago, the one whose reading had prompted me to run away from home once and for all? The one who had promised me a greater destiny than I could even imagine.

"How do you know about that?" I demanded.

"Come," she said, turning and walking away. "I shall explain over a nice hot meal. I find myself quite famished."

Four years later, I'm amazed she didn't run screaming from the filthy, tattered girl who tried to attack her with a broken bottle. Instead, she took me in, told me about my destiny and trained me to fulfil it. There's nothing on the books about our arrangement, and nothing about it that would pass a Child Welfare Services sniff test.

As long as I keep my nose clean at school, we can go on as we are. That suits me fine. But one red flag in the wrong file and I'll be in the foster care system before you can say 'unfit guardian'. Or, worse, back with Phil and Barb. No thank you. Twelve years with them was enough to last a lifetime.

I pull myself up at my desk, straightening my spine to improve blood flow to my brain. Rubbing the backs of my hands against my eyes, I allow myself one last yawn before focusing my attention on the lecture.

I grab a pen out of the pocket of my cargo trousers,

click the top, and start to write the date in the corner of my blank sheet of paper.

The classroom door creaks open as I underline the date for the third time. I continue my doodling, covering the left margin of my page with diagonal stripes. I assume the visitor is an office aide come to request the presence of someone less adept than me at keeping below the radar.

The hush that falls across the room is my first clue.

Usually, an interruption by an office aide means an excuse for the sheep to start talking. They snatch the opportunity to trash-talk each other or trade juicy stories while the teacher is distracted. That they've fallen into silence means this isn't an ordinary office aide visit.

I glance up.

"Class, this is Nick," Mrs Knightly explains, gesturing at the boy standing next to her desk. "He's new at Euclid. Please welcome him."

The sheep erupt into chatter, instant gossip about the new boy. He looks fairly ordinary: on the tall side; short, wavy blonde hair; dark, unreadable eyes; features that look carved from stone – okay, not so ordinary. But not so exceptional among the male half of the herd.

I go back to my doodling.

Mrs Knightly looks out over the classroom before telling Nick, "You can take the seat behind Gretchen."

That regains my attention.

Nick's dark gaze follows the direction she's indicating

and stops when he sees me. Maybe I'm imagining things, but I think the corner of his mouth lifts up into the tiniest fraction of a smile.

As he makes his way down the aisle, I pretend not to notice, or care – keeping my attention on my paper when in reality it's killing me not to sneak a glance to see what colour those dark eyes actually are.

Nick swings into the desk behind me, and I force myself to relax. I've never got this tight and twisted over a boy at first glance. He hasn't even said a word to me yet.

"Gretchen, huh?" he asks, as if reading my thoughts. "Can I borrow a sheet of paper?"

"Um, sure." I reach down into my bag, pull one out and hand it back to him. "Here you go."

"Thanks." Our fingertips brush as he takes the paper, and I suppress a little shiver. He leans closer, so close I feel his warm breath as he asks, "How about a pen?"

"What?" I blurt. "Forget you were coming to school today?"

"Something like that."

"Problem, Miss Sharpe?" Mrs Knightly asks.

I shake my head and sink into my chair. Intent on not causing further distraction, I grab another pen out of my cargo pocket and drop it over my shoulder onto Nick's desk.

"Thanks again," he says.

I sense him leaning back into his chair, away from me.

But I swear I can feel the skin on the back of my neck tingling the whole period.

"Aargh!" I end the call and punch instant redial on my phone. I listen as the phone rings several times before Ursula's voicemail picks up. Ursula's *full* voicemail. I hang up again. I've been trying between classes all morning, with no success. "Where is she?"

"No answer?"

To my credit, I don't scream or jump or even swing a punch at the sound of his voice. I have every right. Not only has he found me in my favourite hiding spot – a vending machine alcove around the corner from the cafeteria, left empty since the school decided to remove all junk food from campus – but he is also the reason for my desperate call to Ursula. The way he kept leaning forward to ask me questions all through biology, each time a little closer than before. The way his fingers tickled across my palm when he gave me back my pen. The way he managed to cross my path between all my classes since. Something's not right about his presence, I feel it, and Ursula might know what to do. If only I could reach her.

Deep breath, Gretch. You can handle this.

Quickly pocketing my phone, I turn to face Nick.

Big mistake.

I'm not usually a sucker for a pretty face, but this one…

Well, let's just say he's a little too handsome for my own good, especially now that I can tell his eyes are a midnight shade of blue, the exact colour of the water beneath my balcony on a moonlit night. An image fills my head, of the two of us standing together, looking out over the inky bay. In the image, I lean against his side and he wraps a strong arm around my shoulders. The idea is more tempting than it should be.

Where did that come from?

"Who were you calling?" he asks innocently. "Boyfriend?"

I almost snort. My life is beyond too complicated for boy interest, even in boys with midnight-blue eyes. I need to nip this in the bud before it goes anywhere, even in my own head.

Throwing on my best huntress glare, I snarl, "What's it to you?"

Without waiting for a response, I stomp away towards the cafeteria. That should scare him away nicely. Only an idiot would want an angry, aggressive girl who makes it clear that she's not interested.

What I need right now is a trayful of carbs to get my energy up. All the recent late-night hunts are catching up with me. Too bad the school removed all the vending machines, because a caffeine-and-sugar-filled energy drink would sure come in handy right about—

"I thought cell phones were off limits at school."

Nick falls into step beside me.

Are you kidding me? What kind of guy follows a girl after the face-flat rejection I just served him? He should be running away to the nearest cheerleader for consolation. With a face like his, he'd have no problem scoring the queen bee.

Not exactly sure how to react to his pursuit, I say, "They are."

"I get it," he says with a gut-tugging laugh. "You're *that* kind of girl."

Stopping in my tracks, I know I shouldn't rise to the bait. But I can't help demanding, "*What* kind of girl?"

He steps ahead of me, pushes open the door to the cafeteria and nods me inside. I move forward because I'm hungry, not because he's holding the door like a real gentleman. I couldn't care less if he's got manners.

As I pass by, he whispers, "The kind who ignores the rules."

The hairs on the back of my neck stand up at that display of arrogance. Easy as that, he thinks he can read me. Thinks he can put me in a little box as a certain type of girl. Well, guess what? He has no idea. *No* idea.

Stopping and spinning so fast he almost runs into me, I say, "I don't ignore *all* the rules. Only the ridiculous ones." Then, as a smile starts to spread across his face, I add, "But I *do* ignore all the boys who think they can figure me out in under five seconds."

As I turn and blend into the crowded lunchroom, I think I hear him say, "Oh, it's been more than five seconds."

The boy is obviously a wackadoo. It's not that boys haven't hit on me before. I'm no beauty queen, but I'm no hideous harpy either. Freshman year, I almost went out on a date with a boy from my English class who played basketball. Right before our date, a cyclops popped into town and I had to bail at the last minute. Thus ended my dating life. That night I realised how impossible a relationship would be for a girl who hunts monsters. I've been doing my best to drive the boys – everyone, really – away ever since.

Besides, it's not that hard when you wear combat boots, fall asleep in class and make yourself scarce as much as possible.

That makes Nick a bit of an enigma. He came back for more, even after my straight-up attempts to scare him away. I shove aside the tiny part of me that wishes he'll come back for more again. I don't wish that. I want him to stay beyond arm's length.

Really, I think.

"Really," I repeat out loud.

I grab a tray and get in the line for the pasta station. Hunting always leaves me starving the next day, and a nice heaping plate of pasta with extra meat sauce is just what I need. Forgetting Nick, I focus on filling my tray.

I toss on a fruit salad, a couple of chocolate puddings – every little bit of caffeine helps – and a glass of apple juice before heading to the checkout. As I hand the cashier a five, I sense a presence at my side.

"That's quite a meal," he teases.

Out of the corner of my eye I can see his tray, with practically identical choices, right down to the double pudding.

This guy can't take a hint.

I suppress the little thrill at knowing he hasn't given up. I need him to give up, even if a part of me doesn't want him to.

I pocket my change and head out into the sea of tables, away from Nick, beelining for my regular table in the furthest corner. The outcast table. On any given day there are between six and ten of us who chow together because we have nowhere else to eat. We don't usually talk, but it kind of alleviates the stress of having to squeeze in at a pre-established table.

I slam my tray on the speckled grey surface, taking the spot between the witch and the manga boy. I'm sure they have names – I just don't know them.

If I thought squeezing in between two other outcasts would keep Nick from following, I was wrong. He walks around to the other side of the table and takes the seat facing mine. He doesn't look at all fazed to be sitting next to the gamer boy whose console never leaves his hands.

In fact, he's smiling.

Clenching my jaw, I focus my attention on my food and ignore Nick.

I'm just forking a giant bite of pasta into my mouth when he says, "You're not exactly the welcoming committee, are you?"

Manga boy and the gamer are oblivious, but I can sense the witch's attention on us. Boys like Nick don't usually hang out at the outcast table. They never hit on the outcast girl.

I chew quietly, keeping my eyes on my tray.

When I don't respond, Nick shrugs and then digs into his own plate of pasta. Guess he finally got it.

I suck down an entire pudding, trying to pretend I'm not disappointed that he's giving up. It's not like I want him to pursue me. I *can't* want him to pursue me. My own ego liked the attention, I suppose, the interest in me as nothing more than an average girl.

Don't be dumb, I tell myself. *You're not average. You don't get the normal life with the BFF and the boy. You're destined for more than that. And your destiny is a solo adventure.*

Still, I allow myself a brief moment of sadness when I stand to take my empty tray to the dish line and Nick doesn't move. Doesn't even react. And just like that, *poof,* I'm forgotten.

"You're being ridiculous," I mutter quietly. I drop my

tray and dishes into one of the big tubs. "You want him to forget you."

I turn, eager to get out of the cafeteria, away from Nick and my irrational feelings. Only to walk smack into his chest.

"Careful there," he says in a charmingly – I mean, annoyingly – teasing way. His hands come up to steady me, wrapping around my upper arms. "Look both ways before crossing the cafeteria."

The two spots where his hands hold me burn with a warmth I'm not used to. I don't get much human contact. Monster contact, hell yeah. I've had enough monster contact in the last four years to fill a century. But actual direct contact with a human being? Not so much.

Ursula's less the touchy-feely type and more the this-is-how-you-handle-nunchucks-so-you-don't-knock-yourself-unconscious type. Maternal and cuddly she is not.

So it's no wonder that I kind of want to lean into Nick and get even more contact. I want more of that warm feeling that's spreading from my arms up to my shoulders and down through the rest of my body.

"I—"

Maybe it's the way his eyes soften as I start to speak. Or the way his head tilts a little to the side. Or the way his hands tighten a tiny bit. Whatever sets me off, in an instant I jump back out of his grasp, shaking my head to lose the spell his touch put on me.

I hear Ursula's voice in my head, reminding me that I'm a huntress. I have responsibilities that the human world cannot even begin to comprehend. I can't afford moments of weakness.

And right then, with Nick's hands on my arms, I felt a whole world of weakness.

With some distance between us, my thoughts clear.

Nick has no trouble reading the scowl on my face. "Whoa," he says, throwing both hands up in surrender. "Just trying to keep you off the floor."

"Look," I say, stepping forward into his personal space, jabbing a finger to his chest for emphasis. "I don't do friends."

I give him a quick shove, with more strength than I should but not enough to send him flying across the room. The more space I put between us, the less effect he has on me. I'd put a continent between us if I could.

As I storm out of the cafeteria, I hear him shout, "You think we're friends? That's a start."

Stupid boy. Can't take a hint. Can't take a megaphone blast to the ear, either. I made it completely clear that I want nothing to do with him.

Which doesn't explain why, when I slip into my seat in fourth period, I'm fighting a grin at our parting exchange.

CHAPTER 5

Grace

"Right click on the download link. Choose 'Save As',"
Miss Mota says, "and save the file to your desktop."
The trial version of Web Code Wizard is downloading
to my station in the computer lab before she finishes her
instructions. I'm excited that our first unit is on web
programming. Most of my coding experience is with
software, not internet design. This will be a fun chance
to play around with something new, even if I have to go at
the slower pace of my less geekified classmates. I can find
ways to fill my time.

While Miss Mota helps a boy who has somehow got
into a never-ending cycle of pop-up ads, I create a hot key
to clear the desktop in a single keystroke – in case Miss
Mota comes by to check on my progress – and then open
a new browser window.

Since last night I've been trying hard not to think
about what happened in the dim sum restaurant. When
Thane and I got home, I took a steaming shower to wash
away the stink, then collapsed into bed. This morning
I missed my alarm and had to rush to get ready in time.

Every time the thought popped into my mind, I slammed the mental door in its face. Until now, my brain's been pretty good at blocking out the memory, but while I'm waiting for my classmates to catch up... it's starting to wander.

The image of that creature walking into the restaurant burns in my mind. The nausea returns.

I need a shiny new distraction.

I have every intention of finding a bad-thought-erasing game to play. Or maybe a tech-obsessed gadget blog to read. Instead, my subconscious takes over and I find myself typing *man* and *bull* into the search engine box at the top of the screen.

Anxiety washes over me. My palms start to sweat and my heart shudders as I wait for the results to appear.

I almost close out the browser, not ready to face whatever answers show up in this list.

"No," I whisper to myself. "I have to face this sometime. If I'm going crazy, it's better to find out now."

I reluctantly scan the screen. The results are all about some comic-book character, so I refine my search to say *man with the head of a bull.*

The first link is a Wikipedia article about the Minotaur.

As the article loads, an image shows up on the right side of the screen. It's an ancient Greek statue of a man's body with the head of a bull. His arms and horns are kind of broken off, showing the wear and tear of the statue's age, but it's still crystal clear what the sculptor was trying to convey.

"No way," I mutter.

It looks exactly like the creature I saw in the dim sum place last night.

There are a few differences, of course. In real life, the bull head was much bigger and much more slobbery. And way scarier.

A quick scan down the page refreshes my junior high mythology lessons. Minotaur: a hideous, murderous monster that King Minos plopped in the middle of his crazy labyrinth so it would eat anyone who ventured inside. All the details match up to my imaginary creature sighting.

"This can't be."

"Everything going all right, Grace?" Miss Mota asks.

Without thinking, I quickly punch the hot key. My browser – along with the Minotaur article – disappears. I restore the download window, and then spin around.

"Yes, I…" I resist the urge to check over my shoulder to make sure the Minotaur is gone. "Fine."

Did she see what I was reading? Maybe I didn't clear the screen fast enough. What if she saw that I was off task? *Don't panic*, I tell myself. Even if she did, I could pass it off as research for English class. According to our syllabus, our second unit will be about mythology. If Miss Mota asks, I can just say I'm trying to get ahead.

She pulls up a plastic chair and sits next to me. "I know you are more advanced than the other students in this class," she whispers conspiratorially. "But I think you will find the work interesting. We can always arrange independent projects if you aren't feeling challenged enough."

"Okay," I say, letting out a sigh of relief that she didn't notice the Minotaur. "I'm sure it will be great."

"You know," she says, eyes wide and a big smile on her face, "when Ms West first showed me your application, I nearly cried."

"What?" I ask, confused. "Why?"

"Because I've never had a student with your level of experience and interest in Computer Science." She claps her hands together excitedly. "I absolutely insisted they give you a full ride."

"Really?" Ms West made it sound like *she* was the one to get me my scholarship.

"Well…" Miss Mota kind of rolls her eyes. "Okay, so I begged. But still! You're here and I'm going to make sure you get some valuable training in this class."

"Oh, thanks," I say. "That's great."

"And," she leans in close again, "I have a great connection in the Computer Science programme at Stanford." She pushes herself to her feet. "But we can talk about all that next year, when you're applying for college."

Wow, first day of class and she's already working

on getting me into a good college Computer Science programme. I'm impressed.

"Okay, class," Miss Mota announces to the room, "now double click on the downloaded file to begin the installation. A window will pop up, asking you to confirm that you want to run the file. Click 'Yes'."

Before she's done, I've started the installation, clicked through all the security questions and acceptance of terms and have the programme open to a new web document.

I hope Miss Mota comes through on her promise to give me challenging work soon. Otherwise I'm going to start hoping for a minotaur to walk through this door.

By the time Thane gets home from soccer try-outs that afternoon, I'm finished with my second-day of-school homework. Not that I'm usually the do-your-homework-immediately kind of girl – more like the do-your-homework-at-the-last-minute kind – but the possibility that Milo might come home with my brother again is enough to make sure I have nothing in the way of whatever comes up.

I've also swapped my standard schoolwear T-shirt for a slightly girlier turquoise one with a ruffle along the neckline and some kind of drawstring thingies up the sides. I'm not exactly sure how to operate the drawstrings, so I leave them as is. My Converse lose out to a pair of dark purple flats that I usually save for weddings and birthday parties.

And, for the finishing touch, I pull out my ponytail and swipe a glob of tinted lip gloss over my mouth.

All very out of the norm for jeans-and-T-shirt me. I'm just collapsing into a trying-to-be-casual heap on the couch when I hear a key in the lock. I quickly flip open the fashion magazine I borrowed from Mom to use as a prop. Thane, who walks through the front door disappointingly alone, takes one look at me and gives me a silent, raised brow.

"What?" I demand, more irritated that I've obviously girlied up for nothing than by his questioning look.

He shrugs and shakes his head, giving me a silent *I didn't say anything.*

Thane has such an expressive face, he always manages to say more without words than most people do with an entire monologue. And after all these years I can interpret his expressions so easily, I might as well be reading his mind. He drops his bag next to the front door and starts down the hall to his room.

I want to throw something at his retreating back. Mom's magazine could do the job. At the last moment I decide to fight the urge. Obviously I can't *ask* Thane about Milo without completely revealing my crush on his new friend. He doesn't say much and I know he wouldn't break my confidence, but I don't want him feeling weird or awkward around Milo. Thane needs new friends as much as I do. I know he's taking the move pretty hard, even if he doesn't say anything.

He didn't want to leave Orangevale. Not that I can blame him – nobody wants to move in their senior year. Thane becoming friends with Milo can only be a really good thing. And I'm not just saying that for selfish reasons.

Well, if Milo's not coming by, there's no point in hanging out in my uncomfortable girliewear. The flats are already pinching my toes.

Pushing myself off the couch, I swing through the kitchen and grab an oatmeal-raisin cookie and a glass of pineapple Fanta. On second thought, I grab another cookie. I'm going to need it. I'm friendless in a new city and my only prospect for Friday-night entertainment is a no-show.

Heading to my bedroom, down the hall from Thane's closed door, I realise that the anticipation of seeing Milo tonight had been keeping my mind occupied. Now, alone in my room with the door closed against the outside world, there's nothing to keep away thoughts about last night and what I discovered in Computer Science earlier.

Shoving a bite of fortifying cookie into my mouth, I step out of my uncomfortable flats and kick them into my closet.

"Time to be rational," I tell myself.

But with my mouth full of cookie, it sounds more like, "Mime moo mee mwathonal."

I force myself to do a quick mental recap. First, I smelled and then saw a man with the head of a bull in a dim sum restaurant last night. Then, this afternoon, I discovered he was a minotaur, identical to a statue dating from ancient Greece. What does that mean?

I swallow the cardboard that was once my cookie and try to reason with myself.

"Let's consider the logical options here," I say, flinging myself back onto my bed to stare at the too-white ceiling. I miss the rainforest canopy Mom painted when I was in third grade. This could be anyone's ceiling. "Option one, maybe it was a really elaborate Halloween costume."

Given that Halloween is almost two months away, a pretty unlikely scenario. Although this is San Francisco, and I've heard some wild stories. Still, every detail, down to the matted fur, the thick drool and the repulsive smell, was too real to be fake.

"Option two, maybe I'm insane."

I don't feel crazy. Then again, don't they always say that the crazy people are the ones who think they're sane? But no one has ever commented on me being delusional or anything. Someone should have noticed if I was a raving lunatic.

Since I don't know who my birth parents are, I can't exactly check for a family history of madness. Still, if there was anything, wouldn't Mom have mentioned it? I know she has some documents she's saving until I turn eighteen. Maybe I should ask now.

"There's still option three," I tell myself, shaking my

head against the idea even as I allow myself to say the words out loud. "Maybe I saw an actual, real-life minotaur in the middle of Chinatown last night."

If the fact that I'm even considering that possibility isn't a sign of complete and total lunacy, I don't know what is. When you look at the facts side by side, though – me having no history of craziness, the nauseating smell burned into my brain and the identical image on the Wikipedia page – it almost seems… plausible.

Anxious, I jump off the bed and start pacing.

I must really be going off the deep end. Am I actually considering this possibility? Maybe I should ask Mom to take me to a shrink. Or I could talk to Ms West – she did say we could talk about anything, and there's probably some kind of student-counsellor confidentiality rule, right? So word of my craziness wouldn't get around.

That would mean I'd have to wait until Monday morning, though. Who knows what kind of state my brain might be in by th—

Knock, knock, knock.

I jump and spin to face my door, my heart pounding violently up into my throat. It's not until I try to yell at Thane for the intrusion that I realise my hand is clamped over my mouth to stop a scream. I drop my hand. Clearly, I really am losing it.

Grateful for the distraction, even if I am annoyed at Thane, I yank open the door and blurt, "What?"

"Hey Grace," Milo says.

I gasp at the sight of him filling my doorway.

It's a miracle I don't collapse into a puddle on the floor. Or slam the door in his face. Or both.

"H-hi," I manage.

"Thane and I are going to Synergy," he says, gesturing at my brother, skulking against his own bedroom door a few feet away. "Wanna come?"

"Syner-what?"

"Synergy," he repeats. "It's an under-age club. Pretty lame most of the year, but first weekend of school is always hot."

"A club," I echo.

Loud music, flashing lights and stifling crowds of people trying to forget their daytime lives. Exactly what I need to get my mind off the fact that I'm probably crazy. With any luck I can hold the insanity at bay until Monday morning, until I can talk with Ms West.

"Definitely." I take a deep breath. "Just let me get a sweater."

Milo smiles. Yep, I think I can keep it together for a weekend.

Synergy is not like any of the under-age clubs in Orangevale. Okay, so there *weren't* any under-age clubs in Orangevale, but I always imagined they would be like a school dance with fancier lights.

This is a far cry from any school dance I've ever been to.

There's a big, scary bouncer at the door who made us show our school IDs to get in. Which doesn't make any sense, because it's an *under-age* club, but whatever. Inside, everything is black. The walls, the curtains, the ceiling, the floor. And judging from what the bouncer, the cashier and the cloakroom attendant we passed on the way in are wearing, the club uniform is pretty much all black too.

After walking along a short corridor, we emerge into the main room.

It's a total crush of people, like pictures of Times Square on New Year's Eve. Teens of all ages – and a few creepy older folks – are filling most of the room and the raised stage that runs the length of one wall.

"Wild, right?" Milo shouts in my ear.

I just nod. He won't hear me above the blaring music anyway, and I'm hyperventilating a little at how close his mouth came to my ear.

On the plus side, I'm definitely *not* thinking about a bull-headed man. I'm not thinking of much besides Milo at the moment.

He leans back in and shouts, "Let's get something to drink."

He motions at the opposite wall, where a bar – with no alcoholic drinks in sight – seems to be the only spot to find a bit of breathing room. Thane and I follow as Milo weaves his way through the crowd.

When we get to the bar, he rises up on tiptoe and surveys its length. He throws me a grin over his shoulder and gestures for us to follow him. He makes his way to the far end, where a lone stool sits empty.

"Seats are like gold dust in here," Milo says, not having to shout as loud in this corner of the club. He pats the black vinyl cushion. "Hop on."

I glance at Thane, who rolls his eyes at me.

"Before someone steals it," he mumbles.

The stool is a little tall, so when I try to lift myself onto the seat I come up short. I'm about to turn and make a leap for it when I feel warm hands around my waist. I can't help the little gasp of shock as Milo effortlessly lifts me onto the stool. His hands linger for half a second, long enough to send a shivery tingle through my body.

"There you go," he says, releasing me like it was nothing, before turning to flag down the bartender.

The only reason I know that little moment wasn't a total figment of my imagination is the lingering tingle at my waist and the protective scowl creasing Thane's forehead. Right now, his expressive face is saying, *I'm not sure I want my new buddy making moves on my sister.*

A girlie giggle bubbles up inside me. If Thane thinks Milo is making a move, then maybe he actually is. Maybe this crush won't turn into an unrequited lovefest like all my previous ones.

While Milo orders us three sodas, I grin and try to

ignore Thane. If I attempt to reassure him or let him know that I welcome Milo's moves, well, then he'll know how I feel and it'll be all over. Instead, I concentrate on not girling out over the cute boy and pretending like the club scene is totally my average Friday-night agenda.

I turn my attention to the crowd and study some of the more colourful characters. Club attire is a broad spectrum of styles. I see girls wearing ankle-skimming maxi dresses and others wearing miniskirts shorter than anything I've seen even on reality TV. Some boys sport ultra-tight skinny jeans, while others wear theirs so baggy that they're falling off. Thane and Milo blend in perfectly in their everyday wear, but I feel a little underdressed. I'm really glad I'm still wearing the ruffled T-shirt and the flats, despite the pinched toes. At least I don't look like a complete slob.

"Here we go," Milo says, handing me and Thane tall, thin glasses of bubbling pop. When Thane starts to reach for his wallet, Milo says, "These are on me. Consider it my San Francisco house-warming present."

Thane nods.

I smile like an idiot.

Thankfully, neither boy seems to notice. Or care.

I'm about to take a sip of my drink when I'm overwhelmed by an awful smell. A vaguely *familiar* awful smell. I place the glass on the bar before it slips from my hand. Eyes clenched, I focus my thoughts on something else, anything else. The horrifying image of the minotaur won't go away.

"Not again," I whisper.

Milo leans in. "What's that?"

Thane looks worried.

Do not *be the crazy girl in the room.* If I'm going to wind up in a nuthouse Monday morning, I want to enjoy my last days of freedom. I want to enjoy Milo. Forcing a normalish smile on my face, I say, "Nothing."

But that doesn't make the smell go away. In fact, it's getting worse. My eyes start to water and my nostrils sting. I'm not far from the limits of my gag reflex when, over Milo's shoulder, I see him. I see *it*.

This one isn't a man with a bull's head. Nope, I don't see a single manlike feature on the thing. The body looks like a lion's, complete with furry paws and a thick mane around the neck. The head, on the other hand, belongs to some kind of bird of prey. A pair of red-and-gold-feathered wings spreads wide above the grinding crowd.

Another memory from mythology lessons springs to mind, but I force it away. Clearly my mental state is deteriorating at warp speed. I shouldn't have come to the club. I should have gone straight to Mom and insisted she drop me at the nearest insane asylum.

Anything would be better than going through this right here, right now, in front of Milo.

I squeeze my eyes shut as tight as possible – so tight

I start seeing little blue flashes of light. Tears tingle at the corners and I take a fortifying breath. I can't shut my nostrils, though, so I lean closer to Milo and inhale a lungful of his yummy-smelling cologne.

It's enough to let me convince myself the lion-bird is a figment of my imagination. Which, of course, it is. It has to be, no matter how sane I feel.

"Are you okay?" Thane whispers in my ear. In those three words I clearly hear the concern in his voice. I want to tell him what's happening, to confess the monster sightings and my failing grip on reality, but not as much as I want to pretend everything's fine. Not as much as I don't want to spoil this night.

I can only nod.

I sense him pulling away. He's always super-protective, but he's also ready to back off when I need him to. The best possible kind of older brother.

"I have an idea," Milo says cheerfully.

He leans away from me, taking his lion-bird-smell-neutralising cologne-cocoon with him, and I open my eyes to see if he's trying to put distance between himself and the crazy girl. Instead, I see him placing his glass on the bar.

He holds out his hand to me and asks, "Wanna dance?"

A cooler girl would hesitate and then coyly accept. A girl with more boy skills wouldn't want to look so eager. Or desperate.

Not me. Nope, I break out in a goofy – and grateful – grin and blurt, "Yes!"

As his hand wraps around mine, all thoughts of the creature hallucinations disappear. In this moment, there is only my hand in Milo's as he leads me out into the centre of the dance floor. Just as a slow song begins to play.

And as he tugs me close and guides my arms around his neck, I can almost convince myself that everything is perfect. I can almost completely ignore the feathered serpent I see slinking after the lion-bird into the back room of the club. Almost.

CHAPTER 6

Gretchen

If a member of the monster squad is going to pull me out on a Friday night, the least it could do is pick a better club than Synergy. It's bad enough I have to spend all day with the hormonal sheep at school, I'd rather avoid them in the off-hours. But this seems to be a favourite freakazoid haunt lately. I'm practically a resident.

Nightclubs give me the snooze in general, and Synergy is more nondescript than most. It's on a side street in the industrial section of Potrero Hill – which might as well mean *completely sketchy after dark* – and from the outside it looks like any other warehouse building. The big, thuggy-looking guy at the door and the occasional line along the sidewalk are the only clues to the raging party inside.

Leaving Moira double-parked behind a Hummer in the empty lot next door, I do my mental gear check as I stifle a yawn. Hunting three nights in a row is tough, especially on back-to-back-to-back week nights. I feel like I might never catch up on sleep again.

My boots crunch on the gritty sidewalk as I head for

the front door. I hand my ID to the bouncer. He's six four, about two eighty, with a buzz cut and bug eyes that indicate one too many steroid cocktails. A dead ringer for the Gegenees giant I took out a few weeks ago, only without the two extra pairs of arms. Even though I've been here a lot lately, he scrutinises my driver's licence like he's trying to read Plato in the original Ancient Greek.

"Gretchen Sharpe?" He eyes the photo, then me, and then the photo again.

This one is my actual ID. Synergy is all ages, which means my sixteen-year-old self is perfectly legal. On occasions when I have to track into an alcohol-serving, twenty-one-and-over club, I've got a collection of fakes to get me in the door, with my hypno powers as a convenient backup.

Bug boy takes his job a little too seriously. If I were in search of underage drinking opportunities, I wouldn't be here. They don't even serve alcohol.

"That's me, Jocko," I say, giving him my best I'm-not-trying-to-do-anything-even-remotely-illegal smile. He probably wouldn't appreciate my I'm-just-trying-to-get-rid-of-the-deadly-monster-you-let-inside smirk.

After cross-checking my licence and my face a few more times, he hands back my ID and says, "Ten dollars. Pay inside."

I breeze past him and push open the door. The nauseating rotten-garbage scent of the griffin is worse than the overused fog machine. It's so strong, I can't immediately pinpoint the source. Guess I'll have to rely on other senses this time.

After handing my cover charge over to the cashier, I step into the giant black box that is Synergy. The space is wall-to-wall people, most of them under twenty-one. It's a sea of bumping and grinding, penned in on one side by the virgin-beverage-serving bar and on the other by a raised stage that is a favourite of PVC-trousers-and-eyeliner-wearing boys who like boys. And the occasional girl who likes boys who like boys, despite their obvious lack of interest in what she has to offer.

Tonight there's a DJ set up at one end of the stage, shouting out dance instructions and tweaking the bass on the unidentifiable music pounding through the speakers. Permanent eardrum damage in the making.

With the added filter of my sunglasses I mostly make out shapes and outlines. The lights hanging from the ceiling grid turn the throbbing masses into a sea of yellow, teal and hot pink. A normal girl would be nauseous. I've never claimed to be normal. Putrid eau de griffin and the revolting colour combination are everyday hazards of the job.

"If I were a bloodthirsty half-lion, half-eagle, where would I be?" I muse.

Being a few inches taller would definitely be a benefit at this point. I need line of sight, which means I need a better vantage point. Higher ground.

Shoving through the labyrinth of bodies, I make my way to the elevated stage. I place one hand on the front edge and vault myself up onto the platform. From my new perch I can see the entire room. I lift my shades to get a better look.

Plenty of gyrating hips, glitter-enhanced cleavage and titanium body piercings, but no griffin.

After winding across the stage to the back wall, I leap down, landing Doc Martens-first in the doorway that looks onto the techno room. It's almost as full as the main room, but with a tenth of the lighting.

"Why do they always go for the back rooms?"

Easier to lure some lonely, heartbroken or otherwise desperate human into a dark corner, I suppose. Synergy's back room is darker than the deepest corner of Hades. Even if the monsters had no veil, no one would notice them standing two feet away in this black hole.

I sniff test the room and discover that the smell is coming from outside, from the open door leading on to the small courtyard to the right. As soon as I step out under the stars, I see it. Prowling around a pair of girls at a picnic table who look like they've been drinking something that didn't come from the alcohol-free bar.

They're sitting ducks.

I'm about to step through the doorway and introduce the griffin to a shiny pair of fangs when I catch a new scent.

I stopped my scan of the courtyard when I spotted the griffin and the party girls, but as I complete my survey, I see the second beastie. A great big serpent thing covered in dark green and brown feathers.

"What?"

Before they spot me – or notice that I've spotted them – I duck back into the techno room to regroup. Two monsters? That's impossible. They can only get out of their realm one at a time. It's one of the first things Ursula taught me when I followed her out of that warehouse four years ago.

She'd led the way to a nearby diner, not uttering another word to me until the waitress placed a steaming bowl of stew in front of me. Ursula waited until I had a spoonful in my mouth before saying, "I know you see monsters."

My only response was a brief hesitation before swallowing and taking another bite. If this lady was going to tell me I was nuts, just like Phil and Barb always did, I'd just take the hot meal and then take off.

"I also know you are not insane."

At that point I didn't think anything could shock me more. I put down the spoon and asked, "How do you know that?"

"Because," she said with a warm smile, "I see them too."

I was wrong. That shocked the life out of me.

"You—" I couldn't even speak. Someone like me. I never knew how much I wanted that – needed that – until right then. I balled my fists in my lap and asked, "What *are* we?"

"You belong to an elite lineage of guardians," she explained. "Destined to hunt down the monsters that escape into our realm and send them back to theirs."

I can't remember how long we sat in that diner, me asking questions and her answering. It felt like years. Sometimes her answers were cryptic; some questions she refused to answer at all, promising all would be revealed in time.

As she explained about my heritage, about my destiny to keep the human world safe from the kind of monsters most people think exist only in ancient myths, I was scared. Fine, terrified. How could I, a lone twelve-year-old girl, stop all these awful things from prowling the streets?

She smiled at me, her grey eyes full of caring and compassion – two emotions that had been in short supply when she found me living on the street – and said, "You are stronger than you think."

"But what if they surround me?" I asked. "What if a bunch of them gang up on me? I could never win."

She reached out with her elegantly wrinkled hand and gently patted mine. "Millennia ago, when your ancient ancestor Medusa was slain, the doorway to the abyss was left inadequately guarded and the world faced the great danger of being overrun by monsters. The gods convened a council to decide how to proceed."

The gods. Like the ones in action movies and old myths. She said it like they were real, like they were sitting around somewhere deciding people's fates. And, as crazy as it sounded, I somehow knew she was telling me the truth.

"Some wished to see that realm sealed completely," she continued, "though doing so would have caused the death of every creature inside."

"What's wrong with that?" Didn't seem like such a bad plan to me, considering the kind of nasty beasts I'd seen prowling the streets. "The monsters are bad. Why shouldn't they die?"

Slowly shaking her head, she said, "Things are not that simple." She let out a small sigh. "Others thought the gateway should be thrown open, allowing monsters of all varieties to walk free among humans."

What morons thought that was a good idea?

"To appease all sides, the gods left a gap." Ursula smiled at me. "A tiny and ever-moving window that allows but a single monster at a time to leave their realm. The gods knew there would always be one of our kind on hand to defend the opening."

I sighed with relief. That was somewhat reassuring. One at a time seemed a lot more manageable than all at once. For the first time, I believed that I could actually do this, I could actually be the huntress. For the last four years, Ursula has been right. The rules have remained in effect, and I've never seen more than one creature per night. Ever.

Until tonight.

"Something's out of whack." First Ursula takes off out of cell phone range without leaving a note. Now two monsters are prowling the same club at the same time. "Something is definitely—"

"Gretchen!"

For the love of Medusa. I'd forgotten number three on my list of out-of-the-ordinary. Nick. The boy who won't leave me alone.

At least this one doesn't have anything to do with myth.

My first instinct is to ignore him. Any normal male would read that as a neon sign saying *Go away!*, but Nick has proven himself incapable of common male normality. If I ignore him and get on with my fight, he'll probably follow me out into the courtyard and wind up getting himself killed.

I need to throw him off the scent once and for all so I can go about my business in peace. Direct orders don't seem to work. Instead, I try for disdain.

"What do you want?"

"Nice to see you too," he teases, unfazed by my verbal

venom. "Funny running into you here. I didn't know you—"

"Yeah, it's a riot." I jab my fists to my hips. "Look, I was just—"

"Can I get you a drink?"

My brain screams. Nothing works with this boy.

"Are you deficient?" I ask, throwing off all pretence of any kind and being as straightforward as I can without telling him my secret. "What about me has ever said, 'Yes, please keep hitting on me'?"

A slow, suggestive smile spreads across his frustrating lips.

"Your mouth may not say that," he says, stepping close. "But your eyes... well, they're saying something else altogether."

I roll those eyes behind my sunglasses, resisting the urge to knock him out with a solid punch to the left temple and be done with him. "You can't even see my eyes."

"Can't I?"

"No, you—" Then it hits me like a thunderbolt. My *eyes*.

I am such an idiot. I can't believe I haven't thought to use my hypno powers on him. That only proves the boy messes with my brain. He needs to be gone, now, before something terrible happens.

In a heartbeat, I flick my shades up, stare deep into

Nick's dark gaze, and say, "You have somewhere else to be."

His brows fall and he gets a blank look on his face. Success! Finally he'll be out from underfoot. What good is having super-hypnotic power if I don't use it for my own benefit every now and again? Consider Nick a memory.

As I turn away, ready to forget him and figure out how to face the pair of monsters outside, Nick grabs my arm.

"Nope," he says with that annoying smile on his utterly unhypnotised face. "I think I'm exactly where I need to be."

You have got *to be kidding me.* The one guy who won't take the hint that I'm not interested, *and* he's the one person immune to my hypno-eyes? Something is not right about that.

I add it to the list of recent abnormalities and then file it away. No time to dwell on that at the moment. Right now, I have a pair of beasties with hungry eyes outside playing with their party-girl food. I need to take care of them before they decide they're ready for their meal. And Nick needs to be gone before I do.

Pushing him away doesn't work, and knocking him out would draw too much attention, so I'm left with only one option.

"Fine," I say with a sigh, as if I'm giving in to his advances. "You can get me a drink." I try to think of something that will take the most time, giving me the biggest window to send my unwelcome friends back to where they belong. "A virgin strawberry daiquiri."

Surely the mixing and the blending will take more than half a second.

With a wink, he's gone, and I'm heading through the courtyard door.

Thanks to my hesitation at seeing double, the pair of monsters has now bracketed the two drunk girls, and the critters are practically salivating at the prospect of a juicy snack. There are quite a few other people out in the courtyard, which means strategy is going to be critical. I evaluate my targets and quickly decide that, between the two, the serpent thing – ophis pterotus is its official name, I think – will be the easier fight. No limbs or claws to fight back with. Fangs, of course, but I've got a pair of my own.

What I don't need is a bunch of teen party hounds thinking they need to break up a fight. Or, worse, stepping in to defend me. Now is not the time to let the ordinary humans think for themselves, so I fold my sunglasses into a cargo pocket and walk over to the nearest group.

"Hey guys," I say with a bright smile. Scanning my gaze over the several pairs of eyes now looking at me, I instruct, "Whatever you see going on over there," I gesture towards the beastie-occupied picnic table, "you don't need to get involved. We'll just be playing around."

Their blank faces nod, and I hurry on to do the same

to the handful of groups scattered around the courtyard.

As I move to the last, a gaggle of giggling girls in the far corner, my heart begins to race, not out of fear but out of anticipation. This is going to be a good fight.

Not that I'm thrilled about the sudden change of rules, but monster hunting has become pretty routine lately. Sniff, find, fight, bite. Go home and take a shower. Repeat.

This fight should present a welcome challenge.

Everything will be fine as long as I follow the two carved-in-stone commandments of monster fighting.

First rule, never let them bite the right wrist, or the super-healing powers of the blood in that artery will give them a period of enhanced abilities and invincibility. The last thing I need is a monster that can't be sent home. The left wrist is fine, because blood from that artery is deadly. But because humans are so often annoying bystanders, it's best to keep that one protected too. Hence the Kevlar wrist cuffs.

Second rule, go for the pulse point. It's different on every monster, but there is always a critical vein, one that feeds directly to the heart – or hearts – and assures an instantaneous trip back to their murky abyss. Other blood vessels work too. Eventually. But who knows what might happen to me or the innocent humans involved in the time my monster-transporting venom takes to make its way to the pumper. One stab in the key vein and the fight is over in a heartbeat. Literally.

I've put in my time studying the ring binders full of monster files Ursula has in the loft library, to memorise the target on every creature I might encounter. But I can't remember everything. And they must be reproducing like bunnies in their realm, creating hybrids and mutant freaks no one has ever seen before, because there are always new, unknown and unidentified monsters showing up. Keeps the job interesting, anyway.

Before tonight, since it's only ever been one monster at a time, knowing the pulse point never seemed imperative. Now, as I turn to face the pair, I kinda wish I remembered where to chomp down.

"No!" I shout as I watch the serpent thing bite down on the blonde girl's neck.

No time for strategy. In a flying leap, I launch myself onto the serpent thing's back. It releases the girl with a shove, sending her to the ground. Twisting to get a look at its unwelcome passenger, the serpent thing unwittingly gives me a choice opportunity to introduce it to my fangs.

Reaching my head around what I can only guess is its neck region, I aim my bite right below its jaw. Before I can sink my fangs, the two girls formerly known as dinner start screaming. Arms clamped around the serpent's writhing body, I struggle to make eye contact with the girls, hoping to quiet their attention-drawing screams before the un-hypnotised masses inside catch wind of the trouble out here.

Even if they did, though, all they would see is me hanging on the back of some beefy slimeball, not some feathery snake.

I focus on the monster prey, trying to get the girls out of harm's way. Not an easy task while clamped onto a giant snake that's trying to violently dislodge me from its body. I hold on with a death grip and keep my eyes trained on the screaming girls, waiting for one to look at me directly.

Finally, one of them throws her wide-eyed gaze at me. Score one for eye contact. Before she can look away, I say, "Run! These guys were about to assault you. Get out of here!"

She screams louder. "They tried to assault me!"

The other girl looks totally confused, like her friend has gone instantly insane. Kind of true. But the hypnotised girl grabs her by the arm and drags her out of the courtyard at full speed.

By now, monster number two has realised what's going on and has circled the picnic table vacated by the fleeing girls. It tries to grab me off the serpent's back, but the serpent is moving too wildly for the griffin to grab hold. Besides, lions' paws aren't exactly dexterous. Still, it has poisonous claws I'd rather avoid.

The griffin clamps both paws around one of my ankles, yanking hard to pull me off the snake's back. I manage a fierce kick to its beak with my other foot, sending it reeling back. It doesn't lose its grip on my ankle.

"Come on," I mutter, wondering if maybe I should have let one or two of the human guys help me out.

No, of course not. They'd end up getting hurt or killed, and I'd have to do a lot of hypno clean-up. And since the hypno power isn't permanent, eventually there would be questions.

Telling myself to stay on track, I ignore the lion-bird behind me and try again for the serpent's feathered flesh. If I can get one of them gone, I'll be able to focus on the other. As I'm about to bite down, the griffin snatches my other ankle and tries to twist me around. My spine feels like it's going to snap from the torque.

"Hey!" Nick shouts, running back into the courtyard. "Let her go!"

I should send him away too. Normally I would. But I'm feeling at a bit of a disadvantage – my training has never covered how to face two attackers, because we never thought I'd need to know. If Nick wants to save me from this pair of goons, then maybe I should let him. Can't save the world from beasties if I become monster food tonight.

"Get the one off my feet!" I shout. If Nick can keep himself from being eaten for five seconds, I can get rid of snake thing and then take out the griffin before things get really out of control.

In a flash, Nick is across the courtyard and landing a solid punch in the vulnerable spot between the griffin's eyes. Pretty good aim for someone who can't see the monster's true face. Stunned, the griffin lets me go. I take the opportunity to bite the snake's neck. It disappears out from under me, flashing back to the prison realm where it belongs, and I fall to the ground, barely getting my feet under me to land in a crouch.

Guess I got that pulse point right.

I don't understand all the details about the process. Ursula's tried to explain it to me, but there's too much magic and physiology involved for it to make any sense. All I really know is that something in my venom is a GO DIRECTLY TO JAIL card for monsterkind. Don't really need to know the details, do I? I'm fine with calling it a mystery of mythology, so long as they go away for a good long while. Too bad there are always more to replace them.

With the serpent creature gone, I turn to help Nick.

He's actually holding his own pretty well for a guy fighting an eagle-headed lion. The griffin is pinned beneath him, roaring and lashing out with four paws full of skin-slicing, poison-tipped, razor-sharp claws.

How on earth am I going to explain this crazy fight away? Especially since Nick appears to be the one and only human immune to my hypno magic.

"A little help!" he calls.

No time to worry about the aftermath at the moment. The griffin gets some leverage and flips over, reversing their positions so that Nick is pinned to the ground. The giant beak is heading for Nick's beautiful face. Nick is holding it off – barely – but his arms are beginning to shake. He's weakening.

No wonder. He's battling a superpowerful mythical creature.

I push off and leap onto the creature's back, trying to remember the illustration that shows a griffin's most vulnerable spot. I know I've studied this one – it's a classic. Distracted away from Nick's face, the eagle head whips around and tries to peck me off its back.

Why can't I picture the drawing?

In a flash, Ursula's diagram of the griffin pops into my mind. I see a bright red circle around the beast's right rear thigh. Bingo! Target acquired.

In a feat of acrobatic wonder, I spin round on the lion's back, wrap my arms around its waist and lunge my head down to sink my teeth into the muscular spot just above the bend in its leg.

The griffin has just enough time to scratch its beak across the back of my neck before vanishing into the dark.

"Ooof!" I land, half on Nick, half on the concrete, with a thud that knocks the wind out of me.

This was the hardest fight I've had since… well, ever. Even my very first – a giant turtle that was attacking tourists down at the maritime park – was a piece of seaweed-wrapped cake compared to this.

With the adrenaline flooding my bloodstream, I can't feel any of the aches and pains I know will be there in the morning. But not even a morphine drip could kill the searing pain burning across the back of my neck.

"You okay?" Nick asks.

He doesn't even sound out of breath.

I roll off him. "Bastard scratched me."

"Gretchen," he asks, "are you—"

"I need to go."

I can't stick around to answer Nick's questions because, well, there aren't any good answers, are there? Besides, thanks to the griffin's last-ditch effort, some nasty monster venom is now making its way through my circulatory system. Wait too long before treating it and I'm in for several days of excruciating pain – which I know from an up-close-and-personal experience with a cynolycus.

The clock is ticking.

Without waiting for Nick to say or ask or do anything, I jump to my feet and run from the courtyard. As I shove my way through the crowd inside, I wonder how on earth I'm going to explain the fight and the disappearing guys to Nick come Monday at school. I've never dealt with a hypno-immune human before, didn't even know they existed. And I know he's not the kind of guy to let this go without explanation.

Hopefully Ursula will be back before I have to face him again. She'll have some suggestions.

I'm halfway through the main club room when I'm hit

with the smell of burning sulphur. Another monster? Not just any monster, either. Sulphur means a fire-breather.

"You have *got* to be kidding me," I mutter.

That makes three in one night. What is this, the freakin' monsterpocalypse?

Thankfully, I don't have to look far to spot the lizard with a spiked tail and smoke curling out of its nostrils. It's dancing by itself in the middle of the room. Even if they disguise their true appearance, some beasties are less than welcome in a crowd. Bad body odour is bad body odour, no matter the species. I kind of empathise with its loneliness.

"Poor thing."

Still, it has to go.

I step up behind the lizard, ignoring the throbbing pain in my neck, and grab it by the wrist. It whirls around to face me, sending its spiked tail whipping through the crowd.

Most people don't react, since all they see is a kind of homely woman in bondage-worthy stilettos and a floral sundress. But as I force its wrist to my mouth, I see the girl behind the creature leap out of the way of the swinging tail.

As I stab my fangs into the creature's wrist – not the pulse point, apparently, because the lizard doesn't go anywhere – the girl turns around.

With a gasp, I drop the creature's wrist. Standing there, in the middle of a dance floor surrounded by dozens of ordinary teens, is a girl who looks exactly like me. I mean *exactly* like me. And, I realise as we blink at each other, she saw the lizard's tail.

Just then, a stab of pain sears across my neck. *Tick tock, tick tock.*

Without stopping to think, I step forward, grab the girl by the waist and fling her over my shoulder. I don't wait for anyone to notice or even for the lizard to disappear. It will. I race for the front door, knowing that eventually my venom will reach the creature's heart and send it home. Right at this moment my two bigger concerns are the monster juice making its way towards *my* heart and the Gretchen lookalike hanging limp as I run out of the club.

CHAPTER 7

Grace

Maybe I should have screamed, or kicked my legs, or struggled to keep from getting shoved into the black Mustang. On any other day I probably would have. Maybe this is another manifestation of my insanity, letting some random girl kidnap me from a nightclub without saying a word. But the truth is, I'm curious. I'm totally freaked about the girl who looks like me and the monster she bit on the wrist. Because she obviously saw the fire-breathing lizard too, which leaves limited explanations.

Either she's another figment of my imagination — though the bruise on my left hip suggests otherwise — or we're both equally insane (What are the odds of that?) or… the monsters are real.

I know which option I'm rooting for.

As she jams the car into gear and squeals out into the street, I study her profile. It's like looking at a photograph of myself. We are virtually identical; the only differences I can see are cosmetic. Her long dark-blonde hair is woven back in a tight French braid. Her face is clear of make-up and there are no earrings in her unpierced lobes. And her jaw is set in a rigid clench, with tension that follows the lines of her throat, around to the back of her neck where—

"You're hurt," I blurt.

She flicks me an annoyed glance. "I know."

"You need to go to a hospital."

She shifts gears, speeding through a yellow light.

"No hospital can fix this."

I nod, somehow instinctively understanding what she means. A monster caused that wound. It couldn't have been the lizard I saw right before she hauled me over her shoulder, because I'd have seen if it had been able to attack her. So it must have been one of the other two.

"Was it the eagle-headed lion?" I ask as we crest a hill and spend a couple of seconds airborne before slamming back onto the street. "Or the feathered snake thing?"

"The griffin and the Ophis pterotus." Her knuckles turn white on the steering wheel. "You saw those too?"

A silent cheer erupts in my brain.

"Actually, I…" As weird as it feels to say out loud, it's an amazing relief to know I'm not going insane. Or, at least if I am, this girl is going with me. "Yes. And I saw another one last night. At a dim sum parlour."

She snorts. "The minotaur."

"Ew, right?" I shove away a mental image of the drooling bull's head. My attempt at shared grossness gets no response, so I admit, "I thought I was losing my mind."

The girl swerves the car along some winding street and guns it as we pass the lower slope of a big green park. "Unfortunately," she says, turning at an old Spanish-style gatehouse, "the monsters are all too real."

I have a second when I wonder if maybe I still am going crazy. I mean, maybe I'm imagining this identical twin I never knew I had. This identical twin I always wished I had – what little girl doesn't? She could be as much a mental trick as the monsters. An expression of an adopted girl's wishful thinking.

But then she cuts the wheel hard to the left, sending me slamming against the passenger door, and races towards the end wall of what looks like a giant warehouse building. No way am I making up the throbbing in my shoulder. Or the fact that we're barrelling towards a completely solid wall.

"Watch out!" I scream.

Before I can finish my warning, a hidden garage door glides up in the middle of the wall, and the Mustang flies into the building. She slams on the brakes, sending the car squealing across the concrete. I scream again, convinced we're going to skid into the corrugated metal interior wall.

We don't.

The car screeches to a halt with a good ten feet between us and the wall. Heart racing and breathing heavy, I stare wide-eyed at my double.

She doesn't say a word, just yanks the handbrake, turns

off the car, and climbs out. I've barely unbuckled my seatbelt with shaking hands when I see her march across the empty space and climb a set of metal spiral stairs in the far corner. As I manage to pull myself out of the car, my legs as wiggly as wet noodles, I see her disappearing from the balcony through a rusty metal door.

"Quite the welcome," I whisper.

Not knowing what else to do, I follow her.

My foot is on the first step when my cell phone rings. I pull it out of my jeans pocket and check the screen.

Thane.

Oh shoot, I totally forgot about him and Milo. Meeting a long-lost twin tends to have that effect, I suppose. I need to come up with a believable explanation – emphasis on the believable bit – for my disappearance. I am so not good at coming up with cover stories, which is probably one of the reasons I've never snuck out of the house. I'd have no way to talk myself out of trouble if I got caught.

If I don't answer his call, though, things will only get worse. He would call Mom and Dad, and they would probably call the police, the fire department and every hospital in the Bay Area. And that's *if* he didn't see me get hauled out of the club over another girl's shoulder. Who knows what he saw or what he thinks happened.

Since he's waited this long to call, I hope that means he thinks I got lost on the way to the bathroom or something.

With a deep breath, I punch the answer button. "Hey,"

I say, trying to sound un-freaked out. "What's up?"

"Are you ready to go?"

Whew. He must not have seen me carried away like a sack of apples.

"Am I ready to go?" I ask to buy time.

"It's not a trick question."

Cover story, Grace. Come on, you're a smart girl. You can do this. "Um, I... er, ran into a new friend."

"New friend?"

"From school." For the first time, I'm really thankful Thane and I are not at the same school. Otherwise he'd know I haven't met a single person I could call a friend. "Yeah, she lives nearby and invited me over to watch movies."

"You left?"

The heavy silence after his question tells me he's angry. Rightfully so, since I bailed without telling him and can't exactly share the real reason.

"Sorry," I say, glancing up at the rusty door. I don't have time to deal with Thane right now. Not when I have a mysterious, monster-fighting twin upstairs who has answers to my burning questions. "I should have told you first."

"Grace—"

"Look, I gotta go," I said, partly because I don't want to risk answering any more questions, but also because my curiosity is killing me. I need to know what's up with the monsters and why no one else can see them and who the lookalike girl is and a million other things. Thane will be waiting at home. I can only find my answers upstairs. "I'll call home to let them know what's up."

I hang up before he can argue.

I allow myself a few seconds of rest against the railing before gathering the courage to call Mom. Before gathering the courage to *lie* to Mom. In the end, the call isn't as stressful as I feared. I give her the story about running into a friend and going over to watch movies. After assuring her that my friend's parents would bring me home before midnight, she lets me go without an interrogation. She's probably thrilled to think I've made a friend.

"Little does she know," I whisper, pocketing my phone and following my double up the stairs.

As I push open the squeaky door, I'm shocked to step into an entirely modern space. All the surfaces are gleaming black and white, polished metal and shiny glass. The complete opposite of the dull beige exterior and the rusty metal garage area.

"Wow," I can't help but say to the expansive room.

It's such a huge, open space. I sweep my gaze around the room, taking everything in. Directly in front of the door is what looks like a living room, with black leather sofas and armchairs around a metal-and-glass coffee table. Along the right wall is a trio of doors, maybe bedrooms and a bathroom, on either side of a flat panel TV the size of my bed. Across the living room is a glassed-in space lined with full bookshelves and with a giant conference table surrounded by chairs in the centre and a computer workstation along one wall.

To my left is another door next to a black granite and stainless-steel kitchen and an equally sleek dining room.

Despite all the slick and shiny covering every surface, the thing that enthrals me is the far wall. Floor-to-ceiling windows, with sliding glass doors and a balcony beyond. Both the dining room and the library have unobstructed, picture-perfect views.

I make my way past the kitchen towards the balcony. I slide open the doors and step out into the chilly air. The view of the Bay and the houses, boats and other lights twinkling all around is breathtaking. I'm so caught up by the sights before me that I don't hear my double walk up behind me.

"What's your name?" she demands.

My heart jump-starts and I whirl around with a gasp, clutching my palm to my chest. "Omigosh, you scared me."

She lifts her brows.

She's pulled off the long-sleeved black T-shirt she was wearing at the club and is now in a black tank top. One leg of her cargo trousers is rolled up to the knee, and her ankle is wrapped in white gauze. She's dabbing at the back of her neck with a cotton pad soaked in a blue liquid that smells like mouthwash.

"Grace," I say, leaning back against the railing. "My name is Grace."

"Grace what?"

"Whitfield," I answer. "What's your name?"

She turns away, walking back inside. I follow her through the living room and into a brightly lit bathroom, a little annoyed that she ignored my question. Twisted around with her back to the mirror, she's trying to secure a second gauze bandage to the back of her neck.

"Here," I offer. "Let me help."

She gives me a sceptical look but doesn't argue when I brush her hand aside and hold the bandage to her wound. As I tear off a piece of first-aid tape, she mumbles, "Gretchen."

"Gretchen?" I echo, securing a second piece of tape.

"Sharpe," she says, almost reluctantly.

I release the bandage, and it seems like it's going to stay in place. I step back and around to face Gretchen. With a smile, I say, "All patched up."

She mutters a quiet "Thanks," and then turns to put away the first-aid supplies.

I would offer to help, but I have a feeling she's not interested.

"So, Gretchen," I say instead. "Wanna tell me what's going on?"

She closes up the first-aid box, slides it under the sink

and then leans back against the counter. It's hard not to squirm as she scrutinises me with eyes the same silvery grey as my own.

"That depends," she says, crossing her arms over her chest. "How much do you know?"

I laugh. A big giant guffaw just bursts out, I can't help it. It's a slightly hysterical reaction to an extremely ridiculous question. "How much do I know?" I ask, still laughing. "I know that yesterday I started seeing monsters from Greek mythology come to life, and you look like my twin."

She looks at me, like she's waiting for me to say more. When I don't, she asks, "That's all?"

"To the syllable."

"And before yesterday you never saw a monster?" She uncrosses her arms and tucks her hands into the back pockets of her black cargo trousers.

"Not once."

"What happened yesterday?" she asks.

"I told you," I say, getting a little frustrated that she's doing all of the asking and none of the answering. "I saw the minotaur in the dim sum parlour. And then I—"

"No, before that." She shifts her weight to the other foot. "What was different about yesterday? What's changed in your life recently?"

Well, there's only been one really big change.

"We moved to San Francisco," I say, using up the last

of my patience. "Yesterday was my first day at the new school."

"That explains it," Gretchen says, as if now everything should be clear. "Monsters don't get far from the city."

Without another word she walks out of the bathroom, leaving me standing there like an idiot, facing my own reflection. That explains it? That doesn't explain *anything*.

"Grrr," I growl at the mirror.

I let myself get kidnapped by a stranger and then lied to my family about it. I at least deserve some answers in exchange. Obviously, she's not going to give them to me. I have to go after them.

I stomp out of the bathroom.

"Look," I say, finding her in the kitchen. "I want to know what's going on. You obviously know a lot more than I do."

"It would be hard not to," Gretchen says, pulling an energy drink out of the giant silver fridge. "Want one?"

"No. I want answers."

"Fine," she says with a sigh. She pulls the tab on the energy drink and throws back half the can before continuing. "Here's what I know. I'm a descendant of the gorgon Medusa, and—"

"Medusa?" I gasp. I don't have to think hard to remember that character from mythology. "The snake-haired monster who turned people to stone with her eyes?"

"Same one." She finishes off her energy drink and

tosses the can into a recycling bin. "That's not the real story, though."

She acts like that's the end of it, like that's all the info I'm going to get. I jab my hands onto my hips and give her my best scowl.

Finally, she sighs and says, "Medusa was a guardian, not a monster. Along with her two immortal sisters, she kept monsters from terrorising the human world."

My arms drop. *The human world.* The earth tilts a little beneath my feet. Why do I feel like, from this moment on, that's going to have a slightly different meaning?

"And the eyes-to-stone thing?" I force the question out around my shock.

"Pure myth." Gretchen starts to rub her neck and then winces with pain. "Her eyes had the power to hypnotise – temporarily. Totally harmless."

"Wow, that's…"

If it weren't for everything I've seen in the last twenty-four hours, I would think she's lying. I shake my head, realising that everything I thought I knew – about myth, about Medusa, about whether monsters might really exist – is wrong.

"How…" I begin again. I have to swallow before I can finish. "How did that happen?" I ask. "How did the real story get so twisted?"

"Ursula, my mentor, says it began with Athena's jealousy." Gretchen shrugs as if it's no big deal. "She thought Medusa seduced Poseidon, and she wanted revenge."

More mythology lessons resurface. "That's why she helped Perseus kill Medusa, right?"

Gretchen nods, and I feel a little surge of pride.

"Ever since her assassination it's been up to her descendants to keep the monster population in check," she explains. "Something I've been doing for the past four years."

Four years? That's a long time, a quarter of my life. I wonder if it's been a quarter of her life too. As much as I might want to believe she's my long-lost sister, just because we look alike and see the same monsters doesn't necessarily make it true.

But I have to ask.

"And do you think... ?" I can't bring myself to finish the question.

In truth, I'm not sure what I want the answer to be. There are pros and cons either way. If it's yes, then I'm some kind of mythological monster hunter, destined to fight the disgusting creatures I've been seeing for two days. If it's no, then Gretchen isn't my twin and that empty spot in my heart stays wretchedly empty.

"That you're one too?" she finishes for me. "I guess it's possible."

As I look at the girl who might be my sister, I realise the cons don't matter. Blood matters. Family matters.

"I'm adopted," I blurt, suddenly *wanting* everything to

be true. *Needing* it to be true, needing Gretchen to be my real flesh and blood, even knowing what that means. As much as I love Mom and Dad and Thane, we don't share any genes. It's not the same. "I don't know anything about my birth parents."

Gretchen hesitates, freezing like a statue. I try to tune in, to sense some kind of twin connection. But she's like a brick wall. Finally, after a long exhale, she says, "I was adopted too."

There's something in her tone, in her use of the past tense about her adoption, that makes me think that she wasn't quite as lucky as I have been. I wouldn't trade my mom and dad for anyone. I know things could be so much worse, that other kids wind up in awful homes all the time.

My heart goes out to her.

"Are you sixteen?" I ask, knowing this is the only way to be anything close to certain right now. It's a very *Parent Trap* moment, only without the summer camp and the prank war. When she nods, I say, "My birthday is July thirtieth."

I hold my breath, waiting. Hoping.

It feels like a lifetime before she says, "Mine too."

My mind reels. Literally reels. I've always wondered about my birth parents, imagining what they might look like or what kind of people they are. Where did I get my silver eyes and my crooked pinky fingers? I used to spend hours at the mirror, studying every little detail and wondering where it came from. The identity of my birth parents has never been something I desperately needed to know, though. Mom and Dad are my parents in every way that counts. Maybe by the time I turn eighteen and can get access to my records, I'll be ready to investigate.

But now, finding out that not only am I a descendant of some mythological guardian, but I also have a sister. A *twin* sister. It's a little—

"I think I need to sit down," I say, feeling a little bit light-headed.

Gretchen pushes herself away from the counter. "Let's go to the library. You can sit and I'll try calling Ursula." She leads the way into the room lined on three walls with books and ring binders. "There's been something seriously weird going on lately, and she might know why."

She yanks open the sliding glass balcony door, and I suck in a breath of salty night air as I drop into a chair at the conference table.

"Weird how?" I ask.

"Like three monsters showing up in one night." She drops into the desk chair and spins around once.

"That doesn't usually happen?"

"No," Gretchen pulls out her phone and starts dialling. "There is supposed to be a one-beastie-per-night rule in place."

That's a relief. Or it would be if it were still true.

"What about during the day?" I want to ask as many

questions as possible while she's answering. Who knows how long this opportunity will last.

"They don't come out when the sun is up." She dials the phone and holds it to her ear. "They're nocturnal, I guess."

With Gretchen's attention fully on her phone call, I turn mine to the room around me. I instantly forget the crazy news that just moments ago threatened to overwhelm me, the news that I have a sister and a heritage and, apparently, a destiny. Instead, I am hypnotised by row after row of books.

I'm not really such a bookworm – my academic speciality veers more towards the digital – but I appreciate the amount of data and research contained in these volumes. It lures me out of the chair and towards the shelves.

My fingers trail respectfully over their spines as I scan the titles. There's an entire case of books on martial arts and fighting techniques. Another two full of books on mythology and ancient Greece. The rest are titles on a variety of minor subjects, like computers and technology and geology and cartography. What those have to do with monster fighting I'm not sure, but they must be useful.

I'm a little gaga over all the books, but it's the final case that captures my attention. Its shelves are full of white three-ring binders. Not so unusual, I suppose, but the spine labels promise something very unusual inside: MINOTAURS, HYDRAS, SERPENT HYBRIDS, CHIMERAS, LAELAPSES, UNIDENTIFIED SPECIES.

With a quick glance at Gretchen, who has left her chair and is staring out over the Bay, I pull the one labelled MINOTAURS off the shelf and flip through. There are sections on history, traits and characteristics, preferences, sociology, physiology and battle tactics. There are myths and legends about the minotaurs. A table of reported sightings. A detailed anatomical drawing, with a big red circle around the back of the neck.

"Come on, Ursula!"

Gretchen's boots squeak on the sparkly white tiles as she starts pacing back and forth, dialling and redialling her phone. With no luck, judging from the curse that punctuates the end of each attempt. With a final curse, she throws the phone onto the table in the middle of the room.

I slide the minotaur ring binder back into place. After a quick estimate, I conservatively calculate that there must be more than two hundred ring binders. Two hundred different kinds of monsters, with valuable hunting information trapped inside the pages. The whole collection should really be digitised. Maybe even made into a smartphone app so Gretchen can get the info she needs anywhere, anytime. That could be a lifesaver sometime.

"Where is Ursula?" Gretchen snaps. "It's not like her to disappear for days at a time without letting me know."

She sounds really worried, and she doesn't seem like the worrying sort.

"How long has she been gone?" I ask.

Gretchen spears me with a look, and I'm pretty sure she forgot I was here. Or maybe thinks I'm to blame for the weirdness going around and her missing mentor. I hope it's the first, because I spotted what I thought was a knife handle sticking out of her boot when she carried me out of the club. I confirmed it when her trouser leg was rolled up earlier. I bet she knows how to use it too.

Finally, reluctantly, she says, "A few days. Maybe a week."

"Does she leave often?"

"Yes," Gretchen answers. "But she usually sends me an email or a text so I know she's okay."

"She could be somewhere with no signal," I suggest.

"Yeah, maybe," Gretchen agrees.

I think she's humouring me.

For what feels like an hour Gretchen stares blankly at the table and I stare blankly at Gretchen. Like I'm staring in the mirror. I mean, it's a little freaky. Our faces are identical. And even without an adoption record or a DNA test, I know without a doubt she's my sister. My twin. I can *feel* it in the same way I feel Thane when he sneaks up behind me. I just know.

"So…" I finally say to break the silence. "What do we do now?"

"How should I know?" Gretchen barks.

I jump back a little at her harsh tone.

"Everything's going sideways at the moment. Ursula's missing, monsters are breaking the rules," she spears me with a glance, "you show up in the middle of it all."

Even though I didn't do anything but move to a new town, I feel a little guilty. Gretchen obviously thinks these changes might have something to do with me, and how do I know that they don't?

"I'm sorry, okay?" she says before I can apologise, still sounding agitated but a little more calm.

I cut her a little slack. "No problem," I say. "You're worried about your mentor. I understand."

It's a lot to take in all at once. Multiple monsters, missing mentor, long-lost twin. No wonder she's a little snappy.

She runs a hand over her hair, swiping her bangs back across her braid.

"Look, I think the best thing you can do," she says, her tone final and far more mature than our sixteen years should have made her, "is to go back to your world. Forget about this one. Go back to your life. You'll be safer there."

What? "I—"

"I'll drive you home."

"No, Gretchen," I argue. "I don't want to—"

She stomps out of the room without another word. I don't want to follow her. I want to stay here, to talk and get to know her and ask more questions. Does she sneeze in threes too? Does she hate cherries and love avocados? What's her worst subject in school? I can't just walk away from all of this. I can't just walk away from her.

If we're twins, like I have to believe we are, then her heritage is also mine. Her duty to hunt monsters is also mine. Is it fair to let her continue to carry that responsibility all on her own?

But as much as I want to embrace this new part of myself, I'm a little scared. I can see that her lifestyle is dangerous. I mean, she took down three mythological monsters by herself tonight. They probably don't go down without a serious fight. She got injured on her ankle and her neck, and I bet that's nothing compared to other injuries she's had. It's dangerous and probably potentially deadly.

Maybe Gretchen is right. Maybe I should go back to my safe world, with parents and a brother who love me very much and would be devastated if I got eaten by a chimera. If I stay and try to help, I might even get Gretchen hurt in the process.

My heart sinks at the thought of going back to my ordinary life and pretending this night never happened, but it might be for the best. For both of us.

Quietly, I follow Gretchen down to the car. As I drop

into the passenger seat and she revs the engine, I can't help feeling like a total coward. That somewhere, wherever she is, our birth mother is ashamed. Buildings blur by my window as I wipe a tear from my eye. But I don't say a word.

Coward it is.

CHAPTER 8

Grace

After a night of horrible and heartbreaking dreams, I finally drag myself out of bed Saturday morning with only an hour to spare before it turns into afternoon. As I face the mirror in the bathroom Thane and I share, I'm amazed I still look like myself. So many things changed last night, it seems impossible that I haven't.

I squeeze a dollop of toothpaste onto my brush. While I scrub back and forth across my teeth, memories flash through my mind. The minotaur. The griffin. The feathered snake and the fire-breathing lizard. Gretchen. Her Mustang. Her loft. Her library. The tight feeling in my chest when she told me to get lost. The look I imagine was on my face when I surrendered to my fear.

I spit into the sink.

"It's not like she wanted me around anyway," I say, trying to convince myself. "She wanted me gone."

As much as I might want to know my sister, she obviously doesn't want to know me. And I'm perfectly happy to pretend that monsters and Medusa are figments of myth.

"Minotaurs don't exist," I tell my reflection.

Maybe if I pretend hard enough, I'll actually believe it.

I stare into my silver-eyed reflection, willing myself to embrace the lie. To forget about Gretchen and minotaurs and my mythological heritage. To never see a monster again.

I sigh. "No such luck."

"Trying to will yourself bigger boobs?"

"Thane!" I gasp, spinning and throwing a hairbrush at his privacy-invading head. "Get out of here."

He ducks, avoiding death by hairbrush, and grins. I should be angry, but it's hard to be mad when he's in such a good mood. Especially after he was so angry at me for ditching the club.

"About last night," I say, knowing I need to apologise. "I should have told you before I left." Although it's hard to say your goodbyes when you're hanging over someone's shoulder. "I'm sorry."

He bends down to grab my brush, and when he stands back up, his entire demeanour has changed. "You should be."

"I…" How can I explain this without *explaining* this? "I was just so… excited to see my friend. She's really the only person I've connected with in San Francisco." True. "I didn't stop to think."

His expression doesn't change, but I can read the silent *obviously* as clearly as if he'd shouted.

"I'm sorry," I repeat. "It won't happen again."

He nods, accepting my apology, and I'm relieved. As much as I hate lying to my family, I hate being in fights with them more.

"Family breakfast," he says, handing me my hairbrush. "Mom made pancakes."

Mmmm. "I'll be right there."

He vanishes as silently as he appeared.

I take a few minutes to wash my face and run the brush through my hair. From the outside, I look like my normal self on a normal day, ready for a normal family breakfast. Well, at least one of the above is true.

I feel like I'm being pulled between two different worlds. On one side, there's the only family I've ever known. The mom and dad and brother I love more than anything and who love me back just as much.

On the other side, there's the family I never knew I had. The family I always dreamed about finding. A sister who, whether she wants to accept it or not, is as close to me as a person can get genetically. Somewhere, maybe, a biological mother who has answers about who and what we are. And a biological father too.

I don't even know which side my mythological lineage comes from, but it's a lineage that dates back thousands of years, to ancient Greece and beyond, to prehistoric myth.

How can I just pretend I don't know about any of those things?

"Gracie!" Dad calls down the hall. "Hurry your behind out here before your brother eats all the pancakes."

"Coming!" I shout back.

There isn't another option. Gretchen wants less than nothing to do with me – she made that a thousand per cent clear. And I have a loving, normal family waiting for me out there, expecting me to be the same old Grace I was yesterday. That's who I have to be right now.

Normal, I tell myself as I drop my hairbrush back into the drawer and slide the whole thing shut. *I can do this.*

In the dining room, I find Mom, Dad and Thane sitting round the table. There's a steaming pile of pancakes, a pitcher of warm maple syrup and a platter of greasy bacon. I force myself into the routine of an ordinary family breakfast. As I drop into my chair, Mom hands me the pancakes.

"Delicious," I hum, inhaling the tasty aroma. So much better than eau de monster.

No! I'm not going there.

I fork a short stack of pancakes onto my plate, smear them with butter and smother them with maple syrup. Thane waves the plate of bacon in my direction.

"Ha ha," I say, pushing it away.

He dumps half the bacon onto his plate. "Oink, oink."

"Thane," Mom chides.

"It's okay," I insist. "I'm used to it."

"That's my girl," Dad says. "Now, kiddos, tell me

about week one. Any horror stories to share?"

Horror stories? Absolutely. To share? Not on your life. Even if I can accept the fact that I'm not insane, there's no way I can tell anyone about seeing monsters. Or meeting my sister. As much as I believe it to be true, I don't think anyone else would.

"Nothing exciting," I say between bites of pancake. Ignoring the topic of my unwelcoming fellow students, I focus on academics. "Alpha has some awesome elective choices. Tae Kwon Do and Operatic Singing."

"Very impressive," Dad says with a nod. "And which classes are you electing to take?"

"Computer Science," I say.

Thane mutters, "Duh."

I throw a piece of pancake at his forehead. He dodges it, like the hairbrush, and it flies past him and onto the floor.

"And I'm thinking," I say, as if my brother isn't acting like an idiot this morning, "maybe... Yearbook."

Even though I've already picked my electives, part of me can't help protecting myself against potential disapproval. Ms West did say I could still change, and if Mom and Dad think Yearbook is a bad idea, then maybe I should.

Mom fills my glass with orange juice. "That sounds like fun," she says. "It'll be good for you to have something less academic."

Dad smiles, and I release a relieved sigh.

"I agree," he says as he grabs a piece of bacon off Thane's plate. "And what about you, Thane? How was your first week at Euclid?"

Thane shrugs, his entire body stiffening at the question. He hates talking about school because it inevitably leads to talking about his non-existent plans for the future. "Met a cool guy. Made the soccer team."

A cool guy. As if that's all there is to Milo. As if he's not beautiful and sweet and fun and... Okay, so maybe Thane wouldn't say all those things, but they're true.

Of course, by now Milo probably thinks I'm a flake for disappearing last night. Imagine if he knew I'm a descendant of a mythological monster too. Full-scale freak.

"You know," Dad says to Thane, "my company has a highly respected internship programme." He takes a sip of coffee. "You should consider applying."

My head drops and I keep my eyes glued to my plate. Dad and Thane have this continuing battle about Thane's future. My brother has no plans to go to college, and for environmental-engineer Dad and retired-lawyer Mom, that's a little hard to swallow. Thane doesn't like to talk about his future at all. He's more a live-in-the-moment guy. I know Dad has the best intentions, but whenever he goes down this path, it never ends well.

"No thanks," Thane says.

Even without looking, I can feel his tension. Dad should really let this go.

"I wish you would consider it," Dad says. "It's an excellent opportunity to—"

Thane shoves back from the table and stands, sending his chair crashing to the floor. "I said I'm not interested."

He's out the front door before anyone can say a word. I give Dad a sympathetic look, even though I wish he would leave Thane alone about the future planning. Thane will figure things out eventually. None of us can make that happen any faster.

Mom takes Dad's hand across the table. "It doesn't help to push him, Sam," she says.

Dad shakes his head. "I know, but I wish…"

We sit in silence for a few minutes, letting our breakfast get cold. When I can't stand it any more, I say, "He'll come around, Dad. You know he has stuff to figure out."

"I know." Dad gives me a sad smile. "But I'm his father. I feel responsible for helping him do that."

I get up and give Dad a hug.

"You are helping him," I say, squeezing extra tight. "He just isn't ready yet."

"Thanks, Gracie." Dad pats me on the back.

We go back to eating our breakfast in silence. Unfortunately, the lack of conversation gives my mind the freedom to dwell on everything that happened last night. I don't know why I do this to myself – go over and over stuff I can't do anything about – but it's like a compulsion. When Mom and Dad get up, I leap at the chance to busy myself with clearing the table.

I'm helping Mom with the dishes when Thane returns.

He nods at us and then goes to find Dad. Thane may have a temper, but he also has an acute sense of integrity. He'll apologise, and everything will be back to normal.

Everything except me, of course.

Nothing can fix that.

Thane and I ride the same city bus to school, even though I stay on for several stops after he gets off. It's packed in the morning, and I'm penned in by people on all sides. The bus takes the corner on the street that runs by Thane's school, and I swing hard towards the window, over the lap of a man in a business suit who is busy checking email on his phone.

The businessman scowls at me, and before he can say something nasty, I look away, glancing out at the sidewalk to see how many people will try to cram on at the next stop.

That's when I see the woman.

She could almost pass for fully human, except for the dark-red exoskeleton and the scorpion tail trailing behind her.

I squeeze my eyes shut. This is not happening. I mean, I *know* it's happening – after everything that happened Friday night, I'd have to be completely delusional to pretend that monsters don't exist, and Gretchen assured me I'm not insane – but it *shouldn't* be happening. It's against the rules or something. Gretchen said monsters don't come out during the day. They're supposed to be nocturnal, according to her and her missing mentor. So why is scorpion lady strolling down the street in the early-morning sun?

Well, you know what? Not my problem. Gretchen didn't want me involved – and I walked away willingly – so I won't be involved. It's not like I can fight the monster, anyway. I wouldn't even know how to try. I'm going to turn away from the window, open my eyes and act as if the lady I saw was heading to an early-morning costume party.

Hey, it could happen.

The bus jostles down the street, slamming to a sudden stop and knocking me forward into a woman with a baby stroller, then back against Thane's shoulder. He stares blankly out of the window at the row of pastel buildings.

What's wrong with him? I know he's still a little upset about my nightclub disappearing act, but he said he was over it.

"Hey, are you okay?" I ask, not wanting to start the week with things weird between us. "I'll apologise again if—"

"It's nothing," he snaps.

"Thane, seriously." I lean around so I can look him in the eye. "I'm sorry I left without telling you. If I could go back and do it differently, I would." Then, just in case humour will fix things faster, I add, "Hurry up and invent that time machine already."

He cracks a grin and I release my breath. He says, "Working on it."

We both laugh.

The bus jerks back into motion. I tighten my grip on the bar to keep from swinging into someone's lap.

"So," I ask tentatively, "we're okay?"

"Yeah," he says as the bus pulls up in front of his school. "We're fine."

I guess that's as good as I'm going to get from Thane this early in the morning. By the time we get home after school, things will be back to normal. Considering everything else going on right now, I need as much normal as I can get.

The bus stops in front of the main gate with a squeal of brakes, and everyone on board lurches forward a step. As the doors open, Thane nods at me and says, "See you later."

I smile and give him a small wave as he heads towards the door.

Half the bus empties out and I drop into the nearest available seat. I'm glad it's one with a view of the school, because if Thane is arriving at school, then maybe Milo is too. There is a whole ocean of students funnelling into the central courtyard. If Milo were there, though, I know I'd be able to find him. I'd see his head of dark curly hair above the crowd.

I haven't seen him since Friday night and I'm having

Milo withdrawals. Okay, that's an exaggeration – I realise I've barely met the boy – but I am worried that he might be mad at me too. One minute we were dancing, the next I was gone. Even though I'm nothing but a new buddy's sister to him, he has every right to be annoyed about being abandoned.

I scan the mass, searching for a mop of dark messy curls.

Instead, I spot a long dark-blonde braid.

Gretchen?

She goes to Thane's school? Well that's one of my questions about her answered. As the bus pulls back into motion, I wonder what will happen if Thane sees her – or, considering my life lately, *when* Thane sees her. Instant mess. Great, another thing to worry about. Exactly what I need on a Monday morning.

"Good morning, Mrs Deckler," a woman's voice says about fifteen minutes into homeroom.

I look up and see Ms West standing in the doorway.

"I need to see Grace Whitfield."

"Certainly." Mrs Deckler scans the room for me and says, "Your presence is requested."

I push myself up from my desk and make my way down the aisle. As I pass Miranda's desk, she slides her leg into my path. Luckily, I see it in time and manage to leap over it, saving myself from a face-plant. Miranda laughs, but I ignore her. I stiffen my spine and follow Ms West into the hallway.

She has a very serious look on her face. "Are you having a problem with Miranda?"

"No. No, it's fine," I insist. The last thing I want is to make a bigger deal of it than it already is. If I ignore Miranda's taunts and jabs, then maybe she'll eventually give up. She'll decide I'm no fun to mess with, because I don't fight back.

Hopefully.

"Are you certain?" Ms West's eyes narrow. "We do not tolerate disrespectful behaviour here at Alpha. If another student is—"

"Really." I appreciate her concern, but I want to handle this problem myself. "It's fine."

I force a cheery smile.

"All right then," she says, shifting her focus. "I wanted to check in and give you one last opportunity to change your elective choices."

"Change them?" I ask. "Why?"

"Your deadline is tomorrow," she says. "I thought I should give you one last chance to trade Yearbook for something else, something more… challenging."

My schedule is full of challenging. Yearbook seems like it's going to be fun, and it will give me a chance to meet lots of other students in the process.

"Actually," I say, "I think I'll stick it out with Yearbook."

"Very well." She clasps her hands behind her back. "As long as you're happy with your choices."

"Oh, I absolutely am."

"Wonderful," she says in a less-than-thrilled tone. She glances past me, into the classroom. Maybe at Miranda. For a moment I'm afraid she's going to make a bigger deal out of that situation after all, but in the end she just says, "You should get back to your class."

Then, without waiting for me to respond, she turns and walks away.

As I make my way back to my desk, wondering at Ms West's disapproval, I avoid Miranda's leg again and swing into my seat.

"Ms West is pretty harsh," I say, kind of to Vail, but kind of to myself in case she ignores me.

She doesn't.

"Guess so." She shrugs. "Never really talked to her much myself."

"Oh," I say, a little surprised to hear that. Why am I the lucky one? "Maybe she takes a special interest in new students."

This time Vail does ignore me.

"Grace," Mrs Deckler calls out, "can I see you for a moment?"

This time I circle round to the next aisle and bypass Miranda completely. As I reach Mrs Deckler's desk, she hands me a book.

"We'll be starting this in class today," she says with a sunny grin, "but I thought you might like a head start."

I inspect the book, a brand-new-looking copy of *Poetics* by Aristotle. "Thanks."

"I always begin the year with the origins of Western literature," she explains, "with Greek myth and drama. Aristotle is the perfect introduction."

An image of the griffin pops into my head, followed immediately by the feathered serpent, the fire-breathing lizard and – of course – the minotaur. Like I need *more* Greek myth in my life at the moment. Not that I say that to Mrs Deckler, because she seems very enthusiastic.

Instead, I say, "Cool." And try to look as excited as she does.

She winks at me. "There are perks to being in both my homeroom and my English class."

Back at my desk I glance over at Vail and see that she's busy colouring in the letters on the cover of her calculus textbook with a black permanent marker.

I'm not rebellious enough to doodle the cover with marker, but when I flip open *Poetics* to the title page and find a line drawing of an old Greek guy in a drapey dress, I take my pencil and shade in the fabric of his toga. Still light enough that I can erase it before returning the book, but I feel a little daring for the effort.

Now, if only I could be more daring in everything else. Too bad real life isn't erasable.

CHAPTER 9

Gretchen

Monday morning comes too early and too hard. I ditch first period to catch an extra hour of sleep in the third-floor janitorial closet and to avoid running into Nick in biology. After what he saw on Friday night, I need to come armed with a reasonably believable excuse for two guys vanishing out from under me in that courtyard. I've got a marginally lame one, but I'm in no rush to feed him the story.

Instead, I snooze until the bell and then slip into the between-classes crowd in time to make second period. Mr Alioso's lecture on the Constitution lulls me to sleep, and since it's a PowerPoint presentation and the lights are off, I get to catch a few more winks.

But the power nap must dull my senses, because when I head for my third period, I forget to take the long way and wind up slamming right into Nick as I round the corner on my way to the stairs.

"Gretchen," he says with a huge smile. "I thought you weren't in today."

Stupid, Gretchen. Top-notch stupid.

Can't exactly pretend the full-on body crash didn't happen, so I might as well face him now instead of later. It's not like he's the type to let things go anyway.

I back up a step. "Nope, I'm here."

"You're not trying to avoid me, are you?" he teases.

"Whatever gave you that idea?" I ask with full-throttle sarcasm. "I've been nothing but nice to you since we met."

He laughs at my joke, but his grin quickly turns into a scowl of concern. "I really was worried about you all weekend. After what happened at the club, I thought—"

"Nothing happened," I interrupt, ready with my stupid story.

"Nothing happened?" he says with a humourless laugh. "You beat the hell out of two creeps and they disappeared right out from under—"

Before he can finish his sentence and blurt out everything right in front of the stream of students swarming around us, I grab him by the T-shirt and yank him through the crowd, across the corridor and into the empty computer lab. I don't want to deal with a school full of red-flag-raising questions and gossip. I'm not messing around any more.

Once inside, I push him against the breeze-block wall and slam the door shut. Nick needs to be off my trail once and for all.

"Look," I say, squaring myself in front of him with my hands on my hips. "I don't know what you think happened on Friday night—"

"I know exactly what happened." He crosses his arms over his chest. "You were fighting with two thugs and then, in a flash, they were gone. They evaporated."

I clench my jaw and roll my eyes behind closed lids. There goes the hope that maybe he didn't see anything truly wacky or that he might have convinced himself he was seeing things. Why couldn't I be lucky with him just this once?

Why couldn't he think he's delusional?

No, he has to just stand there with his dark eyes fixed on mine, one hundred per cent confident in what he saw that night.

Fine. The lametastic lie it is.

"I heard it was something in the drinks, made you hallucinate," I say, giving him the only conceivably plausible line I could think up to explain what I know is unexplainable reality. "Somebody spiked the water supply with something way worse than alcohol."

"Gretchen," Nick says in a disappointed tone, "we both know it wasn't something in the water."

From the intensity in his eyes, I almost believe he really does know exactly what's going on. But that's impossible, isn't it?

He pushes himself away from the wall, advancing on me in such a way that I have to back up and turn at the same time. In less than three steps he's manoeuvred me against the door, penning me in place with his long body and his arms braced at either side of my head. I'm trapped like the monsters I usually hunt.

My heart rate and my breathing pick up and I feel my cheeks warm. I don't know if it's because of his nearness or his tactical dominance or the possibility that he knows more than he should about this situation. Whatever the reason, as he leans in close, his dark eyes growing bigger and bigger in my vision, my self-preservation instincts kick in.

I'm about to execute a sharp knee to the tenders when he bobs to the left and whispers, right next to my ear, "You know you want to tell me what really—"

Before he can finish, the door handle by my hip turns and I'm shoved into Nick as the door bursts open. His arms clamp around me as we both stumble away from the doorway. I try to jump away, but he holds me tight.

"Let me go," I insist, pushing against his chest. "Don't say a word."

He lets go and I turn around to explain to the interrupting teacher why I'm in an empty room alone with Nick. No one ever said I couldn't use my hypno-eyes for personal gain.

Only I don't find myself face-to-face with a teacher. Or even a human.

The thing barging into the room has the head and arms of a woman, but that's where the resemblance ends. Everything from its shoulders to the floor is covered in an armour-like shell, and behind it swings the long, curving tail of a scorpion. A nasty skorpios hybrid. Ten to one that stinger is coated in poison.

My fangs drop into place automatically.

What the hell is this thing doing out in the daytime?

"Huntress," the beast spits.

It obviously came in here after me.

"How did you—" I sense Nick start to move. I swing my arm out to keep him safely behind me. "Uh," I glance sideways at the normal – but unhypnotisable – human boy behind me, forcing my fangs back into their hiding spot, "my name is Gretchen. You must have me confused with someone else."

The beast's eyes follow my glance and focus in on Nick. For a second I almost think I see a glimmer of recognition. Then I don't have time to think any more as the beast lunges past me, grabbing for Nick's throat.

The monster-hunting side of me goes into autopilot. Even without my gear, even with it coming after me on my turf, even in broad daylight when monsters should be nowhere in sight, I'm instantly in fight mode.

With a powerful spin, I land a roundhouse kick to the beast's belly, using my momentum to push Nick away with a shove that sends him flying backwards.

"Watch out!" he shouts.

I turn just in time to see the beast's giant scorpion tail swing down at my head. I drop and roll to the left.

The foot-long stinger pierces the yellowing linoleum, and for a second the beast is anchored to the spot. I use the opportunity to jump to my feet and race around to the beast's back, pulling out the ABS plastic dagger that never leaves my right boot and plunging it in between the exoskeletal plates covering the torso. It sinks deep into the vulnerable interior flesh.

The beast lets out a howl of pain that I'm sure can be heard on the other side of school. Great. Someone's going to call the cops. I need to finish this quickly.

There's no way I can get my fangs in through any of the armoured parts of the body. My best chance is the spot where the neck meets the exoskeleton.

I leap onto the beast's back, trying to get high enough to reach the unprotected flesh, when it pulls the stinger free. Suddenly it's like I'm riding a bucking bull, holding on with a death grip to keep from getting flung into the nearest wall.

As I get spun around, I see a blonde blur rushing towards the monster. Before I can yell for him to stop, Nick grabs a metal desk-and-chair combo and swings like he's trying to hit a home run.

But apparently skorpios hybrids are Olympic-weightlifter strong. The beast forgets me as it grabs the desk midswing, lifts it and Nick into the air and tosses them away like they were crumpled newspaper.

"Aaargh!" I scream.

A wave of adrenaline pumps through me. Tightening my legs around the creature's waist, I lever myself up to eye level with the neck.

Before I can drop my bite, the beast twists around and, using its tail for leverage, slams back-first against the nearest wall. The impact stuns me and I lose my hold on the smooth exoskeleton. I crumple face-first to floor in a giant splat.

"Ugh."

With the wind knocked out of me, I take a few seconds to recover. I sense the beast moving past me, through the door and into the hall. My body processes the adrenaline and my lungs struggle to suck in great big gasping breaths of air. There is a throbbing pain in my ribs where the beast must have gotten in a blow in the heat of battle. I hadn't even noticed.

Can't stop for pain. There's a monster on the loose, and it has a head start.

I'm halfway out the door, checking the hall just in time to see the skorpios hybrid round the corner out of sight, when I hear a faint moaning from across the room.

"Nick," I gasp.

He sounds hurt. I hurry back between the rows of desks to where he landed. I fling aside the desk he tried to wield against the monster.

"Stupid fool," I mutter, leaning down to check his pulse. His neck feels hot and full of life, with a strong and steady beat. What kind of idiot throws himself into a fight with a giant scorpion? Can't he tell I can take care of myself? I don't need anyone to save my skin, especially not a mortal human with zero clue that monsters are more than myth.

But he does have an uncanny ability to know just where the beastie's bad parts are swinging.

Nick groans and turns his cheek towards my palm. I let my thumb brush gently over the soft skin beneath his eye. He looks so sweet and innocent and just... beautiful. I know it's not a typical word to describe a guy, but there is something about the smooth texture of his skin, long blonde eyelashes and chiselled cheekbones that brings the adjective to mind. Without stopping to think, I lift my hand from his pulse point to trail shaking fingertips across his temple.

"Gretchen," he whispers.

I jerk my hand back like his skin has turned white-hot. What am I thinking? I'm definitely cracking up. This boy has been nothing but trouble since he shoved his way into my life. I can't go getting soft feelings for him. Or *any* feelings for him.

And I have a runaway monster to catch.

Shaking off the weird moment, I grab his shoulder and shake hard. "Wake up!"

His dark eyes blink open and find me immediately. He smiles weakly. "Gretchen." Then, as if the memory of moments before hits him, he bolts upright. "What happened?"

"You, uh…" I hate to do this, after he was trying to be the hero and all, but it has to be done. It's for his own protection, really. And mine. "You came on to me. I pushed you away, and I guess I don't know my own strength, 'cause I sent you flying."

His dark blonde brows scowl. "No, that's not what—"

"Sorry." I push myself to my feet and pretend to dust off my jeans. "But don't get so close next time."

I'm already at the door when he makes it to his feet. "Gretchen, I know there was a—"

"Stay away from me, okay?" I ask, glancing back to make sure he's not wobbling on his feet or anything. Then, before I can check myself, I add, "Please."

I'm in the hall before he can answer.

Pushing Nick and my pathetic plea from my mind – I can't believe I just begged like that – I break into a run after the creature.

I'm blind to the mostly empty halls around me. So I'm shocked when I round the corner and skid into a boy. You'd think I'd learn to watch where I'm going around corners, especially after last time, but I'm not exactly thinking straight at the moment.

"Sorry," I mumble, sidestepping and moving on.

But the boy calls after me. "Grace?"

No, no, no.

Am I really still surprised at this point? It's not as if nothing's been going to hell in a flaming handbasket lately. From now on I should just expect the worst-case scenario on a regular basis.

I kick into full speed and am down the hall and out onto the sidewalk before the boy can say another word. No sign of the skorpios hybrid. Lifting my nose to the breeze like a dog, I inhale a big sniff and... nothing. Not a hint of monster on the air. How is that possible? It can't have just vanished. I need to grid-search the area.

"Things can't possibly get any worse," I mutter as I reach the spot two blocks from school where I park Moira. I probably shouldn't have issued a direct challenge to the universe like that but, really, what else could go wrong? As soon as I pull out into traffic, I voice-dial Ursula's number. As I listen to ring after ring after countless ring, I drum my hands on the steering wheel.

"Come on."

I keep trying as I circle the block around school and gradually radiate my search out to surrounding blocks. A dozen fruitless circles, a dozen phone calls and a dozen this-voice-mailbox-is-full messages later, I pull Moira into our building and cut the engine. I drop my head against the lovingly worn steering wheel and close my eyes.

"There's some seriously bad stuff going on," I tell Moira as if she were not a car but a confidante. She is the closest thing I've got at the moment. "Monsters out in daylight, monsters coming to my school, monsters out in pairs and threes. Monsters getting away from me.

My twin, who can see them too. Ursula needs to know about all of this. I need to know what's going on, and she's the only one who might have the answers." I take a rough breath. "So where on earth is she?"

Is it just a coincidence that all of this is happening right at the time when Ursula disappeared? Or when Grace and Nick show up?

I'm pretty sure Nick is more than he seems. When the beastie's scorpion tail was about to spear me, it was almost as if he saw it coming. It shouldn't be possible – just like he shouldn't be immune to my hypnosis – but if he hadn't warned me, I'd be Gretchen-on-a-skewer right now, instead of sitting here, confused, in the dark.

This is getting to be too much. There are so many questions and I don't have any answers. I'm the huntress, the hired gun who fights the creatures that go bump in the night and then reports in to the boss. Only the job isn't that simple any more and the boss is MIA. What am I supposed to do?

I throw my head back against the seat and ask the heavens, "Okay Ursula, where are you when I really need you?"

Standing outside Ursula's door, I know there's no other choice. She's been gone for too long and things have gone too sideways for me to keep pretending her disappearance is normal.

Still, I hesitate as I reach for the doorknob. One of the things I love most about living with Ursula is the freedom. The autonomy. She doesn't question when I go out late at night or whether I've done my homework or if my room is clean. She trusts that I take care of business, that I'm mindful of my duties and responsibilities. She lets me have however much privacy I need, and she gets her own privacy in return.

Which only makes me feel worse for what I'm about to do.

"I have to."

Taking a deep breath, I turn the knob and push open the door. It swings open silently, revealing a pristine room that hasn't been touched for days.

Her bedroom is in the corner of the loft, so she has windows along two walls, with a sliding glass door in the middle of one, leading on to the balcony. Sleek white built-in drawers line the third wall, while her bed is pushed up against the wall with the door. The stark platform number, covered with steely grey sheets and pillows, is perfectly made. There is a full glass of water on the bedside table, next to a book with an ancient Greek statue on the cover.

It feels like an invasion to be in here without her permission.

"I don't have a choice."

I take a quick breath and then begin the search.

Starting with the drawers, I pull open each one and sift through the contents. Lots of soft and flowing clothes in elegant neutrals, like camel and ivory. Ursula always looks soft and elegant, in sharp contrast to my dark and hard wardrobe. As I process each drawer, I make sure to leave it just as neat and organised as I found it. Ursula's gone, but that doesn't mean I get a free pass to mess up her stuff.

I slide the final drawer shut and turn to evaluate the rest of the room. The only other furniture is the bed and bedside table.

Dropping to the floor, I peer under the bed frame. Nothing but empty space. A clear view over the flat carpet to the balcony on the other side.

I quickly flip back the bedding, checking under the duvet and the pillows. Nothing.

Same thing under the lamp and the book on the bedside table. With only one place left to look, I tug open the bedside-table drawer.

Inside, in a neatly organised drawer divider, are Ursula's essentials. Lip balm, nail file, reading glasses. A tube of her lemongrass lotion. No note.

I grab the lotion, twist off the top and squeeze a tiny drop onto the back of my hand. As I rub the silky lotion into my skin, I'm overwhelmed by the scent memory.

She smelled just like this that night four years ago when she first brought me back to the loft. I was scared out of my mind, afraid to trust this woman who seemed to know things about me and my history that no one should know, but even more afraid to go back to the street life I'd been living since I'd run away.

"Welcome home, Gretchen," she said, gesturing one arm in a wide circle, sweeping over the sparkling surfaces and furniture of the loft.

Home? My whole life, I'd only ever had two homes. The filth hole of dirty clothes and broken junk where Phil and Barb slept and the abandoned warehouse where Ursula found me. As much as I hated both, I belonged in both of those more than I belonged here. With my ratty clothes and filthy hair, I shouldn't even have stepped inside somewhere as gleamingly pristine as this heavenly space.

"I…"

I couldn't say it. As much as knew I didn't belong here, I *wanted* to even more.

"Come," Ursula said. "Let me give you the tour."

As I followed her around from room to room – a training gym, a library, a kitchen with a refrigerator full of fresh, delicious-looking food – I found myself inching closer and closer to her side. As her fresh scent of lemongrass enveloped me, I found myself hoping I could belong here someday. Wanting to be good enough for a place like this.

"And here," she said, leading me to the final unopened door, "is your room."

The door swung wide, revealing a place I had only

dreamed about before. There was a big bed with fluffy bedding, a tall dressing table, a closet full of fresh, clean clothes.

"Go on," Ursula said, urging me forward. "Look around."

"I c-can't," I'd stammered. "It's too…" I bit my lip and shook my head, unable to finish.

"It's yours," she insisted, pushing gently on my back until I stepped inside.

A bed of my own. A whole room, without a stack of dirty laundry or torn upholstery or broken floorboard in sight. The opposite of everything I'd ever had.

In that instant, I was determined to make myself worthy.

I spun around to face her. "Tell me what to do," I said, full of a courage I was only beginning to feel. "How do I earn my place?"

It feels so long ago now. Ursula insisted I didn't need to earn anything, that the room was mine without conditions.

But I was eager to prove myself. We started training the next day. Everything from martial arts to weapons to memorising mythology. Ursula has been my guide and mentor in everything about my heritage.

I drop the tube of lotion back into the drawer and slam it shut. "Where are you?" I shout to the empty room. "How could you just disappear?"

Frustrated, I throw myself onto her bed. As I bounce, a pillow lurches to the side, knocking the book off the nightstand. With a groan, I roll to the side, leaning down to pick it up.

When I do, a small white envelope falls to the ground. My heart rate triples.

I place the book back on the bedside table, snatch the note off the floor and sit up, holding the crisp paper in both hands. Scrawled across the envelope is a single word: *Gretchen*.

My breathing shallows as I lift the flap and pull out the folded notecard covered in Ursula's elegant script.

Dearest Gretchen,
If you are reading this note, then I must have been gone for some time already. I feared this might happen. Since your sixteenth birthday some weeks ago, things have been changing. Perhaps you've begun to notice. I knew this time was coming and have been making preparations for the upcoming events, but there are still some mysteries I must solve first. The hunt for answers may take me into danger. Do not worry about my safety — I assure you I am fine. But if I am kept from you at this critical time, you must find my sister. Although we have remained out of touch in recent years, I do know she is living and working in the city. I wish I could give you more

*information to go on, but our separation has been
essential for your protection. Find her, as she can
help guide you into this next phase if I cannot.
I apologise for the cryptic nature of this note,
but if it is discovered by someone other than you,
I must guard our secrecy at all costs.*

*Yours ever,
Ursula*

"What. The. Hades?" I reread the note, not believing it could be as mysterious as it first seems. But after four passes, it still makes no sense. My birthday, changes, new phase, secrecy. She's in danger, but she's safe. Her sister? Does she know that I have a sister too?

I flop back onto her bed. Great. I found a note, exactly what I was hoping for, but I'm even more lost than before. I'm used to knowing exactly what to do – sniff a monster, find it, send it home. I'm at a total loss right now. And I don't like the feeling.

CHAPTER 10

Grace

Standing in the cafeteria line, waiting to pay for a bottle of kiwi-strawberry juice to go with the hummus-and-spinach wrap and baby carrots already in my reusable lunch bag, I'm not really excited to spend another lunch period in the library. Last week was bad enough, and I could at least claim new-girl status as my excuse.

But by day three, shouldn't I have someone to sit with?

Maybe not. This whole new-girl thing is totally foreign to me. I try to remember new students at Orangevale, and how long it took them to assimilate. I only remember one who—

"You're up," a gruff female voice says from behind me in line.

I twist around. "Oh, Vail. Hi."

She jerks her head towards the checkout.

I step forward and show my juice to the cashier. After handing over my money, I turn and say, "Thanks."

She shrugs, sliding her tray of lumpy school food forward.

I turn, ready to head out the side door for the library and another lunch hour alone with the books. It could be worse, I guess. I could have to eat lunch with Miranda.

"You can sit with us," Vail says as she walks by with her tray.

Did she just say what I think she said?

"What?" I hurry to catch up with her. "Really?"

She gives me a duh-are-you-stupid? look. I just grin and follow her to a table in the centre of the cafeteria.

There's a handful of other kids at her table. The group at the far end looks like vamp-loving goths, dressed all in black, with deep purple lipstick and heavy-duty eyeliner. Two empty seats separate them from Vail's diverse trio. Next to Vail sits a girl who looks like Marilyn Monroe, with platinum-blonde hair, ruby red lipstick and a low-cut vintage dress. Across the table is a boy with turquoise-blue hair and matching eyeliner. He's wearing a black HELLO KITTY T-shirt, black skinny jeans and a wide, white studded belt. By comparison, Vail is almost tame. Over the weekend, she dyed her hair tips lime green, a shade that perfectly matches her baggy cargo trousers and the bleeding smiley face on her tight black T-shirt.

With blah-coloured clothes, hair the colour I was born with and nothing but a dab of organic lip balm on my mouth, I definitely feel like the outsider in this group.

"This is Lulu," Vail says, nodding to the girl at her left. "And that's Jax."

Better the outsider *in* a group than the outsider *without* a group.

I smile at the boy, Jax, and place my tray down next to him. "Hi," I say as I slip into the seat. "I'm Grace."

"Charmed, I'm sure," Lulu drawls, offering her hand across the table like I might want to kiss her ring. I gingerly take it and give it a quick shake.

"Lay off," Vail grumbles, swirling her fork around her plate.

"I think we have Computer Science together," Lulu says, in a completely normal voice.

"Yeah?" I reply, wondering why I didn't notice the retro bombshell in class on Friday. Right, because I was too busy researching minotaurs.

Jax turns to me. "You're very eco-chic, aren't you?"

"Uh…" I look down at my yellow TREE HUGGER T-shirt.

"I like it," he says. "You make a subtle statement."

"Um, thanks?"

"Oh, making a statement is always a good thing." He sticks out his tongue, revealing a shiny black piercing. Then he nods to the girls. "We're not usually subtle about it. It's refreshing."

"I…" I smile, a little confused, but I think that was a compliment. "Okay, cool."

My ears feel a little warm as I open up my lunch and pull out the recycled foil-covered wrap. For several minutes, I eat in silence, listening to the rapid-fire chatter of Jax and

148

Lulu with occasional interjections from Vail. They are all so comfortable with one another, I kind of envy that. I wish I could have that with someone. Maybe with Gretchen.

I shake my head and pop a baby carrot into my mouth. No point wasting time on that daydream. That's not going to happen. She wants me as far out of her way as I can get.

At least I can sit here and enjoy not being alone at lunchtime for once. Not having to sneak my food into the back corner of the library. I can eat in relative, non-lonely peace.

Maybe things at Alpha won't be so bad after all.

"Nice to see you've found others of your kind," a snooty voice whines from behind me.

I don't have to turn around to know who it is.

"Get lost, Miranda," Vail says, glaring over my right shoulder. "Don't you have a Botox appointment? Your forehead is looking a little wrinkly."

"Funny," she says, without humour. "I wanted to congratulate Grace on finding the loser table. You make a nice quartet, like four best girlfriends."

Vail's gaze flicks to Jax half a second before she pushes herself to her feet. Lulu grabs her by the arm and tugs her back down. "Don't."

"Do you think that's an insult?" Jax laughs. "I'd rather be called a girlfriend than a stereotype any day."

I whip around to see Miranda's reaction, but before she

can say a word, Ms West walks up, looking all elegance again in a lavender blouse and khaki trousers.

"Everything all right here?" she asks, running her gaze over the whole table.

Her eyes settle on me, and I feel compelled to answer. Flicking a nervous glance at Miranda, I say, "Yeah. Fine."

"Excellent." Ms West turns to Miranda and asks, "Would you mind helping me prepare some handouts I need to distribute in seventh period?"

"Of course," Miranda replies, turning instantly into a perfect ray of sunshine. I hadn't realised she was such a suck-up.

As she follows Ms West away, she turns back and gives our table – *our* table – a sneer. As if they've preplanned it, my three lunch mates simultaneously flip her the bird. A little more extreme – and detention earning – than I am. But since Miranda huffs and storms away, it's obviously effective.

Lulu gives Jax a high five over the table.

"Such a waste of perfect hair care." Jax sighs. "Lowlights that beautiful should only go to the most deserving."

"You might not have noticed," Lulu says to me, "but Miranda is Vail's archnemesis."

Yeah, I've noticed. "She's been pretty awful to me too," I say, glad to have found something in common with Vail and her friends.

"She was born bad," Jax add.

"You give her too much credit," Vail grumbles. "She's insecure. She makes herself feel better by belittling anyone with confidence and picking on those without."

"Isn't that what I said?" Jax asks with fake seriousness. Lulu laughs.

Vail rolls her eyes and goes back to her mush.

My mind processes what Vail said. Is that why Miranda picks on me? Because I don't have any confidence? I definitely don't have the courage Vail has to stand up to her, but I didn't think of myself as such a total weakling. Maybe I can absorb some confidence from the group around me.

I look around at the three friends with wonder, amazed at their ability to confront Miranda as a unified team and bounce right back from her attack. Strength in numbers.

For some reason, that makes me think about Gretchen again. I keep picturing the three monsters in the nightclub and how she's out there fighting them all alone. I keep thinking about how she pushed me away, and I let her.

My wrap becomes a little hard to swallow, and I take a big swig of juice to wash it down. If a unified front can take down Miranda, it can't hurt when fighting mythological monsters.

Have Gretchen and I made a big mistake? And will I get a chance to fix it?

Thane and Milo are already at the dining table doing

homework when I get home. I try to act all nonchalant, dropping my backpack casually by the door and heading for the kitchen, as if I'm not dying to sit down at the table with Milo.

Playing it cool is so much harder than it looks.

I pull open the refrigerator and let out the breath I've been holding since I first saw Milo's dark curls at the table. I take my time choosing from the array of pop on the second shelf, when I already know I want pineapple Fanta. What if Milo thinks I'm a freak for disappearing from the club on Friday night? Which is nothing compared to what he might think if he ever knew my mythological truth, but it's bad enough. Besides, Thane is still kind of mad at me, so there's no telling what he said to Milo today.

No, no way. I delete that thought as soon it clears my brain. No matter how mad Thane is at me, he would never bad-mouth me or anyone else in the family. He's loyal, first and foremost. He could want to strangle me one second, but would still lay down his life for me the next.

Maybe he's so devoted because he was adopted at a late age, long past the time most kids are unceremoniously dumped into the vicious foster-care cycle. When I was seven, Mom and Dad decided they wanted another child. They might have started out looking for a baby, as most adoptive parents do. Then we met Thane.

Everything changed.

He had been picked up off the street, found sleeping

in an alley with a mangy mutt curled up against his belly for warmth. We went to see him at the adoption agent's house where they were keeping him until a foster home could be found. He was sitting in the chair next to the fireplace, feet pulled up in front of him and chin resting on his knees. He didn't say a word, just looked up as Mom and Dad approached, not betraying an ounce of the joy I knew had to be bursting inside. I'm sure he didn't want to get his hopes up, only to have his heart broken again.

I think it was those big grey eyes, a few shades darker than my own, that drew them in.

The agent said a lot of couples weren't interested because he was so quiet. They worried he might be brain damaged or mentally deficient. Their loss, because we are so lucky to have him.

Besides getting adopted myself, he's the best thing that ever happened in my life.

Even when he's mad at me.

"Hey, stranger."

"Ack!" I jump at the sound of Milo's voice, knocking my head against the underside of the freezer door. "Ow."

"Sorry," he says, reaching out to gently rub the place where I hit my head. "You okay?"

"Yeah," I whisper. I lift my hand to the spot, careful not to touch his but hyperaware that our fingers are only millimetres apart. "Just fine."

I might have a massive knot there in the morning,

but for right now I am absolutely fabulous. He's standing oh so close, with his hand on my hair, his pale eyes gazing into mine with worry. I could melt into the floor.

"Didn't mean to startle you." He pulls his hand away, and my head suddenly feels cold.

"No problem." I drop my hand too, even though my skull is throbbing as if the blood is going to burst out at any second. I don't want to look dumb, standing there holding my head.

"Wanted to grab another soda." He reaches around me into the fridge and pulls out a can of Coke.

I'm grinning and nodding like a fool as he turns away.

Then he suddenly turns back. "Hey, I saw you in school today."

"What?" I shake my head. "You were at Alpha?"

"No, at Euclid." He looks adorably confused. "I got a library pass in third period and I saw you in the hall. You didn't even say hi. Why'd you take off like that?"

"That's im—"

Holy goalie. Gretchen! He must have seen Gretchen.

I knew this was going to be complicated.

As soon as I saw her walking into Thane's school, I should have known this would happen. But no, I was too caught up in my hurt feelings over her dismissal and my guilt over slinking away like a coward. Sometimes I'm such an idiot.

I'm probably lucky they haven't run into each other

before. If Milo weren't a year older or their school weren't so big, I'm sure they would have already met.

"It must have been someone who looked kinda like me," I finally say. "I was at Alpha all day."

Both statements are true. I just leave out the part where I know exactly who he saw, and that she looks more than *kinda* like me.

"Must have been." He shakes his head, like he knew it couldn't have been me but he was sure it was. "Weird."

"Yeah," I say with a forced laugh. "Weird."

He heads back into the dining room and I close the refrigerator door. This can only get worse. If Milo can run into her in the hall that easily, then Thane can too. Eventually he is going to see her, and he won't be as easy to convince as Milo. We've sat across the dinner table for almost ten years. If he and Gretchen wind up face-to-face, he'll know.

I need to talk to her about this.

Plus, this is the perfect excuse to go see her again. Because if there is anything I've realised in the days since she dumped me back home on Friday night – especially after seeing that scorpion thing out in the daylight today – it's that I'm not content to walk away and pretend that she doesn't exist.

It might be complicated and dangerous and completely out of my comfort zone, but I have a sister and I'm not losing her right after finding her. I'm tired of being the gutless doormat. It's time I found a spine and figured out how to use it.

"Mom," I call out as I walk into the master bedroom. "Are you in here?"

"In the bathroom, honey."

I follow the sound of her voice and find her squeezing grout around the edge of the bathtub. The painting is done, and now she's doing finishing touches in the bathroom. I'm not sure what's left on her to-do list, but it can't be much.

"It's looking great," I say.

"Thanks." She beams, with a smear of grout across her cheek.

I motion for her to wipe it off, and as she grabs for a rag I ask, "Is it okay if I go over to a friend's house to do homework?"

"What's her name?" Mom's efforts only make the grout smear worse. "Where does she live?"

"Gretchen. And not far," I fib. Nothing's far in San Francisco if you catch a bus. "We're in a lot of the same classes, so it will really help as the school year goes on."

I'm a little surprised at how easily the lies fall out of my mouth.

"Okay," she relents after a moment of hesitation. "Be home for dinner."

"Mom," I whine. "We won't have time to get anything done."

She heaves a sarcastic sigh and drops her rag. "Fine, be home by ten. And call when you're on your way."

"Thanks."

I'm gone before she can change her mind. As I dart through the dining room, I throw a glance at the boys. Milo's dark head is bent over a book. Thane catches my eye and lifts his brows in question.

"Going to a friend's," I explain quickly. "See you later."

"Grace," Thane says, and I spin back to face the table. "Be careful."

His dark-grey eyes are guarded and intense.

"I…" For some reason, I can't just give him a glib reassurance that I'll be fine. "I will."

He nods, apparently satisfied with my answer, and turns his attention back to his book. I grab my backpack to make it look good, even though I have no intention of studying with Gretchen, and hurry to the closest bus stop. I've been putting this off for three days, but now that the decision is made, I'm anxious to talk to her – just to *be* with her again, and to feel like I belong to something, even if she doesn't want me there.

I'm not sure which buses to take to get to her pier, but I'll ask the drivers. They should know, right?

My heart starts pounding at the thought of seeing Gretchen again. I'm not big on confrontation, and I have a feeling she's not going to be too thrilled to see me again. But for once in my life, I'm going to stand up for something. For myself. I hope she doesn't slam the door in my face.

"It'll be fine," I tell myself. "I mean, we're obviously sisters. She can't dismiss that. She can't shut me out forever." A wave of doubt washes over me. "Right?"

I sense another person stepping up beside me at the bus stop, but I keep my eyes straight ahead. After only a few days in the city I've learned that making eye contact can be dangerous. When Thane and I went to the grocery store the day after moving in, we ran into a woman on the street who shouted at us and shot an imaginary pistol in my face. I was terrified. Thankfully, Thane grabbed my wrist and dragged me down the block.

Since then, I keep my eyes averted as much as possible.

"Which bus goes to the Presidio?" the person asks.

"Um, I'm not sure," I say, unable to ignore a direct question. "I'm new in town and I haven't really—"

I freeze when I look up at the person next to me and see that it's not a person at all, but a woman with the shiny head of a cobra. A pair of yellow beady eyes peer at me from opposite sides of the triangle-shaped head, and wide, scaly flaps spread out beneath each ear. Maybe if I'd played it cool she wouldn't have noticed, wouldn't have realised that I saw her true form. But I'm not cool and I can't stop the scream that bursts from my throat.

A sickly sly smile spreads across her dark-green lips. "Must be my lucky night."

Before her forked tongue can slither out between her lips, I turn and run. I make it only a few steps before I feel her human hands clamp over my shoulders. Our momentum thrusts me face-first into the pavement, and her weight crushes against my back, knocking the wind out of me.

As soon as I recover my breath, I struggle to pull myself away, out from under her, my fingertips scraping raw on the rough concrete. There is nothing for me to grab, no traction to drag myself out of her grasp. Still, I reach, desperate to find purchase.

Her weight lifts, but before I can scramble away, she flips me on to my back and pins my arms and legs with her own.

A thin line of serpent drool dangles from her scale-covered chin.

"Ew!" I struggle to shake off her grip, but she's too strong for me.

The ridiculous thought floats through my mind that, if I survive the night, I should totally change one of my electives to Tae Kwon Do. Ms West will be so happy. If I'm not dead.

Her snake head slowly lowers towards my face. "I've never tasted a huntress before." The tongue darts out, flicking my nose. "You don't need to be whole to earn me my freedom."

What?

As her fangs descend towards my neck, I squeeze my eyes shut against the sight of her yellow eyes. Bleak, empty eyes. Hungry eyes. I can't believe I'm going to die like this. Move to the big city and the fears are rapists and murderers and even doomsday cults, but death by giant snake bite?

Mom is going to be very upset.

The weight suddenly lifts away.

"Ugh," I grunt as I lift my free arms to my head.

"Grace?"

I blink my eyes open to find Gretchen standing over me, looking like I'm the burning bag of dog poo left on her porch on Halloween night. Why would she look at me like that when she obviously just saved my butt from snake-head lady?

"Thank you, I…" But as I sit up and look around, I see that I'm not on the sidewalk around the corner from the bus stop. I'm on the metal steps above Gretchen's garage. Halfway across town, without a snake-headed lady in sight. "How did I…?"

Did I… *teleport* here?

That's ridiculous. It's not only physically impossible, it's also… well… I don't know, *impossible*! I must have hit my head too hard against the concrete. And then maybe a bus driver found me and…

Oh, who am I kidding? The only reasonable no-matter-how-crazy-it-sounds explanation is that I somehow beamed across town to Gretchen's loft.

"What are you doing here?" she demands, clearly unhappy to see me. "I thought I made it clear that you needed to stay in your safe little life."

Now that makes me angry. Who is she to tell me what to do? She has no right to give me orders. And she doesn't know anything about my life.

My emotions are running a little high from my snake attack. I need to get this under control before I make Gretchen even angrier. We need to talk about this – about my popping to her doorstep and her seeing Milo at school – and we need to do it calmly and rationally so we can figure out what to do.

Deep breath, Grace.

Besides, my 'little life' isn't exactly safe, is it?

"Tell me something, Gretchen," I say climbing to my feet and holding out my hands so she can see my raw fingertips. "Have you ever teleported out of a fight?"

CHAPTER 11

Gretchen

"One second I was about to become snake food," Grace says, barely pausing for breath in her recounting of the day's events as she follows me back into the loft. "The next I was at your door, staring up at you and you scowling down at me. Has anything like that ever happened to you?"

"No."

"Well, have you *heard* of anything like that?" she asks.

"No."

"Think hard," she says. "Maybe your mentor mentioned some—"

"No!" I close my eyes and take a breath. Taking my frustration out on Grace isn't fair. This isn't her fault. She didn't ask to be part of this world. I turn to face her. "At least, not that I can remember."

"There must be *something*." Her voice tightens like she might be on the verge of panic – or tears. "I mean, people don't just teleport across town. It defies the laws of physics."

"I know, but…" Wait a minute. Teleporting… no, *autoporting*. "I do remember Ursula saying something about my powers. That they are gifts from Medusa and her sisters."

Ursula showed me a book in the library once. I don't remember the exact title, but I know it was small and purple.

Grace follows me, saying, "Maybe that's it." She hesitates before adding, "Guess this eliminates any doubts, huh? We're sisters."

I can't tell if she's thrilled or bummed – or which I want her to be – so I focus on searching the shelves. I scan the books, looking for that familiar spine.

"Aha!" I grab the small purple book off the shelf.

Legends of the Gorgons.

Flipping open the book, I scan the table of contents as Grace reads over my shoulder.

"There," she exclaims, pointing to the chapter titled "Powers of the Gorgons."

I shoot her a sideways glare – I am literate, you know – but she's too focused on the book to notice. After turning to the chapter, I step away to read out loud. The first few pages talk about the shared powers, those that all the gorgon sisters possessed. Keen sense of smell, hypno-eyes, monster-biting fangs, and our deadly/healing blood. Grace's autoporting ability must be one of the unique powers, one that belonged to just one of the gorgons.

"'Each of the gorgon sisters was gifted with an extra-ordinary power that aided in their defence against the

163

monster realm. Medusa was the wisest and had the gift of second sight, the knowledge of things unknown and those to come, known as omnicognition.'"

"That's definitely not me," Grace says with a laugh. "If I could see the future, I'd have helped my parents win the lottery a long time ago."

I ignore the little stab of envy when she mentions her parents with such warm feeling. Phil and Barb never did anything to deserve even being called parents.

"Yeah, me neither," I say, then continue reading. "'Stheno was possessed of corposuperiority, a great and unnatural strength, both physical and mental.'"

"You've got that one for sure," Grace says with a grin. "I knew you were super-strong when you threw me over your shoulder like a bag of candyfloss."

I feel a tiny burn of blush on my cheeks – partly because I feel bad for hauling her out of the club like that, and partly because I'm not used to compliments. She's probably right, though. I've never thought much about my strength, and I always figured it was training or mind over matter or something. But maybe it's a little more special than that.

I can't believe Ursula has never told me about this. Maybe I should have read the book when she showed it to me.

"Keep going," Grace urges. "Mine has to be next."

"'Euryale was called *the far-roaming*,'" I read, "'because

of her incredible ability to travel distances, short and far, in the space of a moment. A power known as autoportation.'"

"That's it!" Grace squeals. "That must be what happened." She bounces over and reads the page again. "Euryale," she repeats. "Wow. Just wow."

I look at this girl – my sister, my twin – who has no idea what she's in for. Things seem to be spiralling out of control exponentially. My world is changing so quickly and I'm just trying to hang on. The old rules are out the window, and I'm getting blindsided by new things every day. It's easy to forget that Grace is just trying to hang on too. Where in Hades is Ursula? Is it a coincidence that she disappeared right before monsters started breaking all the rules and this twin sister I never knew I had showed up in my life? No, I'm not that naive. Somehow, all these out-of-the-ordinary events are connected. Only I don't know how. I feel like I'm missing a few essential pieces of the puzzle.

Meanwhile, Grace is excited to find herself part of an ancient legacy. She has no clue what membership will cost her in the long run. Her family, her friends, maybe even her life. How can I initiate her into this world? How can I take on that responsibility too?

I've done fine on my own for this long, and I'll keep on doing the same. I can save Grace from the lonely fate I've chosen. She can have the safe, normal life I gave up a long time ago.

"Listen, Grace," I begin, "I really think you should—"

"No."

She glares at me with hard determination in her silver eyes.

"What do you mean, no?" I ask. "You don't even know what I was going to say."

"I bet I do," she says, stepping forward and meeting me toe-to-toe. "You were going to send me home. Back to my *safe* life – which isn't so safe, in case you hadn't noticed."

She's right.

She holds out her hands, palms first, as if I need the reminder of her brush with a basilisk hybrid. She nearly died – would have died if instinct hadn't engaged her autoporting power – and it's my fault. I thought if I sent her away from me, she would stay safe. As if I am the only reason monsters attack. I fight monsters on the verge of killing humans every day. Even if they didn't know that she's a descendant of Medusa, she'd still be in danger.

Keeping her away from me won't protect her.

"So if you think you can just play the martyr," she continues, "and shoulder all this responsibility on your own," she punctuates her words with a pointed finger at my chest, "then you're mistaken. I need to be part of this and—"

"You're right," I admit.

She opens her mouth, as if she is ready to keep arguing,

but then jerks back as she realises I have just agreed with her. "I am?"

I nod. It was stupid to think that her life could be normal ever again. She needs training, skills and knowledge to help her defend herself the next time she's attacked. I shudder at the thought, but I have to be practical. It's bound to happen again.

"Now that you're in San Francisco," I explain, "there's no turning back. You see monsters, and that puts you in danger."

She looks down at her shredded hands, in a kind of helpless gesture. Yes, this is what she wanted, but maybe she's realising this is a life-changing moment. Good. She needs to have a healthy respect for the seriousness of the situation.

The wounds on her hands – a fresh reminder of just how dangerous beasties can be – still need to be treated. There may not be any monster venom in her bloodstream, but a little antibiotic ointment couldn't hurt.

I head for the first-aid kit in the bathroom.

"Where are the monsters?" she asks, following me. "When they're not in our world, where do they live?"

"In another realm," I explain – not that I fully understand the logistics. "Like a parallel underworld, a dark cavernous abyss full of all the bad creatures ever born." I flip on the water. "Here, rinse off your hands."

"Have you been there?"

She slips her hands under the tap. I'm impressed that she doesn't scream at what must be a burning sting all over her palms.

"No, but from how Ursula has described it," I explain, "I picture a bleak, stinky cave, with nasty stuff dripping from the ceiling and nonstop beastie-on-beastie prizefighting."

Grace snorts a little and I smile.

"How do they get out?" she asks.

"Ursula says the gods had to leave a crack." I grab a tube of antibacterial ointment and twist off the cap. "A window barely big enough for one to get out at a time."

Or, at least, it used to be barely that big. Now it's big enough to let out two or three or who knows how many. Another sign that something big is happening.

I hand her the tube.

"So they're in this parallel underworld, hanging out, until they can sneak through the crack." Grace squeezes a glob of ointment onto her hand. "Why do they come out? Just because their parallel underworld is so bad?"

I take back the tube and replace the cap while she rubs the ointment over her raw wounds. They're looking better already. She probably shares my quick-healing ability, a definite plus for a huntress. I'm – we're – not immortal or anything, but our supernatural genes do wonders to speed up recovery time.

"Partly, I suppose."

"And the other reason?" she asks, proving that she won't let me get by with half answers.

"To hunt humans," I blurt, because there is no way to soften this blow. "They come out to feed on humans, on their life force. It gives the monsters a kind of high."

I leave out the part where it also gives the monster control of the human. Grace is probably freaking out enough already about all this stuff.

"And the ones that escape... do you kill them?"

"I wish. Follow me." I head to the kitchen and grab an apple out of a bowl on the counter. "From what I understand, there's some sort of magical protection so they can't be killed in our world. A little bonus rule that some god or goddess slipped into the ritual when Olympus sealed the realms apart."

"Nice."

"Yeah." We share a wry smile. "Ursula says no one knows who for sure, but everyone suspects Athena."

"Makes sense," Grace says. "Since she's the one who got Medusa killed in the first place, she probably didn't want our jobs made any easier."

I shrug. "Anyway, the best I can do is send them back to where they belong."

"How?"

"With these." I pull back my upper lip, revealing my teeth as my fangs pop down into place.

Grace's eyes widen. "Fangs?" She touches her own

169

canine teeth, as if expecting fangs to suddenly burst through. "Are we, like, vampires?"

"Not even close," I say, tossing the apple from hand to hand. "These babies don't suck, they inject."

She looks concerned, like she doesn't believe my insistence that we're not bloodsuckers. I'm kind of surprised her fangs haven't made an appearance already. Especially during her run-in with the basilisk hybrid tonight. Maybe if her subconscious didn't know about the pair of weapons hiding in her mouth, they couldn't engage. Self-preservation instinct sent her magically to my door instead.

Obviously she needs training, to learn how to defend herself against the creatures that would love nothing more than to send their own nasty venom coursing through her veins. As much as I wish I could send her away, back to the world she's always known, that's not possible any more. Monsters know about her and she knows about them. The floodgates are open, and there aren't enough buckets on the planet to get the water back behind the dam. I'm going to have to train her, for her own protection, and this might as well be lesson number one.

"Here, take this," I say, handing her the apple. "And close your eyes."

I think back to Ursula's earliest lessons. It's been four years since she found me and we started training, but I remember every session as if it were only yesterday.

When you've spent a lifetime feeling like a worthless burden, you tend to pay attention to the person who gives you a destiny.

Grace closes her eyes.

"Now," I say, circling around her as I speak, "think about the monster that attacked you at the bus stop. Picture every slimy, snaky detail."

Her brow creases and her upper lip curls in disgust. Good girl.

"Imagine it has you pinned down. You're trapped." I step close and whisper, "You're scared and helpless and angry."

She starts shaking all over, and I have a feeling I'm getting it pretty close to what actually happened. I'm not trying to freak her out, but she has to learn to overcome the fear. I wouldn't be good at my job if I went out hunting terrified of what might happen.

To her credit, she doesn't open her eyes or beg me to stop.

"You think you're about to die," I say, making my voice as low and hypnotic as possible. "Now," I stop in front of Grace, "picture yourself flipping it over, so you're on top and it's trapped beneath you. You're in control."

Her lips spread into a small smile. Two perfectly white fangs slide into place so smoothly, she doesn't notice.

"Now, pretend the apple is the beast's neck," I command. "Bite!"

Without hesitation, she lifts the apple to her mouth and sinks her teeth into the shiny red skin. She sighs, and my own fangs tingle with envy. When the venom flows, there's a kind of sweet euphoria. I call it the huntress bliss, an amazing feeling that you want to experience again and again. It makes you want to hunt again and again. After four years, the novelty has kind of worn off, but sometimes it catches me by surprise. If I could bottle that feeling, I'd be a billionaire.

I cup my hand around hers and pull it and the apple away from her mouth. Her fangs recede as she opens her dreamy eyes, clearly confused about what has just happened.

"Did I...?"

She doesn't need to finish the question. I hold out the apple, showing her the twin fang holes oozing with the translucent purple liquid, the venom that holds the power to send monsters back to their realm, and the unequivocal proof that she's a huntress too.

She lifts her hand to her mouth, running fingertips over her back-to-normal teeth. "I did that?"

"All you."

"Can I...?" She reaches out and gingerly touches the apple, collecting some of the venom on her fingertip.

"It's harmless to us," I explain. "Taste it. It's kind of sweet, actually."

I don't mention that it's probably sweet in order to

get rid of the nasty taste of monster. She doesn't need to know that yet.

She dabs her finger to her lip and licks a tiny taste of the purple fluid. She looks up at me, amazed. "It *is* sweet."

I turn and toss the apple into the compost can on the counter. If there'd been any doubt before about Grace being my sister, it has just evaporated like a monster back into the abyss. My sister.

For a second, with my back to Grace, I press my palms against the cool black granite and let all the changes of the last few days overwhelm me. For so long, it's been me and Ursula. Two, alone. And before that, only me. I don't know how to have a sister, how to *be* a sister. How to be a *teacher*. Who am I to give lessons to Grace? Just because I can hunt doesn't mean I can teach someone else to do it.

I don't know if I can do this.

"So I'm supposed to… *bite* them?" she asks.

I suck in a deep breath. Whether I think I'm up to the task or not, I'm the only one around who can train her. It's either me or a painful death at the hands of some hideous creature. I'm definitely the better of the two options.

I spin around and lean back against the counter. "Yes. Bite fast and hard. In a vein is best," I explain. "Fastest. But anywhere will work. As long as you don't get bitten or scratched in the meantime."

"What happens if I get bitten or scratched?"

"Monsters have venom of their own. Each one is different. Most only cause unbearable pain if not treated quickly enough."

"Most?" she asks.

Some part of me doesn't want to tell her, wants to protect her from the harsh reality of the world she's been forced into. Born into, I suppose. But shielding her from reality doesn't make it any less true. "Some are deadly," I have to admit. I close my eyes so I don't have to look at her face. "We have antidotes for a lot of them. Not all."

"Like the blue liquid you used on your neck the other night?"

I nod. "Griffin antivenom."

I sense Grace leaning against the counter next to me.

"It's not a bad dream, is it?" she asks quietly.

"No," I say just as quietly. "It's not."

We stand there in silence for a few minutes. I can imagine what's racing through her mind – a swirl of thoughts about monsters and fangs and venom and attacks and maybe getting killed in the process – but mine is calm. For the first time in days, I know what I have to do; I don't have much of a choice. Either I teach her to defend herself, or she's a sitting duck for any monster that pops into our world.

"You need training," I say, turning my stare across the dining area and out over the dark bay. Now that I know what needs to be done, I'm ready to attack it with the same confidence I attack everything.

"You think?" she replies with unexpected sarcasm.

I smile at the spunk I haven't been giving her credit for. She's my sister in more ways than one, I guess.

"Can you be here?" I ask. "Every day after school, and on weekends."

"I…" She hesitates – maybe worrying what her parents will think, since she has parents to worry about her whereabouts – but then says, "Yes. I'll be here."

"Okay," I say, trying to put myself into the mode of teacher. "We'll start with basic defence strategies," I explain. "Ways to protect yourself from an attack."

She looks down at her ointment-covered fingertips. They've stopped bleeding, but they're still pretty raw. "I could have definitely used that tonight."

I try not to think about what might have happened if she hadn't managed to autoport. I'd be back to being an only child in a venom-filled heartbeat. I push the thought aside. No point worrying about that now. Time to focus on the future and not dwell on the past.

"Once you've mastered some basic defence techniques," I say, "we'll move on to offensive strategies."

"Biting?" she asks.

"Biting," I agree. "And other things. It's not always easy to get a bite in, especially on the multi-headed creatures. You'll need backup techniques. Punches and kicks and weapons."

"Like the knife in your boot?"

I turn a surprised look on her. "How do you know about my knife?"

She shrugs. "I caught a glimpse the other night when your trouser leg was rolled up. And when you carried me out of the nightclub."

"Oh," I mumble, suddenly feeling guilty about my actions that night. "Sorry about that."

"No worries." She's surprisingly chipper for someone who has, in the last week, been kidnapped, discovered a long-lost sister, started seeing monsters and been attacked by one.

"I'm…" She dips her head, like she's embarrassed. "I'm glad you did. I'm glad we… found each other. No matter how it happened."

As much as it shocks me to admit it, I say, "Me too."

We stand there, side by side, leaning against the counter, and I'm surprised at how comfortable it feels. I'm not usually at ease around other people, especially not people I've just met. I don't know if it's that I prefer being alone or that I'm used to being on my own. Or at least that used to be true.

That's another part of the strange events of late, because it's not only Grace who makes me feel this way. It's Nick too. Even though I know he has to be nothing but trouble, I let my guard down when he's around. I let myself be a little more… me than I am with other people.

I shake my head to get those thoughts out. There's no place for Nick or any other boy in my life. I have a mission and a destiny and a world of responsibility that no one else can possibly understand.

Well, no one but Grace, now.

"What are we going to do about Milo?" she asks, pulling me thankfully from my thoughts.

"Who?"

"Milo," she repeats. "The boy who thought you were me at school today. You didn't even know who he was?"

"Oh, him," I reply. I forgot that part of my day and Grace's rushed recap of the situation. "Nope, never saw him before. Or at least never noticed him."

"Never noticed him?" she asks in disbelief. "How could you not notice Milo?"

I shrug. "Guess I wasn't looking."

I do my best to stay off other people's radars and to keep anything that's not from the beastie realm off mine.

Grace lets out a snort. I glance sideways at her and find a daydreamy look on her face. Three guesses what – scratch that, *who* – put it there.

I almost ask her about him, almost cross the fine line into girl talk and into the beginning stages of friendship. But that world is as foreign to me as monster hunting is to her. I need to take baby steps in that direction.

Instead of probing for details, I say, "I'll keep a low profile. He'll never see me again."

"It's not really Milo I'm worried about," she says, turning to face me. "He barely knows me. But Thane is another story."

"Thane?"

"My brother."

I must get a confused look on my face, because she quickly adds, "My *adopted* brother."

"Oh." My breath whooshes out in relief. Not that the idea of another sibling horrifies me or anything, but it would be kind of a lot to take in all at once. One sister is enough.

"I won't be able to convince Thane he saw someone who only looked like me," she explains. "He'll know."

"Thane Whitfield?" I ask, committing the unfamiliar name to memory. "I don't think we have any classes in common."

"He's a senior," she says, "but if you pass him in the corridors or—"

"I'll make sure he never sees me, either," I say. For some reason it's important for me to reassure Grace, to keep her life as close to normal as possible. My life has never been normal, I wouldn't even know what that feels like, but I can do my best to make sure hers stays that way.

At first I'm not sure she hears me. She just stares down at her hot-pink sneakers, lost in thought. Finally, she says, "Well, we'll have to deal with whatever comes up." She looks up at me and smiles. "Right?"

"Right."

She pushes herself away from the counter. "I'd better get going. Mom will worry if I'm out too late."

I follow her out of the kitchen, to the living room where she tossed her jacket on one of the leather armchairs.

"Are these real leather?" she asks, nodding at the couches and chairs.

"As far as I know. Why?"

She makes a disgusted face but just shakes her head. "Never mind." As she shrugs into her jacket, she says, "I'll be here tomorrow after school for my first lesson."

I nod, grabbing her backpack off the floor and handing it to her.

"Do I need to bring anything?" she asks. "Or wear anything special?"

I shake my head. "Only if you want to. Monsters don't care whether you're in sweats or a party dress. You can train in whatever you wear every day."

"Makes sense," she says, taking the backpack but not putting it on. Her gaze flicks to the library. "Um, do you think I could take a couple of those monster file ring binders?" she asks. "To study."

I shrug. "Don't see why not. Help yourself."

I've read them all already. And Grace needs to learn what's inside them too.

She hurries to the library and returns a minute later, her backpack on her back and a big smile on her face.

I'm about to give her a smile in return when I catch the faint scent of skunk wafting in off the balcony. Here we go again.

I grab my keys off the table by the door.

"Come on," I say. "I'll give you a ride home."

And after I make sure she's home safe, I've got a hippalectryon to hunt. I should hunt down Grace's basilisk hybrid too. It must be running wild on the streets by now. Not to mention my missing skorpios hybrid from this afternoon. What is it with all the monster escapes today? Can't they give it a break for a night? I've still got hours of homework.

But, I think as Grace follows me down the spiral staircase, I guess a huntress's work is never done.

Lucky us.

While Grace takes off her shoes at the training room door, I mentally prepare myself for the role of trainer. Teacher.

For so long, I've been the student; it's a big adjustment to be on the other side. *But,* I think as I watch Grace nearly fall over while trying to step out of her left sneaker, *there isn't another option.* I spent all night trying to come up with a game plan, a strategy for giving Grace the ability to defend herself.

As I punched the hippalectryon in its horsey face, I decided to start with basic martial arts training. Learning a stable stance and defensive techniques will help Grace stand strong against whatever comes after her.

Never did find the runaway hybrids.

"Ready," she says, her cheeks pink with embarrassment. If she's ready, then so am I.

"Okay," I say, taking a calming breath, "the first thing you need to learn is how to stand properly."

Her brow pinches together. "Standing?" She glances down at her feet and then back at me. "I think I've got that down pretty well."

I'm tempted to roll my eyes. Instead, I step forward and give her shoulder a quick shove. The push throws her off balance and she stumbles to the floor. Her fall is padded by the mat, but it still stings. Especially her pride.

"I said *properly*," I say, trying not to gloat as I reach down to give her a hand up. "A defensive stance can help keep you on your feet."

"Oh," she says when she's upright. She releases my hand and self-consciously dusts at her backside. "Okay. How should I stand?"

"Feet shoulder-width apart." I demonstrate, opening my stance and bending slightly at the knees. "And drop your butt a little. It will give you a lower centre of gravity and the ability to absorb more force through your legs."

She mimics my stance, spreading her feet a little too wide and dropping a little too low. I circle her, nudging her feet inwards and urging her back up a couple of inches.

"Good." I move around to face her and, without

warning, give her shoulder another shove. She wobbles back but doesn't fall.

"Wow." She grins as she maintains her footing. "That's amazing."

I shrug. "It's simple physics."

"But you have superstrength," she argues. "If I can stand up when you—"

I give her another, harder shove that sends her back to the floor.

This time she pops back up before I can offer help. "Okay, point taken."

We spend the next half hour working on her stance, giving her the best solid base before working on movement. I'm pushing against both her shoulders, leaning into the effort, while she resists by squatting deeper and leaning forward into me, when she asks, "Can I ask you something?"

Since I haven't managed to knock her to the floor in ten minutes, I decide her stance is in place.

"Sure," I say, releasing the pressure and proud to see her adjust her balance to stay in place, rather than falling forward. "What?"

"How do you find the monsters?" She starts to put her hands on her hips but must remember that it's better to leave her arms hanging at her sides. "How did you know the minotaur was in that restaurant?"

"For the minotaur, I just followed my nose."

"Oh, the smell!" Her nose wrinkles up in disgust. "It was awful. So you were in the neighbourhood, so to speak, and caught the scent."

"No, I was home."

Her head jerks back. "You smelled it all the way over here? Chinatown is, what, two miles away?"

"I guess."

"How is that possible?" she asks.

"Like a hunting dog," I answer. "My sense of smell is highly tuned to eau de monster."

Grace sniffs the air. "Do you think I can do that too?"

"Maybe." I inhale but can't sense anything over the stink of the sweaty gym. "Let's go to the balcony and try it out."

I feel her practically bouncing behind me as I head through the living room, to the library, and out onto the balcony beyond. Closing my eyes, I take in a deep breath through my nose, searching out anything that sounds warning bells.

Beside me, Grace does the same.

"I don't smell anything but salt water," she complains.

"Yeah," I agree. "Me neither."

"So the streets of San Francisco are safe from monsters at the moment?"

"From the kind that reek. There are some that smell pretty much normal—"

"Like the cobra lady," Grace says. "I didn't smell anything

weird, and she was right next to me. How do you find that kind?"

I turn and lean back against the railing, looking at our reflections in the glass windows of the library. "Good old-fashioned footwork," I explain. "Most nights I take a drive, patrolling the streets in Moira, eyes out for anything non-human."

In the reflection, I see Grace nod. She stares out over the Bay as I stare at us. A few days ago, I would never have imagined discussing my life with anyone but Ursula. It feels kind of good to share it with someone else.

"There's another thing you should know about," I find myself saying before I can think better of it. "Our eyes."

Grace turns, mirroring my stance against the railing. "Yeah, they're the same silver grey."

"No," I say. "I mean, yes, they're the same, but they are special. You remember how I said Medusa didn't turn people to stone, she hypnotised them?"

"Yes."

"Well." I take a deep breath. "So can we."

"What?" She scuffs at the concrete floor of the balcony. "Hypnotise people?"

I nod. "If you look someone directly in the eye, you can make them do whatever you want."

Unless you're the new and mysterious Nick, of course. But that's a puzzle for another day.

"That's…" She shakes her head, like it's too much

to accept. "How do you… How often have you…"

"I try not to use it unless absolutely necessary," I explain, so she doesn't think I'm out hypnotising people left and right. "Usually only during a fight, if a human is in danger or getting in the way."

She's silent for a few long moments before saying, "That must be a very powerful feeling. To have people do what you want. To control someone that way."

"I'll admit, at first it was a little thrilling." I don't need to tell her about the time I convinced the owner of a flower shop I had already paid for the bouquet I wanted to give Ursula for Mother's Day. Ursula made me earn the money and pay the man back threefold.

"It's not a power to be used lightly," I explain. Grace doesn't seem like the type to abuse power, but you never know. "And the effects don't last long. Just enough to get out of a bad situation."

"Oh," she says quietly. "Good."

For some reason, I get the feeling she's thinking about that boy, Milo. I could give her a lecture or well-meaning advice, but I'm not her conscience. That's a moral decision she'll have to make on her own.

"You know," I say, "I think that we've done enough for the first day of training."

"Yeah," she says, shaking off her thoughts. "I've definitely got standing down to a fine art now."

I push myself away from the balcony and head inside.

"You need a ride home?"

"No thanks," she says. "I know which buses to take now."

She grabs her backpack off the conference table and pulls out the monster ring binders she took home last night. After returning them to the shelf, she grabs a few more.

When she has them zipped in, she slings the pack over her shoulder and turns to face me. "So, same time tomorrow?"

"Sounds good." I glance down at her feet. "Might want your shoes, though."

She laughs, but her cheeks flame bright pink. "Probably a good idea."

She's on her way out the door, shoes in place, when she turns back and says, "Thanks, Gretchen."

"For what?"

"For training me, for finding me, for being my sister." She gives me a small smile. "For everything."

I nod and she disappears out the door.

Gretchen the teacher had a good first day. Now it's time for Gretchen the huntress to go out on patrol. Just because I didn't scent any beasties from the balcony doesn't mean they're not out there. Yesterday's missing hybrids are my first priority. I snatch Moira's keys off the counter, grab my leather jacket as I walk out the door, and head back into familiar territory.

CHAPTER 12

Grace

My body is so sore and achy, I feel like I've been beat up by a sledgehammer. Which, I suppose, is pretty equivalent to two days of training with Gretchen. She's mentioned, several times, that I need to get into shape. My strength and stamina are lacking, she says, and that translates into lots of press-ups and skipping.

After dragging myself home, I collapse onto the couch, wondering how on earth I'm supposed to fight a monster if I can't lift my arms. Seems counterproductive to turn me into a pile of muscle mush.

Maybe, if I close my eyes for just a few minutes, I'll…

"Hey Grace," Milo says.

My eyes flash open and my heart spasms. In a single beat, my mind is completely awake.

"Milo," I stammer. "Hi, I didn't know you were here."

"We weren't," he says, jerking his head at Thane, who is stuffing a lemon bar into his mouth as he emerges from the kitchen. "Just got back from practice."

Did they just walk in? Maybe I actually dozed for a minute. Or longer. My sluggish brain is fully refreshed, and some of the painful ache in my muscles is gone. Either I snuck a bit of a nap or those quick-healing powers Gretchen told me about have made fast work of my training pains.

"I'm going for a shower," Thane announces.

As he heads down the hall, Milo drops his duffel bag on the floor by the front door and walks into the living room. Besides the couch I'm crashed out on, there are a couple of armchairs and an ottoman. All of which are perfectly comfortable. All of which Milo ignores, instead circling the coffee table and taking the other end of the couch.

"So," he says, leaning back into the corner of the couch and stretching out his legs so they're only inches from mine, "how are you liking San Francisco?"

My skin tingles at the thought of him sitting only a few feet away. I try to deepen my shallow breathing. It won't do me any good to pass out right now. I want to absorb every moment.

"I, um, it's…" I take a deep breath and force myself to look up. Not quite into his eyes, but at his temple, at the dark curls just above his ear. "Great."

"It's a big change, huh?" he asks.

"You have no idea," I say.

And I'd like to keep it that way. The last thing I want is Milo finding out I'm a freak with fangs, a secret sister and a monster-hunting destiny. My best chance with him is to be a normal, average girl.

"It's different," I say, "but I like it."

My gaze shifts to his eyes, and I find him studying at me. I'm caught in his eyes. Hypnotised by his…

Shoot. I *can't* look into his eyes. I don't want to accidentally hypnotise him or make him think or feel something he really doesn't. If Milo likes me, I want him to like me for real.

"Are you okay?" he asks.

"Yeah, I—"

He pushes himself away from the end of the couch, moving to the cushion directly next to mine. Startled, I start to lean back, until I see him slowly lift his hand. I watch, frozen, as he reaches out and brushes his fingertips against my forehead, right at the hairline.

The contact sends shivers over my skin.

"What happened?" he asks, his voice almost a whisper, just inches away. "You have a nasty-looking bruise right here."

I jerk back and slap my hand to my forehead, connecting with the bruise and sending a throb of pain through my head. Ouch.

"Oh, that." Like I can explain that my long-lost twin accidentally – or so she said – karate chopped me in the head during a monster-hunting training session. "I hit my head on a cabinet," I explain. "I have klutz tendencies."

He laughs softly, and my heart melts.

"It's gonna look worse before it gets better."

"Great," I whisper.

"I like it." His mouth quirks into a dimpled smile. "Makes you look tough."

His pale eyes are so close, I can see the fringe of light brown around the pupil. I'm surrounded by the faint, after-practice remains of his cologne—

A door slams down the hall and I jump back. The movement jars my muscles, and a dull ache radiates through my body.

Thane appears in the living room, a scowl on his face. One brow lifts. He asks Milo, "Homework?"

"Right," Milo says cheerfully.

As they settle in at the dining table to do their assignments, I sink back into the soft couch. I could use a long soak in a hot bath – the tub in the master bath is humongous and has been calling to me ever since we moved in. But for right now, I'm content to sit here, with two of my favourite boys just a few feet away, and daydream about what might have happened if Thane took longer showers.

"Come on," Gretchen shouts, standing over me like a hovering drill sergeant while I struggle with sit-up number forty-seven out of the fifty she has ordered me to do.

I manage to touch my elbows to my knees just before my stomach muscles give out completely. I slam back to the floor, my arms flopping out to the sides.

"Three more." She leans down over me and grabs my hands, stuffing them back behind my head. "You can do it."

"I can't," I pant. "I'm done."

"You're not done." She moves around to my feet, kneels down and braces my ankles. "You can't give up if a Teumessian fox is chasing you down Market Street, and you can't give up now."

"Fine," I huff.

Focusing all my energy on getting my elbows to my knees, I manage two more. My muscles are shaking and I can already imagine the cramps I'll have later. The thought of doing one more is just inconceivable.

"Last one," Gretchen cheers.

I flop my head back and forth, incapable of arguing out loud.

"If you make it," she says, "I'll tell you what I learned about Milo today."

What? With a surge of hidden strength, I force my torso up, barely reach my knees, and then fall back with a thud.

"What?" I gasp. "What about Milo?"

"Nothing." Gretchen jumps to her feet. "I just thought that might motivate you."

Oh, unfair. "If my body wasn't all wet-noodly right now, I'd throw something at you."

Gretchen laughs, a big, full laugh that I don't think

she lets out very often. I smile and am relieved to discover that my cheek muscles don't ache. That's something.

"Here," Gretchen says, extending a hand to help me up. "Let's go refuel."

I let her haul me to my feet, barely contributing anything to the effort. Just as I'm fully upright, I catch a foul smell. Like the stink of melting tyres.

"Ugh," Gretchen says.

"You smell it too, huh?"

"The burned rubber?" When I nod, she says, "It's a satyr."

"A satyr?" I repeat.

"Basically a man with a horse's tail and donkey ears." She rolls her head, like she's working kinks out of her neck. "They're not usually the mean and nasty type, but sometimes they're tricky."

I follow her as she stomps out of the training room and shrugs into her leather jacket. Monster-hunting time.

"Oh." I'm a little relieved that my gruelling physical training is over for the day, but sad that I'm going to lose out on some time with Gretchen. We're still getting to know each other, and I like hanging out with her.

I grab my backpack off the floor. "I guess I'll see you tomorrow then."

"Why?" She spins back to face me. "You're coming with."

I can't help grinning. "Really?"

Then it hits me. I'm going on my first real monster hunt. My stomach turns. And doesn't stop turning. The whole way from Gretchen's loft to the strip of beachfront condos where the smell is originating, I feel like I'm going to be sick. Gretchen's driving doesn't help, either.

"Here," she says, pulling up on to the sidewalk in front of a narrow walkway between two of the buildings. "Put these on."

She hands me what looks like a pair of wide leather bracelets, only they don't feel like leather. "What are they?"

"Kevlar wrist cuffs," she answers without explanation. She nods at the walkway. "The satyr's just at the other side of this building."

Getting attacked by cobra lady – a basilisk hybrid, Gretchen calls her – was bad enough, but at least it came as a surprise. I didn't know what was coming, so I didn't worry myself into a state of freak-out beforehand.

Now I've had the whole drive to play out scenarios in my head. None of them end well.

"I don't think I can do this," I tell Gretchen. "I'm… I haven't had enough training."

"You've had more than I did when I took down my first beast."

"But you're you," I exclaim. "You're strong and brave and I'm… not."

Gretchen lifts her sunglasses and looks me in the eye.

"I know you're scared," she says, "but there's nothing to worry about."

I bite my lips and shake my head. She can't possibly know what it's like to be this terrified.

"You know I won't let anything happen to you."

"I know," I say. That's not my main concern, though. I'm more worried about letting Gretchen down, about discovering that I can't do this and that I'm not fit for my destiny.

"Besides," she says, patting me on the knee as she slides her glasses back into place, "satyrs are cowards. They run more than they fight."

She climbs out of the car before I can argue more. Obviously she has confidence in me; otherwise she would have sent me home instead of bringing me to the fight. And her confidence gives me some too.

I follow her out onto the sidewalk, snapping the Kevlar cuffs onto my wrists as I go. "Tell me what to do."

"It's at the other end of this path," she explains, nodding down the walkway. "You stand at this end, blocking its escape, and I'll come at it from the other side."

"Okay." I nod, trying to give myself courage. "I can do that."

Gretchen gives me an encouraging smack on the shoulder before taking off around the building at a run. I stand at the end of the walkway, feet spread and knees bent. I'm not sure what I expect to happen, but I want to be prepared.

It all happens so quickly.

A figure moves to the end of the path, silhouetted against the late-afternoon sun. At first I think it's Gretchen. Until I see the tail.

He turns, looks my direction and starts running. Right at me. I tense my muscles, ready to block his escape route.

But instead of trying to escape past me, he launches into the air, knocking me off my feet and pinning me to the ground. The breath whooshes out of me and I can't even scream for help.

"I'm sorry," he says, giving me an apologetic look. "I wish it didn't have to be like this."

Like what? I shake my head vigorously. I don't understand.

Then I see it – a dagger clutched in his fist.

"No," I gasp.

"I—"

His weight is jerked off me as Gretchen tackles him. I suck in deeper and deeper breaths, trying to get my wind back.

"What the Hades are you doing?" she demands, practically snarling in the satyr's face. "You guys usually run."

"I know, I know," he says, his face crumpling like he might actually cry. "I didn't want to do it, but—"

"But what?" Gretchen shouts, shoving against his shoulders.

"The bounty," he wails. "I couldn't resist the bounty."

She leans very close to his face. "What. Bounty?"

"Word is going around," he explains, "that any creature who brings back a huntress will earn freedom from the abyss."

Gretchen jerks back.

A bounty on our heads? I suddenly remember basilisk lady saying something about me earning her freedom. At the time I was too freaked out to process it, but this must be what she meant.

"Who ordered it?" Gretchen asks.

"I don't know," the satyr whines. "I swear. It might just be a rumour for all I know."

"Rumour or not," she says, smiling as her fangs descend, "you're not going to be the one to find out."

One second she's biting him in the big furry ear, the next he's gone.

"This is not good," she says.

"Maybe it is just a rumour," I suggest hopefully.

She pushes herself to her feet and brushes the gravel dust off the knees of her cargo trousers. "Considering all the craziness hitting the fan right now," she says, reaching down to pull me up without waiting for me to ask for help, "I'm going to have to go with *not* a rumour."

"Yeah," I say as I follow her to the car. "Probably not."

She guns her engine and takes off before I can buckle my seatbelt. Definitely not good.

CHAPTER 13

Gretchen

"I'm sorry, Miss Sharpe," the assistant principal says, "but all the other first-period science classes are full."

"There has to be something else," I say, verging on desperate. "Like an art class or maybe choir."

I can't sing, but anything would be better than being stuck in first period with Nick every day. I've skipped two more classes, forging Ursula's signature on notes to clear things with the front office. But any more misses and the administration is going to start poking its nose into our business.

They probably won't like the idea that I've been living alone for almost two weeks, or that before that my only guardian was a woman who found me on the street. Authorities tend to frown on things they can't file into a neat little box.

Avoiding Nick isn't worth the kind of trouble that would bring. The best solution is for me to transfer out of Mrs Knightly's class.

"What about Woodwork?" I ask. "I would totally rock Woodwork."

The assistant principal shakes his head. "You need a science class." He leans forward, resting his forearms on his desk. "I'm sorry, but you'll have to stay in Biology."

"Yeah, fine," I say, shoving out of the brown vinyl chair and snatching my backpack off the grimy linoleum floor. "Thanks."

For nothing.

As I weave through the crowd of students, heading for Mrs Knightly's class, I tell myself to grow up. Avoiding Nick is a weak move, and I'm stronger than that. I won't let him affect my life any more than he already has. It's not like me to run away from a problem. I turn and fight instead.

But as I walk into class and see him sitting there in the desk behind mine, my courage fades.

I'm not scared of him, not exactly. I just don't understand him. I don't understand why he's immune to my hypno-eyes, why he won't back off from pursuing me, why he keeps showing up when I'm in the middle of a monster fight. And it's not as if I can ask him any of those things.

I can't run from the unknown forever.

Straightening my shoulders, I march into the room and drop into my seat. I ignore the fact that the hair at the back of my neck prickles to attention. I ignore the fact that I can practically feel his eyes on me. I ignore everything but the process of getting my notebook out of my backpack, pulling my textbook out from under my chair and opening it to the page indicated on the board.

I'm tense, waiting for him to say something. Waiting, waiting, waiting.

The bell rings and he hasn't said a word. There's no indication that he's even noticed that I'm here. Or that I was gone the last three days.

When Mrs Knightly closes the door and moves to the whiteboard, I think I'm home free.

"Nice to see you again, Miss Sharpe," she says. "I do hope your teeth are feeling better."

"Uh," I stammer, remembering that my notes said something about dentist appointments. "Yes, ma'am."

"I trust you can find someone to fill you in on what you've missed."

"I—"

"I'll help her," Nick says.

"Thank you," she says, turning her attention to the board. "Now, if you'll look at the diagram…"

"You're welcome," Nick whispers over my shoulder.

Ignore him. Ignore him, ignore him, ignore—

I feel a tickle against my left ear, and when I jerk around at the sensation, I find a folded piece of paper waving before my eyes. I snatch the paper, throwing Nick a quick glare, and turn back to face the front. I don't need Mrs Knightly calling me out for note passing, especially not because of *him*.

For several long seconds, I sit with the note clasped between my palms, resting in my lap. Don't be curious, I tell myself. It's only going to annoy you anyway.

In the end, of course, curiosity wins out.

Carefully, so I don't draw any attention, I unfold the note and slip it beneath my textbook. When I'm sure Mrs Knightly is focused on the board, I slide it down to read: *can we talk after class?*

Frankly, I'm a little disappointed. My imagination came up with so many better ideas for what the note might say. Like: *you fight giant scorpions often?* Or: *can we be more than friends now?* Or even: *thanks for leaving me with concussion.*

Can we talk? seems so tame in comparison.

I quickly scribble *No* on the paper and slip it under my arm and onto his desk.

Seconds later it comes flying back over my shoulder. I slap my hand down before it sails off to the floor.

Mrs Knightly glances up at the sound, and I force a very interested and attentive look on my face. When she looks away, I open the note: *coward.*

I write back: *brain-dead idiot.*

He chuckles when he reads that, and I find myself smiling in return. I have to admire a guy who can laugh at being called an idiot. He must be pretty self-confident.

When he doesn't return the note right away, I catch myself anxiously waiting for the next instalment.

Get a grip, Gretchen. I turn my attention to the board and start copying the academic notes I should have been writing all along.

I've almost forgotten his presence – almost – when the note slides back over my shoulder a few minutes before the bell.

I nonchalantly open it over my notebook and see that the message is longer this time. Like half a page long.

I'm sorry for whatever happened on Monday. I don't remember the whole thing, but I know you were upset and for that I'm really sorry. It won't happen again. I think you're a different kind of girl

I have to snort at that. He has no idea how different I really am. And he can't know. I keep reading.

and I like that. But if you want me to back off, I will. Even if I don't want to. (BTW, in case you haven't noticed, I don't want to.)

The bell rings. I don't say a word, just fold the note up and slip it into my backpack along with my notebook. I half expect him to stop me as I get up and head for the door. I'm relieved. And, to be honest, a little disappointed.

He's backing off. That's exactly what I've wanted all along, and I refuse to let myself be annoyed that it's finally happening. This is a good thing. And I'm really glad I didn't transfer out of Biology… because I like Mrs Knightly.

CHAPTER 14

Grace

Our next unit in English class is on mythology. Like I haven't had enough myth showing up in my life lately. As Mrs Deckler starts handing out unit outlines halfway through class on Friday, I can't help a giddy giggle at the thought that I *am* myth now.

I accept the papers from the girl in front of me, take one and pass the rest behind me.

"Something funny, Miss Whitfield?" Mrs Deckler asks.

I bite my lips and shake my head. "No, ma'am."

"While you read over the unit plan," she says to the class, "I'm going to set up a quick introductory PowerPoint to prepare you for Monday's lesson."

I scan the topics – everything from Homer to Edith Hamilton to some contemporary fiction about teens descended from gods.

"As you can see from the list," Mrs Deckler says as she walks to the light switch, "we will be studying, in depth, the heroes, gods and monsters of ancient Greece."

I bite my lips again to keep from laughing. Between

Gretchen's training, the creatures I see on the street almost every day and studying the ring binder contents as I digitise them, I think I'll be the definite authority in the class when it comes to mythological monsters.

Not that I'll be able to admit why.

"I think you'll find that Aristotle was a nice introduction." She gives the room a big grin before flipping out the lights. "But now we're getting to the good stuff."

As the PowerPoint begins, my mind kind of drifts. I think about the monsters I've seen and the training Gretchen and I have been working on. I wonder if any of the monsters I've studied, seen and fought will be part of the unit.

"You will learn about hideous creatures."

I look up as the slide changes.

"Like the Minotaur."

There, on the screen, large as life, is an extremely accurate drawing of a minotaur. So exact, I can almost smell the rotten odour of...

I feel something slide against my upper lip. From the inside.

"Shoot," I whisper.

But since my fangs just decided to make an appearance, it sounds more like *Sssoot*.

I slap my hand over my mouth and jump out of my seat.

"Problem, Miss Whitfield?"

This isn't the first time my fangs have dropped on their own. Ever since Gretchen first got my fangs to engage, they keep popping down at really awkward times. Like when Thane snuck up on me while I was brushing my teeth. Or when the Rottweiler down the hall escaped his leash and I barely slammed the apartment door shut in time. But this is the first time at school, and I never know how long they're going to hang out.

I rush to the front of the classroom.

"Misssesss Deckler," I say from behind my palm, "I need to…"

She takes in my horrified look and the hand over my mouth and draws her own conclusions. "Go," she insists. "Don't worry about a bathroom pass."

Thank goodness. I nod and race out of class, heading for the girls' room.

I'm almost there when someone calls my name. I spin around to see Ms West hurrying towards me. My hand is still clamped over my mouth, so I just wave.

"Why are you outside of class?" she demands. "Do you have a pass?"

"No," I say from behind my hand. I try to focus on using words that won't lisp because of the fangs. "Girl twouble."

Shoot.

"I understand." Her eyes widen. "Don't let me keep you."

I nod and turn to dash into the bathroom. From outside,

she calls out, "Please see a nurse if you are unwell."

Gosh, I appreciate the concern. Doesn't she have other students to bug?

Inside the bathroom, I check to make sure it's empty before leaning on a sink to inspect my fangs in the mirror. The bluish glow of the lights above make them shine like pearls. Anyone walking in on me right now would think I'm some kind of vampire wannabe. A freak of a whole different kind.

I guess they do look like vampire fangs, extended canines that narrow down to a sharp – an extremely sharp – point.

"Come on," I tell my reflection. "Retract already."

Gretchen says it will take time for me to learn to fully control them. Now would be a really useful moment. I don't really look like the vampy goth type, so it would be hard to explain why I'm wearing fake fangs.

As if they understand my plea, my fangs slowly slide back up into their regular human-like position. I watch as my canines return to normal. As I return to normal.

"Whew."

I'm not sure what I would do if they stayed put. Hide in the bathroom all day? Mom would get a call when I missed class, and that would be even harder to explain.

Thankfully, I don't have to face that today. I turn the tap handle and am splashing a little cold water on my face when I hear the door swing open.

"Did you vomit?"

I turn towards the sound of the voice I am unfortunately learning to recognise. Miranda. Just what I need.

"No," I reply calmly. "I didn't vomit."

Her eyes scan me from head to toe.

"You look like you did." She makes a disgusted face. "Then again, you usually do."

She heads for a cubicle. I know I should walk out, should leave it alone, be the bigger person and all that. But some desperate part of me can't help asking, "Did I do something to offend you?"

She turns to face me. "You mean other than being alive?"

"Yeah," I say, despite the warning bell in my stomach. "Other than that."

She looks me over again, and I can feel myself squirming under the attention. When her blue eyes return to my face, she says, "Nope, that's enough."

She turns and heads into the cubicle, slamming the door shut behind her. I feel my fangs drop back into view. *If only.*

I wonder what my venom would do to a human. With my luck it would only make Miranda more unbearable.

I head into the last cubicle, quickly shut and lock the door and lift my feet off the floor. While I'm glad my fangs have decided that Miranda is a worthwhile threat – she could rival a minotaur any day – if I don't get them under control soon, if I have to keep hiding in the bathroom to avoid anyone noticing, my grades are going to suffer. And I don't think there's a believable explanation on the planet that could convince my parents of why that's happened.

The last thing I want is for them to decide we made a mistake and move us back to Orangevale. As much as I don't like Miranda and wish I could either stand up to her or avoid her altogether, I couldn't stand the thought of leaving Gretchen. Now that I've found my sister, I'll do whatever it takes to keep her.

"Focus," Gretchen shouts, moving somewhere behind me.

I can't see anything through the scarf tied around my head as a makeshift blindfold. She taps a hand against the left side of my waist.

"That's another kill," she grumbles. "If you don't learn to focus on your surroundings, you'll never survive a night fight. Feline hybrids especially have excellent night vision."

I clench my jaw and resist the urge to mention that we're in a major metropolitan city. There are flashing signs and glowing street lights everywhere. I'll never face a monster in complete darkness. At this point, though, my comment will only earn me some press-ups, which Gretchen is oh-so-happy to demand.

I close my eyes behind the scarf. Pointless, I know, but somehow the physical act of dropping my eyelids tells my brain to switch to the other senses. I listen and feel and even smell – taste is proving to be the only sense that's not exactly an asset in a fight. Actually, the thought of chomping down on a minotaur head or a scorpion tail seems like exactly the scenario in which I'd like my sense of taste to fail altogether. I know I'm going to have to bite one back to the abyss eventually, but I'm not really eager for the first time.

Shoving thoughts of monster bites from my mind, I pinpoint all my attention on Gretchen. She's been silent, which means she's been moving. No longer behind me.

I feel a gentle breeze on my right cheek. I tilt my head that way—

Just as Gretchen delivers a gentle punch to my stomach.

"Dead again," she complains. "You don't stand a chance in Hades of surviving a blind attack. You're going to make a nice meal for a sphinx if you don't focus."

That was an awfully wordy taunt for Gretchen. During training, she usually rivals Thane in the silent-communication department. This must be a distraction technique. I squeeze my eyes harder and catch a whiff of her eucalyptus shampoo. A soft squeak behind me.

I drop to a squat, spinning as I go.

I hear Gretchen's soft grunt as her punch connects with air, sending her arm swinging with unchecked momentum. While her centre of gravity is thrown off, I reach out, wrap both hands around her waist and flip on to my back, using my legs to send Gretchen flying over me as I roll.

"Oooft!" She hits the training mat with a nice thud.

I rip off my blindfold, jumping to my feet to survey my success. "Woohoo!" I shout, twisting around in a happy dance. "I did it!"

"Yeah," Gretchen says, trying to sound all gruff and mean. I can tell she's proud. "But only because I tried to telegraph my moves. I was getting tired of your failure."

"Whatever," I say. Not even Gretchen's grumbling can dampen my success. "I totally did it."

I extend my hand to help her up. Not that she needs it – I've seen her kick up from her back to a squat without using her hands. I'm surprised when she places her hand in mine and lets me pull her to her feet.

"It's not much," she says, reaching back to tug her tank into place, "but it's something."

I can't help but beam. Gretchen's not exactly free and easy with the compliments, so even this reluctant, minor one feels like a major success.

"What's next?" I ask, giddy to continue my training.

She sniffs the air.

"What? Do you smell a monster?" I ask. "What kind?"

Despite the disaster that was my last run-in with a monster, I'm kind of eager to go out on a hunt with Gretchen again. I'm ready to test out my training. It's been only four days, but surely I've acquired some useful fighting skills. Besides, with Gretchen at my side, no beast can get the jump on me.

I try sniffing the air the way she does, searching for the scent of a creature that doesn't belong in our realm. I don't smell a thing.

"Nope," she says with a wry smile. "I stink like sweat. Time to hit the shower."

"Oh." I feel my cheeks burn with embarrassment. Maybe I am a little overeager to go on another hunt. I feel like such a colossal idiot sometimes.

She hesitates, like she's thinking about reassuring me or making me feel better. Then, without a word, she walks out of the training room, heading for her bedroom and the giant glassed-in shower with three walls of massaging jets.

"Don't worry," I call out after she's out of hearing. "I'll amuse myself for a while. No problem."

I take a look around the training room, a massive gymnasium with padded mats covering half the floor and flat industrial carpet underneath. On the walls are a variety of traditional weapons. Long staffs, nunchucks, throwing stars, daggers, swords, foils and tonnes of others I couldn't name if you asked me. Gretchen won't let me touch them yet. She says I need to master hand-to-hand combat, to learn to defend myself with nothing but my hands and feet, which are usually all I'll have.

There are a couple of those wall-mounted ladders you have to climb in gym class sometimes and a long knotted rope hanging down from the ceiling. I can see weight machines and balance balls and even a balance beam, and I'm sure there is plenty more equipment I can't see.

As a non-jock-type person, this is not the kind of stuff that interests me. Well, at least not beyond what it means for my training.

If I've realised anything in the last week since I discovered my heritage and my duty, it's that I am totally ready to embrace this unknown part of my life. The only problem is that, besides Gretchen's training and what I've been able to get her to tell me, I don't really know anything about that side of me.

When I feel lost at school, I head to the nearest computer and pull up as much info about the subject as I can find.

"What I need to do," I mutter, "is research."

The only problem is that everything available on the internet about my ancient mythological ancestor is rewritten history. The results of Athena's full-scale smear campaign. Not exactly helpful.

But I know one place where I can find the research I need. "Gretchen's library."

Quickly slipping out of the training room, I head for the book-filled library. On the way I grab my backpack. The first thing I do is pull out the six ring binders I took home to digitise yesterday and trade them for new ones. I've managed to scan in more than two dozen, converting them into digital format. At this rate, I'll have the whole collection of monster files computerised in a few weeks. There are so many, it feels pretty daunting, but it needs to be done. Paper files provide such limited access. And they're vulnerable.

Besides, when I use the document scanner Mom bought last spring – I finally convinced her to go paperless – the pages are scanned in no time. I can probably get another two dozen done this weekend.

I shove the half dozen new ring binders into my bag.

"Now," I say to the walls of books, "where should I begin?"

At least the collection seems to be organised by subject matter rather than author or title. That would be madness to search through, especially without a catalogue of some kind, which Gretchen assures me does not exist.

"When I'm done with the ring binders," I say, wandering past the laden shelves, "that'll be my next project."

My eyes skim titles, looking for something that strikes my mood. Monsters and mythology? No thanks. Martial arts training techniques? Not right now. Medusa and the gorgons?

I stop at the section of books about my ancient ancestor and her immortal sisters. This is more like it. There are four full shelves of books, everything from collections of myths to anatomy to—

"Bingo." I tug a book off the shelf. *The Truth About Medusa and Her Sisters: Guardians of the Door.*

This sounds like exactly what I need. Not more about the propaganda that turned Medusa – in the public's mind – from a protectress into a monster. Libraries and websites are full of the lies that steal Medusa's noble glory and make her a much-feared beast instead. This looks like a more factual account of her story.

I drop into one of the comfy armchairs and open the book. There is no copyright page, which means that it was either privately published or printed before the first copyright laws. There isn't an author's name, either. The book is attributed to "an anonymous descendant of the great gorgon Medusa." I suck in a breath. One of my ancestors wrote this book.

I trace my fingers reverently over the worn cover, wondering how many generations back this book dates. A few? A dozen? More?

I flip to the table of contents, curious about what topics the book might contain. As I scan the list, I see a lot of chapters I should probably read. Some day. Right now, though, I'm looking for one particular topic. Autoporting.

Since escaping from cobra lady, I haven't been able to repeat my disappearing act. It's a power that could definitely come in handy, so I'd like some hints on how to make it happen.

My eyes skim over the early chapters. History, mostly, detailing Medusa's life from her birth to her death at the hands of the supposed hero – aka Athena's pawn –

Perseus. There are a couple of chapters on the gorgons' roles as guardians and their powers. I'm about to turn to the chapter on their powers when the title of the last chapter catches my eye.

"'Descendants of the Mortal Gorgon.'"

Forgetting about autoporting, I flip quickly to the first page of that chapter and begin reading.

> *Although most of the world believes the only*
> *offspring of Medusa were the great winged horse*
> *Pegasus and the golden-bladed giant Chrysaor,*
> *both born from the blood of her decapitated head*

How disgusting and horrifying and – I remind myself that this is my ancient ancestor I'm reading about – sad. To have your head chopped off and creatures born from your blood? That's awful.

I take a deep breath and plunge forward.

> *Medusa also had a human lover, a husband who*
> *has since been erased from myth and history. His*
> *disappearance was yet another strand in the web*
> *of deceit woven by Athena to justify her rage and*
> *jealousy at the gorgon's supposed bid for Poseidon's*
> *love. But the lie that obliterated Medusa's husband*
> *from all written record provided another, unforeseen*
> *service: it protected the progeny of their union with*

*a veil of secrecy. Their children, who would carry
on the legacy of the gorgon sisters, passing the magic
of Medusa's blood down through the generations,
disappeared from record.*

*At first decried as sacrilege, Athena's fabrications
about the evil murderous monster who turned men
to stone eventually became widespread, accepted fact.
But if their existence was widely known, the mortal
gorgon's offspring would become the targets of self-
proclaimed heroes, assassins and anyone fearful of
Medusa's true legacy and Athena's rage.*

"What a scary time that must have been," I muse.
"I wonder how many of my ancestors and their friends
and family had to risk their lives to keep the Medusa
legacy intact."

I'm in awe of the sacrifice. Their preserving the line
made it possible for me and Gretchen to be here today.
We owe a big thank you to whoever made that happen.

I read on, desperate to know more about my legacy,
hoping to learn something about my autoporting incident.

The next sentence nearly knocks me off my feet. I have
to reread it three times and then read it once out loud to
make sure I'm not imagining things.

Into every generation since have been born three

children, three daughters to carry on the
guardian legacy.

Three children? Three daughters? *Every* generation?
This can't be. Can it?

No way.

Tucking the book under my arm, I sprint to the computer and leap into the desk chair. It only takes a few clicks and taps to do a quick search for adoption records. There are tons of sites designed to reunite mothers and their children. I've seen all of them before, but that's not what I'm looking for. I need to find my official adoption records. I know I won't find that on any of those sites. The documents I need are protected, shielded by strict privacy laws. I need to get inside the Child Welfare Services website – into their internal database of completely top secret and sealed records.

I wouldn't call myself a hacker. Most of my coding skills are used for purely legal purposes. But I've finessed my way into a server or two. And now is definitely not the time to get squeamish about legality. I might have sorta accidentally peeked at my record before, but that was just the individual record of my adoption by my parents. I never thought of searching for any siblings.

Now that I know what I'm looking for, my entire brain focuses in on figuring out how to get what I need.

By the time I hear Gretchen's shower turn off,

I've broken through their firewall, cracked their surprisingly weak encryption and am entering the keyword search to find our record. When my record pulls up, it contains all the details I've seen before about my adoption, but nothing about where I came from. Or who I came *with*.

Next I try searching my name and Gretchen's together. Maybe if our mom named us— "Holy goalie."

"What?"

I jump at the sound of Gretchen's voice. I'm sure my face looks white as a ghost as I spin around in the desk chair to look at her. She's rubbing a towel over her hair and doesn't notice my utter shock.

"I pulled up our adoption records," I explain.

My hands are shaking and I have to take the Medusa book out from under my arm and set it on the desk so I don't drop it. Adrenaline fills my bloodstream.

I've never felt so completely thrilled and excited and terrified all at once. Not even when I saw that minotaur walk into the dim sum parlour. Not even when I saw Gretchen at Synergy.

"Yeah," she says, flipping her hair forward to dry the back. "And?"

How can she be so blasé about this?

Gretchen doesn't talk about her adopted parents. Ever. She just says that she ran away when she was twelve and never looked back. Which, I suppose, tells me everything I need to know.

But this has nothing to do with them.

This is going to knock her to the floor.

"Gretchen," I say, my mouth spreading into a shaky smile, "we're not twins."

"We're not?" she asks, lifting her head and paying attention for the first time.

If I weren't freaking out, I might take a moment to gloat, because she looks a little disappointed, sad, even, at the suggestion that we're not sisters. But there's no time for gloating. This news can't wait another second.

"No." I slowly shake my head, still full of disbelief. "We're triplets."

CHAPTER 15

Greer

"I'm telling you, Veronica, an ice sculpture would be tacky on a colossal scale."

"But Greer," the edging-on-whiny voice of my Immaculate Heart Alumnae Tea co-chair pleads, "can you imagine our school mascot in beautiful crystalline ice, wings spread wide over the buffet? It would positively be a miracle."

"Until it melts." I absently rearrange the sample place settings I've laid out on the formal dining table. The gold cutlery looks cheap next to the aqua china but goes beautifully with the violet-trimmed porcelain. Perfect. "Then we have a big puddle of dragon all over the hors d'oeuvres and petit fours. Less miracle, more disaster."

"We can keep the air conditioning cranked," she suggests, not willing to let her horrid idea go. "If the temperature stays below—"

"The guests will all freeze." I'm bored with this debate. Especially since the main reason Veronica's so married to this idea is that her boyfriend – her poor, starving, tortured-artist boyfriend – has recently taken up ice sculpting to pay the bills. I am not about to let the wealthy, powerful and influential alumnae of Immaculate Heart shiver through afternoon tea so Veronica can indulge her latest fascination with some lowlife guy. Time to end this discussion. "We are not having an ice sculpture."

"But—"

"Final decision." The doorbell rings, giving me the perfect excuse to hang up – not that I need one. "The "petit four samples have arrived. Must go."

Before she can get in one more plea, I end the call and place my phone on the foyer table. That girl seriously needs to find another way to get her parents' attention. Slumming it with that sad, talentless excuse for an artist is only going to turn into a tragic made-for-television movie.

I reconciled myself long ago to the fact that my parents aren't the demonstrative, caring, supportive type. They're too busy running *Fortune 100* companies and making sure they stay on all the right social lists. In a good week, I see them a couple of mornings before school. In a less good week, not at all.

I could wallow in self-pity, indulging in destructive and unproductive behaviour, hoping they'll start paying more attention if my behaviour gets bad enough. Or... I could act like an adult, accept that no one is going to coddle me in this world and forge my life into what I expect it to be.

Not hard to guess which option I chose.

Or that Veronica chose the opposite.

I am long past regretting not fighting her bid to be co-chair. If I had known she'd be such a constant thorn in my side, I'd have made certain Emily won the position instead. Oh well, what's done is done.

Pushing Veronica and her taste for losers aside, I do a quick check in the gold-edged mirror hanging above the foyer table. Not one escapee from my meticulously straightened, crisp chignon; subtle lip sheen still in place; princess-cut diamond studs – real, of course – glinting from each ear. I dust a small speck of lint from my sky-blue cashmere crew neck before deeming myself ready for public appearance. Waving off Natasha, who is only now emerging from the kitchen to answer the door – if she weren't an impeccable chef, my parents would have fired her long ago – I release the dead bolt and grab the handle.

"Henri, you're early," I say with a charming smile, swinging the door wide. "I didn't expect you until..."

My welcoming comment dies in my throat as I see that standing on my doorstep is *not* the most sought-after pastry chef in the Bay Area, bringing me a sample of petit fours to choose from for the tea. Instead, I see two girls, about my age. Who, despite wretched taste in clothes, hair that would make my stylist faint and a pathetic lack of personal style, could be my twins.

Shock does not even begin to describe my reaction.

Not that I allow it to show on my face.

"Greer Morgenthal?" the one on the left, wearing generic blue jeans and a cheap graphic T-shirt, asks.

I rest my hands on my hips. "And who might you be?"

She grins. "We're your sisters!"

When she starts forward, arms wide like she's going to hug me, I step back and thrust my palms out to deflect her approach. Her face falls. Is she certifiable?

"I don't have sisters."

"I should have printed out the records," the over-friendly one says. "I just never thought…" She looks at my face and then the other girl's. "I thought it would be obvious once you saw us."

The other one rolls her eyes, her dark look matched by her grey cargo trousers and fitted black T-shirt. She looks like a walking Army-Navy surplus ad. I wouldn't be surprised to find daggers hidden in her combat boots.

"I'm Grace," the cheerful one says, recovering from her disappointment at my reaction. "And this is Gretchen."

Gretchen crosses her arms in what could be a defensive move, although it is more likely an intimidation gesture. I cross my arms to match her stance. I'm not afraid of her, no matter how many scars and muscles she has.

When I don't respond, Grace continues. "How funny, we all have names that begin with *G-R*. Grace. Gretchen. Greer." She glances nervously from me to Gretchen and back. "Isn't that cool? I wonder if there's some special sig—"

"Stop making nice," Gretchen grumbles, looking bored. "Get to the point."

"The point?" Grace's brow furrows. "Oh yeah, the point." She looks nervously around. "Can we come inside?"

Inside? These girls may look like me, but I don't know them. For all I know, they could be some new high-tech gang of genetically altered thieves who work their way into houses by posing as the owners.

All right, an unlikely scenario. That's what I get for electing to read the collected short stories of Ray Bradbury for my extra-credit English project. Too much science fiction.

Still, these girls are strangers. I'm not about to grant them open access to our silver drawer.

"Um… no."

Grace looks slightly taken aback by that, as if she expected me to swing the door wide and say, "Come on in and help yourselves to our priceless art and antiques."

Undeterred, she repeats slowly, as if I have a hearing problem, "We're your sisters." She takes a deep breath, checks the empty street again and blurts, "And we're also descendants of the gorgon Medusa."

"Excuse me?" I exclaim, losing my well-practised icy demeanour at her outrageous claim. "I'm sorry. Medusa?"

"You might have wanted to build up to that one a little," Gretchen mutters.

They are *both* insane. I curse myself for leaving my phone on the table, several feet away. Since calling for help is out, I nudge the door closed an inch.

"You know, the mortal gorgon sister," Grace explains, as if I'm not familiar with the myth. As if I haven't had an entire semester of college-level classical mythology. Ignorance of the subject matter is not the problem here. "The one Perseus slew by looking at her reflection in his shield."

When I don't respond, she looks to Gretchen for help.

Gretchen, in turn, deepens her scowl.

"Of course, that's not the real story," Grace continues. "She really was a guardian. History has been rewritten to make her look like a monster. Athena's involved somehow. Maybe another god too, but we're not sure who, because Gretchen's mentor has disappeared and we don't know where else to—"

"Stop!" I shout, abandoning my grip on the door and flinging my arm forward, as if I can physically stop her stream of babble. I never lose my calm. But honestly, if the girl strings one more phrase into that outrageous story, I'm liable to go a little insane myself. Maybe a lot insane.

"Look," Gretchen says, "this isn't a game or a prank or a reality TV show. This is very real and very dangerous. You need to know what's going on."

"I don't think so." I reach for the door again and start to close it. "I'm quite busy right now and—"

Gretchen's combat-booted foot wedges between the door and the jamb before I can finish. She pushes against the door and, hard as I try to hold it shut, manages to send it swinging into the wall so hard the mirror rattles. I meet her steely grey gaze, ignoring the fact that her eyes are almost the identical silver shade as mine and – I flick a quick glance to the left – yes, the same as Grace's. That doesn't mean anything.

"Have you ever seen a monster?"

"Of course not." My mind is spinning, but I somehow manage to keep my face emotion-free. My mother taught me well. I don't betray an ounce of how ridiculous this sounds. "What an absurd idea."

Gretchen's eyes narrow. "You need to train," she explains. "To learn how to defend yourself if a hydra attacks you from behind or an ichthyocentaur blocks your way out of an alley."

"You're insane." I shake my head. "Monsters don't exist."

"They do," Grace insists. "And it's our legacy to hunt them. To protect the unsuspecting human world."

"They're dangerous," Gretchen argues, pushing into the doorway. "Now more than ever. If they recognise you as a descendant of Medusa, then they won't stop until you're dead or in their power." She takes a quick breath before adding, "Or both."

That's it. It was bad enough, them trying to convince

me they're my sisters and that we're descendants of some hideous monster, but now they're trying to scare me. I do not scare easily.

When Tommy Willowick tried to frighten the girls at my eighth-grade Halloween party by sneaking into my bedroom closet in a werewolf costume, *he's* the one who ended up running from the room, screaming for his mommy. I didn't let him scare me then and I won't let these two strangers scare me now.

I school my features into a falsely pleasant facade, a skill I learned early on from my mother.

"I'm sorry," I say, not meaning it. "I have a very full schedule today. The pastry chef is delivering samples and then I have to confirm the place settings with the caterers, not to mention finalising the seating chart, the menu and the procession of events."

"But you're in danger," Grace interrupts.

I ignore the sincere fear in her eyes. While she may believe this fantasy tale, I do not. And I will not allow her delusion to disrupt my genuinely busy day.

Still, I can't dismiss our identical faces so easily.

"It's enough to process that you freaks *might*," I allow the possibility, "be my sisters. But you're obviously deranged. And I have appointments."

Gretchen rolls her eyes again, and I sense a moment of distraction. I snatch the opportunity. Giving her a quick shove to send her back a step out of the doorway, I pause only to say, "Thank you for stopping by," before slamming the door in their stunned faces.

I do not have time for this kind of drama.

It's not until I'm leaning back against the door, dead bolt in place, that I realise my heart is pounding, my palms are sweating and I have a truly horrid feeling in the pit of my stomach. A combination of fear and anxiety and nausea. I can remember feeling exactly like this only one other time in my life. Now that's an unpleasant memory… and an unsettling coincidence.

CHAPTER 16

Grace

Gretchen turns and stomps down the steps to the sidewalk below, a boiling look on her face. I hurry down after her. This was not exactly how I imagined our sisterly reunion turning out.

"We can't leave her," I insist, grabbing Gretchen's arm to make her stop and listen. "She's in just as much danger as we are."

"She's a snob," Gretchen says, looking like she wants to spit.

Okay, that's true. I can't deny the blinding reality that she looked at us like we were peasants come to beg favour from the queen. But that doesn't change the facts of the situation.

"She's our sister." I'm still kind of reeling at the thought that in less than a week I've gone from having no blood relatives to having two as-close-as-you-can-biologically-get sisters. I can't let either of them get away. "We have to make her understand."

"We don't *have* to do anything." Gretchen sneers up at the dark-grey door of Greer's house.

It's an absolutely gorgeous building, one of those three-storey gingerbread Victorians you see in postcards, with a big round turret in one corner and classical details trimming every inch. The main colour is a pale grey, almost identical to today's overcast sky, with bright white trim. The architectural details are highlighted with touches of black and gold. Kind of old Hollywood. Everything about it screams classical glamour.

Just like Greer.

I can't imagine anyone more different from me and Gretchen. Greer is poised and elegant and reminds me of photos I've seen of Princess Grace of Monaco. I'm pretty sure her sweater was cashmere. Her high-heeled shoes probably cost more than my entire wardrobe. She is delicate in a way I could never be.

There's no chance she could hold her own against a monster. I may not be a super-athlete like Gretchen, but Greer looks like a porcelain doll. A minotaur would shatter her into a million tiny designer pieces. She needs help even more than I do.

At least I wear sneakers. Greer couldn't even run away in those shoes.

"We have an obligation," I try again, appealing to Gretchen's sense of duty, "to train her, like you're training me. What if something happened to her? You'd feel awful."

She mutters something that sounds like "Hardly," but

then she says, "Look. Nothing's going to happen to her."

"How can you know that?"

"You heard her." She jerks her head up towards the house. "She doesn't see monsters."

"So?"

"If she doesn't see them," Gretchen explains, "then they won't see her."

"But what if—"

"Monsters don't know who we are."

"What about the basilisk thingy that attacked me at the bus stop?" I can't believe Gretchen is being so stubborn about this. It wasn't this hard to convince her to train me. "She knew I was a huntress."

"It knew," Gretchen says with a heavy dose of sarcasm, "that you saw it. You must have reacted to its true appearance in some way. That's how it knew what you are."

I want to argue, but I think she might be right. About that night, anyway. That doesn't mean she's right about everything.

"What about the ones who've seen us," I press. "They could tell others what we look like, and could mistake Greer for one of us."

"Unlikely. It's not like they're uploading pictures to Flickr or passing around wanted posters with our pictures and a big reward offer."

"But there *is*," I cry. "There's a bounty on our heads. You heard what the satyr said. They've been promised

231

eternal freedom in exchange for our lives. Greer is just as valuable to them as we are."

She hesitates. Good, hopefully I've got through to her. Hopefully she'll—

"You saw her," she snaps. "We could be standing side by side and no one could guess we're triplets."

Now she's just being deliberately difficult. I think part of her is jealous, resentful of the obvious advantages Greer has in her life. I think Gretchen's worried too – she just doesn't want to admit it. I need to push the right buttons.

"You said yourself, things are getting weird," I say, trying another tack. "More monsters, monsters at different times. What if other things change?" I grasp for anything that might change her mind. "What if they can start smelling us the way we smell them?"

That gives her pause again. I can see – and almost feel – her considering that possibility. Which only makes me more nervous. Gretchen is a keep-it-together girl. If she thinks that might happen, we could be in really big trouble.

She finally shakes her head. "It doesn't matter—"

"Doesn't matter?"

"We can't make her accept the truth." Gretchen clenches her jaw. "She made her choice. She doesn't want anything to do with us."

"But Gretchen—"

"Forget it," she says, walking away to the street where her Mustang is parked at an alarming angle. "If you want a ride home, let's go. Otherwise I'll see you tomorrow."

I watch, helpless, as Gretchen disappears down the steep hill. How can she be so heartless? I look back up at Greer's house – at our *sister's* house. A curtain on the first floor flutters back into place.

Greer might be a bit of a snob, but that doesn't change our blood. She's obviously been given everything she wants her entire life, so it's not surprising that she has a superior attitude about things. She probably needs to see the proof that we're triplets. Next time I'll bring the records.

At the moment, though, I feel like I need to stay close.

Gretchen might be able to walk away, but I can't. I've only just found my sisters, and I'm not going to leave one of them at the mercy of whatever monster crosses her path. And Gretchen can obviously take care of herself.

Acting like I'm walking away, in case someone is watching through that window, I head around the corner. The house behind Greer's on the side street has a big, six-foot-high brick wall around the property. As soon as I'm clear from view, I break into a run. Circling around the block, I head into the hilly park across from her house. It's scattered with dense bushes and shaded by lush trees. A perfect hiding spot.

I climb the concrete steps to the path that gives me a perfect, unobstructed view of Greer's house below.

As I sink down onto the grassy hillside, next to a thick-leaved bush, I'm not sure about this plan. I'm not sure

I even have a plan. I just know I can't abandon her. Greer may not want anything to do with me, but I'm going to watch out for her anyway. That's my job, isn't it? What kind of guardian would I be if I let my own triplet get eaten by a griffin or something on the day we meet?

Besides the fact that Gretchen and Greer are my sisters, there's a lot more at stake. According to the book, we are the only three girls of this generation of Medusa's descendants. Always girls. Now I know that we inherited our mythological genes from our biological mother, but I've never been able to find out anything about her. There could be aunts or cousins out there somewhere too, I suppose, but the book clearly said there are only three girls born in a given generation.

That means we're it. We're the only ones who can carry on the legacy.

There's a whole mess of pressure that comes along with that realisation. The three of us are the only ones standing between this world and the monsters. There is no way I can leave one of us unprotected and in danger.

As I settle in for however long this security stake-out is going to take, I reach into my backpack for my phone to text home about the delay.

Instead, my fingers brush over the rough cloth surface of a book.

In the craziness of discovering our triplet and the rush to meet her, I must have tossed the Medusa book into my bag. I'd stopped reading at the sentence about three girls in a generation. Maybe there are clues about our other relatives or more specifics about the legacy.

And it looks like I'm going to have plenty of time.

I turn back to the page I was on and continue reading.

> *When the time to break the seal draws near, a time predestined by the fates at the moment of closure, the Key Generation will arrive. It will be a generation born in the same moment of the same womb.*

The same moment? The same womb? That must mean triplets.

> *The Key Generation is safe from neither the forces of supposed good nor those of confirmed evil. It must be protected at any cost, by any measure, separated to prevent their discovery by those who wish to render the scales unbalanced.*

Separated? Is that why Gretchen, Greer and I were separated at birth and adopted out into different families? Our mother must have known we were special – the Key Generation – and that we would be in danger. She gave us up, leaving us with no knowledge of our true heritage in order to protect us. I've always wondered why my mother gave me up. Now I guess I know.

Only when the Key Generation has reached maturity will it be able to join together to break the seal, thus restoring the natural order. There are those on both sides of this war who would prevent this occurrence by any means available.

What on earth does that mean? The only seal Gretchen has mentioned is the one that keeps monsters locked in their realm. If we are the Key Generation, then we're supposed to break the seal? But why? It's supposed to be our job to keep monsters away. Breaking the seal would have the opposite effect.

I skim the rest of the chapter, looking for anything more about the seal and why anyone would want to break it, but it's just more about the danger to all descendants of Medusa. Especially the Key Generation.

Maybe that explains the bounty. But who is it that wants us gone?

There are two sides that don't want us to break the seal, which I'm pretty sure we don't want to do anyway. But I have a feeling they won't pause to ask before going to 'any means available' to stop us.

While I sit, the cold of the ground seeping through my jeans, I keep cycling the thoughts through my mind. Triplets. Danger. Key Generation. Two sides. Break the seal.

It doesn't make any sense, but I know one thing for

sure. Protecting Greer and keeping her safe is my top priority. Whatever the Key Generation is supposed to do, I doubt we can do it as two out of three. Gretchen and I need Greer, as a member of the Key Generation and as a sister.

CHAPTER 17

Greer

I can't stop myself from watching as the two girls – my
sisters, apparently – stand arguing on the sidewalk.
Most of their words are lost to the soundproof windows
and heavy velvet drapes, but I manage to catch a few.
"Duty…" "Sister…" "Snob…"

As Gretchen, the military-looking one, stomps away,
I can imagine which of the words were hers. Her disgust
was apparent.

Which is fine with me. I'm not a fan of *her* personal
style, either.

She's obviously one of those girls who look down on
those who have more opportunity in their lives. That
giant chip on her shoulder is only going to keep her in
her disadvantaged place.

Grace looks up at the house, her face a mixture of
helplessness and determination. She seems nice enough,
despite her insanity, and more the type to envy someone
who has advantages than to despise them for it. The type
to work hard to gain opportunities of her own. Why
she's let herself get sucked into this crazy delusion is

beyond me, but at least there's hope for her.

Finally, after what feels like forever, Grace leaves too, heading around the side of the house. I resist the urge to sprint to the living room, to spy out the side window and see if she is actually leaving.

Greer Morgenthal does *not* spy.

Frozen to my spot, staring out of the window – at the drapes, actually, since I've let them fall back into place – my mind plays over everything they said. I would like to reject the idea that they are my sisters. I'm not adopted, as far as I know, but it also seems unlikely that Mother and Dad would have adopted out my two sisters if we were actually triplets. Not that Mother has ever been the most maternal sort. Quite the opposite. Still, I've always had the feeling that Dad wanted more children. I've spent my life trying to be *enough* for both of them. To be mature and classy and successful enough for Mother. To be loving and childlike and daughterly enough for Dad. If they were around more, I might have a schizophrenic episode from the opposing efforts.

In any case, the idea that they would have given away my siblings doesn't make sense.

Assuming I believe that Grace and Gretchen are my sisters – and I would have to be delusional myself to deny that physically obvious fact – that leaves me with only one logical conclusion: I am adopted.

I am surprisingly unaffected by the realisation. Maybe

Mother has trained all the emotion out of me. Maybe I truly am the ice queen my social enemies and ex-boyfriends so often claim. Perhaps I should cry or scream or feel betrayed in some essential way. A normal person would. Instead, I feel… relieved.

A surprising emotion. At least it is an emotion. I suppose, if I had ever analysed my relationship with my parents in the past, the possibility might have occurred to me. I have never felt the elemental connection many of my friends have with their parents. Even when my friends claim to despise their parents, I sense the underlying indelible links. I've always felt like more of an accessory than an expression of love. I finally understand why.

The ever-present pressure lifts off my chest, and I feel like I can truly breathe for the first time since I took third place in the fifth-grade spelling bee and Mother punished me by sending me to my room without dinner. I'd disappointed her, and I have spent every day since trying to keep that from happening again. All this time, all this pressure, and the feeling of distance. It all makes sense. And it isn't my fault.

I don't know why the realisation that I'm adopted clarifies everything in my mind, but it does. It's like a frosted window has been removed from my vision.

Perhaps I should feel that my world has been rocked. And perhaps I should feel a little more off-kilter, considering the second startling claim my sisters made.

"A descendant of Medusa," I muse, then immediately chide myself for even entertaining the thought.

What an absolutely ridiculous notion. As if such creatures of myth actually exist. They are nothing but stories, fables made up to help ancient man understand the inexplicable. To keep children obedient, lest they be fed to a dragon.

"Monster hunters." I snort. "How ludicrous."

But that resurrected memory floats into focus.

When I was a small child, four or five years old, I slept alone in my turret bedroom, as I do now. I had been tucked in by my nanny some hours earlier and had fallen asleep easily. I remember that I dreamed of ponies and rainbows. In the middle of the night, something woke me.

I don't remember if it was a sound or a smell or some kind of subconscious feeling. I only know that I opened my eyes, my room illuminated by the faint glow of moonlight, and screamed. My closet door stood wide open. Creeping carefully across my room, its hooves tapping quietly on the hardwood floor, was a centaur.

At the time, of course, I didn't know the creature by name. I only knew that a horse with the torso of a man was clomping towards me. And the look in his dark eyes left me with no doubt that he was not interested in making friends.

My scream startled him. I scrambled out of my four-poster bed, getting tangled up in the frilly lace ruffled valance. Certain I would be easy prey, I looked up. Only to find my room empty.

Still terrified, I ran downstairs to the second-floor master bedroom. I burst through my parents' door, flipped on the lights and stood sobbing in the middle of the room.

"What is it, Greer?" Dad mumbled, half asleep.

"A-a-a monster!" I wailed.

My mother sat up in bed and called me closer. I was hoping for a hug and a kiss and maybe an invitation to sleep with them for once.

"Listen to me very carefully," she said, making no move to touch me. "Monsters do not exist."

"B-b-but—"

"No!" Her bark startled the fear right out of me. "Monsters. Don't. Exist."

I knew better than to argue again.

"You did not see a monster," she insisted, calm once more. "And you will never see one again."

Still shaking with fear, I nodded and backed away towards the door. Mother slid her sleep mask back into place. As I turned off the light, my dad mumbled, "Goodnight."

I climbed the long, eerie staircase back up to my room. Standing outside my door, I took a deep breath. I told myself my mother was right, as she always was. Monsters did not exist. I hadn't seen one that night, and I would never see one again.

After the series of hypnotherapy sessions Mother started me on the next day, I never did.

Now, considering what my sisters said, I almost wonder if maybe the centaur was not a figment of my imagination after all.

"Ludicrous." The news of my adoption must have shaken me more than I realised, if I'm even pondering the possibility that mythological monsters actually exist, or that I might *actually* be a descendant of a hideous monster myself.

My phone rings in the hall.

"Thank goodness," I say, relieved for the distraction.

Shoving thoughts of monsters and sisters and other nonsense from my mind, I straighten my spine and go answer the call. Even Veronica would be a welcome interruption at the moment.

"Greer Morgenthal."

"Hey babe," Kyle's surfer-boy voice says. "What's up?"

I close my eyes and mentally count to eleven. I've asked him not to call me 'babe' more times than I can recall. I'm not sure if he thinks it's charming or if the sun has actually cooked so many of his brain cells that he can't remember I don't like it. Either way, I've decided to ignore the transgression for the most part, and make him pay in other ways. Jewellery is always welcome.

The surfer-boy thing is mostly an act. He does surf, but not very well, and he's the son of an internationally renowned oncologist and a tyre heiress. He's as likely to attend a benefit dinner in a tuxedo as he is to hit the surf in a wetsuit. It's all about image.

"Hello, Kyle," I answer, turning on girlfriend mode and trying to sound warm and affectionate. "I'm waiting for Henri to arrive with the petit fours for the tea and—"

"That's great, babe," he says, cutting me off. I'm about to forget my ignore-now-pay-later strategy when he asks, "How'd you feel about dinner at the Wharf tonight?"

I pause. "Where?" I ask cautiously. Last time we dined at the Wharf when he was in surfer-boy mode, we ate clam chowder from paper cups while standing at the end of the pier. I appreciate a good San Francisco chowder as much as the next Bay Area native, but standing up to eat is not my idea of a dinner date.

"Ahab's," he says.

I can hear the smile in his voice, like he knows he'll impress me with his choice. And, to be honest, he has. Ahab's is an iconic institution, and their cuisine is first-rate. Five stars. Their view is even better.

"Sounds delightful," I reply, grinning to myself.

"Great," he says. "Meet me there at seven?"

"Meet you—"

"Yeah, I'm at the beach with the guys." Shouts echo in the background as the guys clamour to be heard.

"Gotta go, surf's up. See ya at seven, babe."

Before I can say goodbye, he's gone.

I put my phone down, close my eyes again and remind myself of why I put up with Kyle. In the year we've been going out, I've got a lot of practice in what my personal trainer calls aggression-reduction techniques – an elaborate name for counting to ten. Or, in Kyle's case, eleven.

He can be very sweet sometimes. Like last Valentine's Day, when he skipped school to bring me two dozen red roses in French class, or when we drive down the coast and park on the beach, watching the sunset from the hood of his Jeep. Those days mostly make up for the other ones.

He's also very handsome, in a lead-actor way. His brown hair is usually too long, but after he spends all summer surfing, the tips bleach to an amber gold that matches his tanned skin, making it hard for me to complain.

And he's the most popular and powerful student at St Stephen, the all-boys partner school of Immaculate Heart. As I'm the most popular and powerful student at Immaculate Heart, it's as if we're destined to be a couple.

Still, sometimes – like when he's been spending too much time 'at the beach with the guys' – he becomes a little less than the ideal boyfriend. I'm not the kind of girl to meekly accept inattention and negligence. Kyle should know that by now.

"That's all right," I say. "I will give him a reason to pay attention."

With a cool smile on my face, I head upstairs to select the perfect outfit to carry out my plan. An outfit designed to tempt and tease, with no promise of fulfilment. By the time the night is over, Kyle will be desperately begging me to forgive him for anything he's ever done.

"I will be in my room, Natasha," I call out as I mount the stairs. "Buzz me when Henri arrives."

Her muffled reply comes through the kitchen door. "Yes, Miss Greer."

Now, should I wear my new strapless shantung silk cocktail dress, in the perfect lilac shade that makes my silver eyes pop, or the silver sequinned tank that is cut a touch too low, and that Kyle can never keep his eyes off? Ah, decisions, decisions.

I will make tonight a date to remember.

Kyle holds out my chair, like the gentleman I know he can be. He's been an ideal dinner date since I crested the stairs into Ahab's lobby a fashionable fifteen minutes late. I do believe I chose the right outfit.

I smile demurely and nod, carefully collecting myself as I sit and he slides the chair in under me. Hands still on the chair, he leans down and whispers, "You know how I love that top, Greer."

I allow myself a brief, pleased smile. Success. I knew the silver sequinned tank would do the trick. It always does. Only Kyle doesn't know there will be no discovering what I'm wearing underneath the top this time.

Not that I've ever let him get much further than that – we haven't been going out *that* long – but since I had to manage my own transportation tonight, he will be lucky to get a goodnight kiss. It would take a complete transformation into future-president mode on his part to get any more than a quick peck.

He slouches into the opposite seat. So much for transformation. It takes all my willpower not to ask him to sit up straight. But I don't want to sound like his mother or a nagging girlfriend, so instead I lean forward over the table as if I want to whisper something naughty. As expected, he sits up and leans in to hear.

"Thank you," I whisper. "This is my favourite restaurant."

His grin is all cocky arrogance. "I know."

The waiter arrives to pour our water and Kyle slouches back against his chair. I can't exactly lean across the table all night, whispering. Sometimes I think Kyle isn't worth all the effort. Maybe he's not future-president – or even future-state senator – material after all. I could be wasting my time on a boy with no greater ambition than following the surf season around the globe.

His parents are wealthy enough that he never has to work a day in his life. I suppose I have been hoping that he *wants* to earn his own way. I don't want to be hasty, though. I've already invested a great deal of time and effort in him. Maybe I shouldn't cut my losses yet.

Gazing out of the window, I decide to give him a few more weeks to prove himself.

The view from Ahab's is amazing. A practically unobstructed wall of windows on the Bay. Depending on how thick the fog is at the time, you can see Alcatraz just offshore and Sausalito across the Bay. The brilliant orange Golden Gate stands out against the rich green foliage of the parks at either end of the iconic suspension bridge. At times I've seen seals, sea lions and even a dolphin or two. And there are always plenty of seagulls, usually flying beak-first into the glass.

The waiter takes our drink orders – mint iced tea for me and orange soda for Kyle – and then disappears. Our table is right up against the window, and with my back to the rest of the dining room, it feels like we're all alone in the place.

I make an effort to forgive Kyle his slouching and ask, "How was the surf today?"

"Wicked," he says, sitting forward. "The wind kicked up right at high tide and there were some killer waves."

I smile, but even I know there aren't really killer waves at Ocean Beach. Down the coast, maybe, but up here the waters are a little less… gnarly, as Kyle would put it.

"Must have crested at six feet or more," he continues. "Yokie took a header and almost cracked his skull on his board."

Yokie is actually Eric Yokelson, and he is my least favourite of Kyle's friends. He doesn't go to St Stephen, doesn't even go to private school, which alone isn't enough to indict him. Despite what my alleged sisters might think, even I'm not snobby enough to think the only people of quality are those who can afford private school. No, it's more that he has hit on me every time we've met. And not a subtle *Hmmm-was-that-a-pass-or-not?* hit, but a full on, get-the-heck-out-of-my-face come-on. I try to avoid being around him.

I wouldn't cry if he had cracked his skull on his surfboard.

Kyle is still going on about today's surfing when the waiter brings our drinks and takes our starter orders. I thank him for the tea and let Kyle order for both of us. Taking a sip of tea, letting the cool earthy taste invade my mouth, I glance out over the Bay.

The fog is thin tonight, and even in the faint light of dusk I can make out the craggy outline of Alcatraz. At night, when the tourists are gone and the only inhabitants are gulls and a pair of National Park Service guards, the island looks positively eerie. A glowing monument to a haunted past.

"Hope you're in the mood for calamari," Kyle says, leaning back in his chair with his arms behind his head.

My lip starts to sneer, but I quickly get it back under control. Kyle knows how I feel about fried foods – or at least he should. In the year we've been dating, I've made it perfectly clear that nothing soaked in oil will ever enter my system to threaten my perfect complexion. My beautician would have a fit.

He must sense my displeasure, because he leans forward quickly and says, "Grilled, of course."

"Grilled," I repeat with a genuine smile. "Sounds perfect."

Thank goodness he got that right. After he made me drive here, I might have to leave if he ordered something he should know I don't eat.

Kyle looks relieved by my pleasure.

"What about you, babe?" he asks. "How was your day?"

How *was* my day? Where do I even begin? School was routine and I spent the afternoon finalising details for the alumnae tea. On any other day, the details of my argument with Veronica would be the perfect dinner conversation, but all I can think about is the doorbell ringing and opening the door to find my lookalikes standing there, telling me crazy stories about monsters and gorgons.

That's not exactly the sort of thing you tell your boyfriend over grilled calamari. Or, at least, that's not exactly the sort of thing *I* tell *Kyle* over grilled calamari.

I haven't even fully processed the information yet. I'm not ready to tell anyone I'm probably adopted, let alone the other ridiculous stuff.

So, in the interest of an enjoyable dinner, I recount the

phone conversation with Veronica about her ice-sculptor boyfriend.

"A dragon ice sculpture?" Kyle asks, his voice a little too full of awe for my taste. "Sounds radical."

I clench my jaw. It's not his use of entirely outdated slang – he's single-handedly trying to bring back the eighties' surfer lingo – that bothers me. He's my boyfriend and he's supposed to take my side. In everything.

Guess who's not getting a goodnight kiss.

"Sorry, babe," he says, trying to sound contrite. "I know you hate the idea, but it might be way awesome."

"Yeah," I say, not wanting to get into another fight today. I've got bigger things on my mind. "Maybe you're right."

"Ah, thank you, my man." Kyle changes track as the waiter arrives with our starter. He grins at me. "Fruits of the sea."

I can't help but smile back. It's hard to stay mad at Kyle for long – his grin is infectious. And tonight I'd welcome having his carefree attitude about everything.

While he squeezes fresh lemon over the plate, I look out the window again. For the rest of the evening I promise to let go of all the things that have gone wrong today. I will sit here with my boyfriend, enjoying a five-star meal, while I look out over the—

"What the—?"

Kyle looks up, a forkful of calamari halfway to his mouth. "What, babe?"

I quickly look away from the scene below. That can't be happening.

"What?" I ask, my voice high and startled. I swallow and try again. "Why?"

"You just said, 'What the—?' like you saw something crazy." He looks down at the water below, looking for whatever startled me.

"It's nothing," I insist in a rush, trying to get his attention away from what I cannot possibly have actually seen. "I was thinking. About the dragon ice sculpture." I resist the urge to glance back down out of fear that it might still be there. "Maybe I'll think about it."

"Right on," Kyle says.

He digs into the calamari, and I struggle to get my breathing under control. This is a perfectly normal date with my perfectly normal boyfriend, overlooking a perfectly normal body of water. The setting sun must have reflected into my eyes because, for a second, I thought I saw...

No, it's not possible. It's the stress of the day, and the news of my adoption and my supposed sisters showing up on my front step. Stress hormones are playing tricks on my mind. Because I can't possibly have seen a woman with long, stringy black hair swimming towards the pier, with a giant serpent's tail undulating along behind her human torso.

Picking up my salad fork, I spear a ring of calamari,

dip it lightly in seafood sauce and lift the bite to my mouth. My attention stays sharply focused on Kyle, our food and the elegantly set table between us.

I'm not afraid to look out the window again. I'm trying to be in the moment, to enjoy my meal and my boy—

Oh, who am I kidding?

I place my fork down on the plate, close my eyes and turn towards the window. *One, two…* On the count of *three* I open my eyes.

Just in time to see the serpent lady climb out onto the deck below and slink into the crowd of tourists.

"Sugar," I whisper.

This is not my problem, I reason. I'm Greer Morgenthal, junior class president, alumnae tea chair and future junior leaguer. I'm wearing Stella McCartney and Jimmy Choo. I can't take on something like, like… *that*.

But as I rationalise with myself, the creature slithers through the crowd, running her abnormally long fingers through women's hair and up men's spines. They react to the touch, but not to the creature herself. Can they not see her?

When the pointy end of her tail makes a big swing, knocking three people off their feet, and the crowd only looks confused, I think I have my answer.

"Kyle?" I ask absently. "What do you see down there?"

I point directly at the creature as she cuts a swathe through the crowd.

"Tourists," Kyle answers. "Loads and loads of tourists."

"Of course." They, ordinary humans – I shudder as I realise what this means – *can't* see her.

I want to stay. I want to ignore the snake lady and whatever she plans to do in the crowd below. But I have nothing if not a strong sense of responsibility. If I am the only person who can see what she really is, then I don't have much of a choice, do I?

"Excuse me, would you?" I push back from the table, leaving my napkin on my chair as I get up. "I need to use the restroom."

"Sure, babe."

Not even wasting time to get annoyed at Kyle for calling me 'babe' – *again* – I turn and hurry for the lobby. Instead of heading through the door with a mermaid sign, I slip downstairs and out the main entrance.

With every fibre of my being, I'm hoping she'll be gone when I get down there.

CHAPTER 18

Grace

Two hours after Gretchen stormed off Greer's doorstep and sped away, I'm beginning to think that maybe she was right. Maybe I was overreacting about Greer being in immediate danger. After I've sat in the park across the street from her house, watching absolutely nothing happen for the rest of the afternoon, Greer finally pulls out of the garage on to the side street. I have to run full out to keep up with her little grey sports car.

Thankfully, her house is at the very top of a hill, so I only have down to go. And she hits a lot of red lights along the way. From the way she revs her engine, I get the feeling she is pretty annoyed about something – either that or she's very impatient. At least it gives me a chance to keep up without dying from the exertion.

By the time she pulls into a car park near Fisherman's Wharf, I feel like I've run a marathon.

"At least it will get me in shape," I pant, sucking in painful gasps of air while I wait for her to emerge. "Gretchen will be so proud."

I lean against the corner of the building, letting my

body recover, as Greer crosses the street to the Wharf, hugs a surfer-looking boy dressed in worn khaki cargos and a slightly rumpled white button-up shirt and disappears up a narrow staircase. I make my way – slowly – after her. The sign above the stairs says Ahab's Fine Seafood. My jeans and T-shirt aren't exactly fine-dining wear. If I try to follow her upstairs, I'll stand out like a fish in a desert.

Besides, they'll probably be up there for a while. Dinner at fancy restaurants always drags by at a snail's pace. For me, anyway.

Instead, I decide to scope out the area. I wander around to the far side of the pier, below the restaurant windows. I can watch out for her from down here, and if anything happens, I can be around the front and upstairs in seconds. Assuming I've recovered by then.

I find a weathered wooden bench and plant myself.

Spending my evening on Fisherman's Wharf, surrounded by a billion tourists and a heavy stink of fish, was not exactly how I planned to spend my evening. Or what I told Mom I'd be doing. She thinks I'll be home for dinner.

I pull out my phone and send her a quick text that says my study session is running over. I add that I'm staying for dinner, so she won't worry. Who knows how long I'll be out?

She replies with a sad face and says Thane's out for dinner too. I wonder if he's with Milo. I text back that

256

I look forward to leftovers tomorrow; with Thane not eating at home, there might actually be some.

Of course, as soon as I send the text, my stomach reminds me that I haven't eaten since lunch. Gretchen's workouts zap everything out of me and I need extra nourishment to keep up. If I were home for dinner more lately, Mom would probably notice a huge spike in my appetite.

Content that Greer will be safe without my eyes on her for a few minutes, I head out in search of food. There aren't that many vegetarian choices in the land of seafood. Most of the vendors give me 'an are-you-crazy?' look when I ask. Pulling out my phone, I open the VegFinder app and do a quick search within a two-block radius. Within seconds it finds a stall with a vegetarian corn chowder on the menu. I gratefully accept the paper container and hand over my cash.

With the chowder warming my hands, I take my time wandering back to my bench.

It amazes me how many people there are in San Francisco. The population of Orangevale was probably smaller than our block's here. So many people from so many different places, a mix-and-match collage of cultures. Between the tourists and the residents, I think every ethnicity, religion and heritage in the world is represented. It's the most exciting place I've ever been.

In Orangevale, you couldn't leave the house without

running into twelve people you knew. With only a couple of grocery stores and one post office, everyone had to run their errands to the same few spots. Here, though, there are dozens of post offices and hundreds of grocery stores. Hundreds of restaurants and boutiques and coffee shops. You could live here your whole life and never run into someone you know.

"Grace?"

I jump at the sound of Thane's voice. I swallow the hot bite of chowder before I choke on it. In that moment, I do a quick glance around to see if Milo is here. No such luck.

"Thane," I gasp. "What are you doing here?"

"Me?" he asks with a scowl. "I thought you were studying at a friend's house."

"I, um, am." Great. Lying to Mom via text is one thing, but face-to-face with Thane is impossible. I need to stick as close to the truth as possible. "I was. I…" I look around, hoping for inspiration but finding none. "I'm supposed to be."

"This isn't your friend's house." He steps closer. "Tell me what's going on. Have you—"

The crowd jostles, knocking me forward into Thane. We both stumble but stay upright, and I take the opportunity of distraction to change the subject.

"What are you doing here?" I ask. "Don't you have practice?"

He scowls more than normal, deepening the creases

across his forehead and a rosy pink floods his cheeks. "Did," he says abruptly. "It's over."

"Oh, then why are you—"

"Supposed to be meeting someone here." He looks around, and I can't tell if he's looking for someone or avoiding looking at me. "She's a no-show."

"She?" I ask, agog. "You're meeting a girl?"

His blush deepens.

Oooh, this is so juicy. It's not like Thane hasn't dated before – he's just really particular – and it's not like he couldn't have almost any girl he wanted. I know he's my brother, but I think I can see him objectively. He's tall, broad shouldered and strong. He has chiselled features, sharp cheekbones and a square jaw. With his brown hair cropped short, his eyes positively glow. He looks like the star of some Hollywood army flick or a cologne ad. Girls definitely go after Thane.

He doesn't often reciprocate.

"Just a… friend," he mumbles, not sounding pleased at all. He shifts uncomfortably on his feet. "I'll see you at home. Be safe."

He turns and disappears into the crowd. How odd. I wonder what set him off? Thane is always a little cryptic, but that was exceptional. I only hope he doesn't plan to tell Mom and Dad that I'm not where I'm supposed to be.

I'll have to ask him later about his girl *friend*.

What a funny coincidence to run into him. At first

I thought it was kind of serendipitous that Gretchen and I were at the same nightclub at the same time. But maybe coincidental run-ins aren't as uncommon in the big city as I thought.

Or maybe, I wonder, it was a little more than coincidence. If we really are the Key Generation, then maybe someone has manipulated things to bring us together. From everything I've read about mythology, the gods love to stick their noses into the affairs of others. And fate is their favourite plaything.

Maybe Gretchen and I were *supposed* to meet at that club.

I take another bite of chowder, letting the steaming goodness warm me from the inside, and weave my way through the crowd as thoughts of fate and coincidence swirl in my mind. San Francisco is much colder than I ever imagined. I'm practically shivering in my short-sleeved T-shirt. If it gets any chillier, I'll be tempted to pull my dirty gym clothes out of my bag and start layering.

By the time I make it back to my bench, it's surrounded by a sea of people. A startled shout emerges from somewhere in the crowd, and the hair on the back of my neck stands up. Relax, Grace. It could be anything. I sniff the air but get nothing beyond the heavy scent of fish and ocean. The people are so thick, I can't see beyond the circle immediately around me. Curious, I climb up on the end of the bench to get a better view.

I almost drop my chowder.

Not twenty feet away, winding through the crowd and knocking people over along the way, is a soaking-wet woman with a serpent's tail. Oh, shoot.

I stand frozen, not sure how to react. There's a snake-woman slithering among the hundreds of tourists filling Fisherman's Wharf, and I have no idea what to do.

For a second, I wish I'd gone home with Gretchen when I had the chance.

No, that's cowardly thinking. I'm done with cowardly. I'm a descendant of Medusa and a monster huntress. *Cowardly* isn't in my blood.

Still, Gretchen is the one with all the knowledge and skills.

"Maybe I should call her," I tell myself.

A guy shouts an obscenity as the serpent's tail slithers around his ankles.

There's no time to wait for Gretchen. It would take her at least fifteen minutes to get here from her loft. Who knows what kind of havoc the snake-lady could wreak in that time?

I glance up at the restaurant windows, where I know Greer is safely eating dinner with her date. Well, I wanted to protect her. This is my chance.

And I'll save a few dozen ignorant tourists in the process.

Jumping down from my bench, I toss the remains of

my chowder into the nearest trash can, tighten down the straps on my backpack so it doesn't get in the way and head off in the direction of the monster. She's moving deeper into the crowd. The first thing I need to do is get her away from all these people. How on earth am I going to—

"Ugh," I grunt as I crash into someone.

"Watch where you're going," my collision victim snaps. "We're not on the dodgems."

I jerk back at the familiar voice.

"Greer?" I ask.

Our silver-grey eyes meet.

"What are you doing down here?" I ask. "I thought you were having dinner upstairs."

"I *was*," she says, not bothering to disguise her annoyance. "Until I saw this… *thing* climb out of the bay. Wait, how did you know where I was? Are you following me?"

"You saw her?" I squeal, ignoring her questions.

She stiffens, like she didn't realise the slip until I commented. But she can't take it back. She saw the monster. She is a descendant of Medusa, destined to be a huntress, just like me and Gretchen.

"That's wonderful!" I scream. I wrap my arms around her before she can push me away. She's got a few inches on me in her heels. "I knew you could see them too."

"Yeah, yeah. It's a flippin' family reunion." She pats me

awkwardly on the back and then leans away. Gesturing to the snake lady's wake, she asks, "Shouldn't you do something about that?"

"Yes!" I jump back, beaming. "Yes, we should."

I stare at her, beyond thrilled that she has admitted to seeing the creature. And maybe that will mean she's willing to accept her responsibility as a huntress. Then the three of us can be reunited as sisters, as the Key Generation, and we can roam the streets, tracking monsters together. We'll figure out what the seal is all about and how we're supposed to be making the world safer for—

"And that something would be… ?"

"Right," I say, jerking myself back to the immediate situation. Tourists. Wharf. Sea-serpent lady. "First, we need to get her away from this crowd."

"Um, we? And how do you suggest *we* do that?"

"Oh, I've got an idea," I say, a plan forming in my mind. A dangerous plan, true, but it's the only one I've got. "You go down to the end of the pier, out of sight behind the building, where there won't be any people."

"And where will you be?"

I give her a shaky grin. "I'll bring the monster."

Greer looks unconvinced but heads off to the end of the pier. I turn and follow the sounds of grunts and thuds to where the snake-lady has almost made it off the pier and on to the mainland. I need to be fast. For a lot of reasons.

Catching up to her serpent tail, I take a deep breath,

tell myself to be brave and stomp my foot down on the scaly flesh as hard as I can.

Snake-lady howls in pain, spinning her torso round to face her attacker.

"Oh, I'm sorry," I say, with mock sincerity and even more mock courage. "Did that hurt?"

"A huntress," she coos, a look of evil delight creasing her craggy features.

"You guessed it," I retort. My hands are shaking so hard, I have to grasp the straps of my backpack to hide obvious signs of my fear. "And people say snakes are dumb."

As she emits an ear-splitting howl, her torso dives forward, the rest of her serpenty body coiling round for the strike. That's my cue.

I turn and run, slipping through whatever space I can find in the crush of people, shoving into bodies left and right if they're in my way. It's a dash for my life at this point. Possibly for a lot of people's lives. Maybe I shouldn't have taunted the evil monster – the lure of the bounty might have been enough to get her attention – but I had to get her to follow me. And making her angry was the only way I came up with.

Now I know why a rabbit's heart beats so fast when you catch it, because mine is fluttering in my chest like a butterfly on a sugar rush.

Finally, after what seems like forever, the crowd thins

and I can sprint straight for the end of the pier. I skid round the corner, where Greer is waiting with a bored expression.

"She's coming," I pant. "Get ready!"

"Ready for what?" Greer asks, a sudden look of sheer panic on her face.

"To pounce." I brace myself into a defensive stance. "Grab on and don't let go no matter what."

I've barely finished my command when snake-lady comes slithering round the corner. Her beady eyes focus on me, so she doesn't see Greer standing next to the wall.

"Now!" I shout.

Without hesitation, Greer dives onto the serpent tail. I give her a little silent cheer. The creature twists to see what has landed on her tail. I take advantage and launch myself onto her back.

I have no idea where the hot spot on this creature is – I'm not even sure what the creature is called – but since I'm not interested in my first taste of monster, I'm hoping a single bite in the torso will do the trick. Since it's a human torso, I'm going for close to the neck.

She's not thrilled to have me as a passenger, that's obvious, and as soon as I wrap my arms and legs around her, she starts thrashing around, trying to dislodge me. I squeeze tight and ride it out, hoping for an opportunity to bite her without knocking my teeth out in the process.

The world around me spins, everything a blur. I hear a big splash.

Oh no, what if she takes us into the Bay? She might be able to breathe underwater, but Greer and I would drown. I have to take a chance and get my fangs into her flesh fast.

Without further hesitation, I pull myself up a few inches, close my eyes and bite. Thankfully, I feel my fangs pop out as my lips brush her flesh. I can only hope my venom is making its way into her bloodstream.

After a few more moments of holding on for dear life – only now accompanied by the eardrum-bursting screams of a monster in agony – suddenly my arms are wrapped around thin air. I fall several feet to the weathered boards of the pier, landing with a thud. My breath whooshes out of me. It takes a few seconds of painful effort to get my lungs working again.

"Holy goalie," I gasp, rolling on to my back and staring up at the overcast sky. "We did it."

When Greer doesn't respond, I call her name. Nothing. I sit up and look around, afraid something awful has happened to her. But then…

I stifle a giggle.

"Uh…"

Well, she's not dead. That's something.

"Guess I know what that splash was, huh?"

"Apparently."

Greer is standing about ten feet away, right at the edge of the pier, completely drenched. Her beautiful hair is hanging down in limp, dripping clumps. The gorgeous sequinned tank and grey skirt have a slightly brownish tint. One of her shoes is missing.

"Oh Greer," I say, scrambling to my feet. "I'm so—"

"Don't." Her eyes squeeze shut. She looks like she's doing deep-breathing meditation or something.

"Can I help?" I offer. Slinging my backpack to one shoulder, I unzip the main compartment. "I have my gym clothes in here. They're not exactly clean, but they're dry."

"This is *all your fault*."

I jerk back, confused. "What? How? How is this my fault?"

"You were following me," she accuses.

"Well, um… kinda."

"Well, um," she says mockingly. "Then that creature must have climbed out of the Bay to find *you*."

"It didn't," I insist, even though I can't really be sure of that. From everything Gretchen has said, I think that's unlikely, but even she admits that things are changing right now.

"If you hadn't shown up on my doorstep today," she continues, "I would still be upstairs, enjoying exquisite shrimp scampi with Kyle and deciding whether he's earned a goodnight kiss. I would still be blissfully ignorant, and monster sighting would just be an embarrassing childhood memory."

"I'm sorry." I don't know what else to say.

"Instead, I'm drenched in stinky, fishy Bay water."

She looks like she wants to throw up but has too much class to do it. "I'm seeing mythological monsters again. I've lost a two-hundred-dollar shoe to the murky depths, and my favourite date outfit is completely ruined."

I feel awful. Especially since my only side effects from the fight are a bad taste in my mouth and getting the wind knocked out of me for a few seconds.

"Maybe, if you take it to a dry cleaner..." I suggest.

She spears me with an annoyed look. A clump of seaweed drops off her head and onto her bare foot.

"Now, if you'll excuse me," she says with a finality in her tone that worries me, "I need to go figure out how to retrieve my purse without my boyfriend – or anyone more than absolutely necessary, for that matter – seeing me in this state."

"But Greer—"

"Good." She turns on her one shoe and stomps lopsidedly away. "Bye."

With sloshy up-and-down steps, she disappears round the corner. Okay, so she's not thrilled. And I feel bad for her getting dunked in the Bay, I really do.

But I can't help but be excited. She saw the snake-lady *and* left her dinner to do something about it. She's not completely immune to our responsibility.

Together, we defeated the monster. It's my first battle victory, and although I know there are tonnes more where snake-lady came from, I feel like I can take them all on.

Gretchen is going to be so proud of me. Of both of us.

Pulling my phone out of my backpack, I'm about to punch the speed dial for Gretchen's ultra-private phone number when I sense a presence. I look up, don't see anyone around, and am about to dismiss the weird feeling when a woman appears right in front of me.

I mean *right in front of me*.

"Gretchen?" she asks, a faint scowl on her sophisticated grey brow.

She's tall and elegant, like a graceful ballerina. Her clothes – softly flowing trousers and a long, draped top made of a kind of stretchy, purple-grey fabric – ripple around her in waves.

I shake my head, uncertain what to say or what is going on.

She reaches out her hand, like she wants to touch my cheek, but pulls back at the last moment.

"There isn't time for that." She kind of flickers, like a holographic image. "Do you know who I am?"

I didn't. But as soon as she asks the question, the pieces fall into place.

"You're Ursula, aren't you?" I ask, even though I already feel the truth of the guess. "Gretchen's mentor."

"I am." She grins. "Good, that means you and Gretchen have found each other."

"We've found Greer too."

Her elegant brows arch up, surprised. "That is an unexpected delight."

"She doesn't want anything to do with us," I feel compelled to confess.

"Give it time," she says.

As if startled by some noise behind her, she looks over her shoulder. Now she seems frightened.

"Listen carefully." She fixes her gaze on me. "You must take a message to Gretchen for me. Tell her I have been taken prisoner. I—"

"Oh no," I gasp. "Are you all right?"

"Yes dear, I'm fine." She smiles sadly. "Well, fine enough."

"But..." None of this makes sense. "If you're being held prisoner, then..."

"How am I here?"

I nod, but the answer is already forming in my mind.

"I think you can guess," she says. "We are connected by power."

"You're..." Is this even possible? "You're... Euryale."

"Smart girl."

This can't be. Euryale was a gorgon who lived thousands of years ago. How can I be standing here talking to her? Of course, I know the answer to this too. She is immortal.

"I wish we had time to discuss this," she says. "But I'm afraid things are quite urgent."

Right. Focus on the immediate problem, Grace.

"Where are you being held?" I ask, wanting to help in any way I can. "We can come get you or—"

"I'm afraid that is impossible." She looks over her shoulder again. When she turns back this time, there is more urgency in her voice. "This is a very dangerous time. Now that you girls are reunited, things are only going to get worse."

"Because we're the Key Generation?"

Her eyes widen, but she recovers quickly. "Yes, in part. Your reunion with your sisters is no accident. It is pre-destined. My sister and I have been waiting for this time. It saddens me that I cannot be there to guide you through it."

There is such longing in her eyes and her tone that I feel the sting of tears in my eyes.

"Do not fret, Grace. I am unharmed." She gives me a forced smile. "But you must find my sister. I do not know what name she uses – we have kept our communication at a minimum out of necessity. I do know that she is here, in San Francisco."

"How are we supposed to find her?" I ask desperately. "There are so many people—"

Ursula jerks back, as if pulled by an invisible hand.

"Tell Gretchen I miss her terribly."

"No," I shout at her retreating form.

"You must find Stheno!"

In a flash, she's gone.

I'm alone on the deserted end of the pier, tears streaming down my cheeks. I can't fully process what has just happened. Gretchen's mentor is really the immortal gorgon Euryale, and she's been captured. She knows about me and Greer. She knows we're in danger and that we're the Key Generation. She wants us to find her sister, the other immortal gorgon, Stheno, but doesn't know who or where she is.

I can't make it add up in my brain.

I do the only thing that makes sense. I call Gretchen.

CHAPTER 19

Gretchen

After spending the last four years risking my life to hunt down freaky monsters and their hybrid offspring, I don't have much tolerance for elitist snobs who care more about the state of their wardrobe than the state of the world around them. Gee, I'm proud to have a sister like that.

I shift Moira into the next gear and floor the accelerator.

If anything, I feel bad for Grace. She's so much more optimistic than I am, so much more hopeful and willing to believe the best in people. She's going to get burned by that eventually. Too bad I can't help her learn that lesson without making her heart break in the process.

And I hope Greer isn't the one who does it.

"Frigid, snooty heifer."

Cutting the wheel sharp to the right, I squeal on to the Embarcadero, heading south.

As if her freakin' tea is more important than her sisters. More important than her legacy.

I could cut her some slack, give her a little leniency for the giant, out-of-the blue whammy we plopped on her doorstep today. But I can't get the image of her out of my head, in diamonds and cashmere, looking down her upturned nose at the pair of urchins who dared to ring her doorbell. As if she's untouchable royalty who can't afford to waste a single second on anyone below her on the social ladder.

No thank you. I'm better off without her. So is Grace – not that she realises that.

Still, I can't suppress a very reluctant grin at the thought that Grace and I are triplets. It makes so much sense, what with there originally being three gorgon sisters. Our ancient ancestors liked cycles and repetition. If I'd thought about it for more than a second, I might have guessed. Grace figured it out in less than a week.

She's a smart girl. I just hope she smartens up about Greer.

I'm just about to make the turn on to Bryant, heading for the loop on to the Bay Bridge, when I catch a glimpse of something small and furry in the shadows of the bridge above.

With lightning-fast reflexes, I slam on the brakes and pull a sharp U-turn. The beastie looks up, its orange eyes widen and it starts to run. Unfortunately – for it – it heads in the wrong direction. I manoeuvre Moira to pen the cercopis, a small monkey-shaped monster, against the dirty brick wall fencing in one side of the empty lot.

When it starts to run back the other way, I swing open my door to block its path.

"Going somewhere?" I ask as I jump out, grab the creature by the shoulders and haul it out into the open.

"No, no, no," it cries, shaking its furry head violently. "Going nowhere."

Not any more.

"Don't send me back," it pleads.

"Back?" I smile sweetly. "Back where?"

"You know where," it says. "Huntress always send back."

"That's the general job description," I agree. "Send bad beasties home."

It must be a sign of my frustration that I'm taunting the monkey. Usually I just get my bite in and go home. But for some reason, I feel like playing with my prey a little.

And besides, I could use some answers about this supposed bounty on our heads. Maybe the monkey knows something useful.

"Not bad." It shakes its head again. "Not all bad beasties."

"What do you mean? I send home every bad beastie I can find." I'm definitely not counting the hybrids that got away recently. Before that my track record was pretty perfect.

"No, not all beasties *are* bad," it says carefully.

I laugh.

It takes advantage of my distraction to wriggle out of my grip, crawling up my arm and heading for my shoulder. Before it can reach my neck, I squat and then jump, flinging myself back in a somersault over the monkey and knocking it to the ground as I land. I press my right foot to its furry little chest, securing it against the crumbling tarmac.

"And I thought we were getting along so well."

"Why you toy?" It lifts up a foot, presenting it for my biting pleasure, I guess. "Do already."

"Not so fast." I shake my head, surprised that the creature isn't fighting back. "I have some questions first. Tell me about the bounty."

"Bounty?" it echoes. "What bounty?"

"Nice try." I press down on its chest. "Talk."

"Ow, okay," it says. "Sillus hear about bounty."

I release the pressure from my foot slightly. From the broken speech, I'm going to assume that *it* is Sillus.

"Word say, big honcho on Olympus want huntress. Any huntress. Any way, live or no live."

"What big honcho?" I think back to Ursula's hushed conversation I overheard a few months ago. "Zeus?"

"Maybe." It pushes against my boot with tiny monkey hands. "May not be. Sillus no go home for many months. No hear first hand."

Many months? "Do you mean you've been here, in San Francisco, for—"

The blaring ring of my phone interrupts my thought. The monkey is instantly forgotten, because I'm hoping it's Ursula.

My cell number is unlisted – not even the school has it – so if things ever get hairy and we need to slip away, I won't need to get a new number. It's been nearly two weeks since I've heard from Ursula. I'm a little disappointed when I answer and Grace is on the other end. I forgot I gave her the number just in case she's ever in danger.

"Everything okay?" I ask.

"No," she says. "Not really."

The hair on the back of my neck stands up. "What happened? Are you hurt?" I swallow hard. "Is Greer—"

"We're fine."

I exhale a huge sigh. I'm not used to having people to worry about, but apparently my sisterly instinct is strong enough to make me panic at the thought of them in trouble. I shouldn't give a centaur's backside what happens to the ice queen, but I do.

Sillus starts to wriggle under my boot, as if I'm so distracted it could just sneak away. I press down harder and wag a finger at the naughty monkey.

Grace says, "We were fighting a monster and—"

My muscles tense up again. "What kind?"

"I don't know," she says. "Some kind of serpent-tailed lady who came out of the Bay, but—"

"A sea dracaena?" I squeeze my eyes shut. "You fought one of Scylla's spawn alone?"

"I guess."

"Idiot." A sea dracaena. Of all things. "Grace, they're

among the most dangerous creatures out there. She didn't scratch you, did she?"

"No," she says, sounding a little exasperated. "But Gretchen—"

"You're lucky." I don't care if she thinks I'm being overprotective. This is serious. "One scratch is all it takes. There's no antivenom for—"

"I saw Ursula!"

I nearly drop my phone. "What?"

"After the fight," Grace explains. "I was about to call and tell you what happened when she appeared right in front of me. Out of nowhere."

"What do you mean?" I shake my head. "Out of nowhere?"

"She materialised," she says. "Gretchen, she autoported."

Autoported? That must mean… "She has your same gift. She has Euryale's power."

A part of me aches at the realisation that Ursula has kept this secret from me for so long. How did I not know this? How did I not figure out that she was a descendant just like me? She sees the monsters, used to fight them. I should have guessed. I feel so dumb.

Sillus struggles again. I'm too stunned to deal with it right now.

"Hold on," I tell Grace.

Reaching down, I grab the little monkey by the scruff of the neck.

"Please," it begs. "Don't send me…" When it sees my fangs drop, it sighs. Lifting up its foot, it says, "Fine. Make quick."

I almost feel sorry for the little monster. With my quick bite to the sole of its foot, it's gone.

"Okay, Grace," I say, my attention back on the call, "so Ursula is a descendant too. What else did she—"

"Gretchen," Grace says, like she's bracing me for something, "Ursula is *Euryale*."

For a second I think I'm going to collapse to the ground. All the air whooshes out of my lungs. I sink to my knees, sitting back on my heels.

"She's… What?"

"There's more," Grace says.

How much more could there be? Not only is my long-time mentor secretly my relative, she's one of my immortal ancestors.

"Wait, why did she come to you?" I ask. "Why didn't she visit me?"

"I'm not sure," Grace says. "At first she called me Gretchen, so she must have been trying to reach you. But I think her situation probably made things more difficult."

"What situation?" I'm so not used to being the one asking questions of Grace. I'm usually the one with all the answers.

"Gretchen, she's been taken prisoner."

I lurch to my feet. "What? Where?" In three quick

strides, I'm pulling open Moira's door and sinking into the driver's seat. As I turn the key in the ignition, I say, "I'll pick you up so we can go get her."

"We can't," Grace says. "She says we can't come get her, but she's safe."

There is a hesitation in her voice. "She said she was safe?"

"Yes."

"But you don't believe her."

"No, I..." Grace takes a breath. "I don't know. Maybe, maybe not. She's trying to protect us, I know. She knew about me and Greer and that we're all in danger right now."

That doesn't surprise me. Those are probably some of the answers she kept promising to tell me. I lean back against the headrest.

"What does she want us to do?" I ask, knowing Ursula wouldn't go to these measures just to not tell me where she is.

"She wants us to find her sister," Grace says. "She says we need to find Stheno."

Her sister. I already know that from her cryptic note. "How?"

"She didn't know." Grace makes a frustrated sound. "They have been out of communication, trying to keep us safe. She only knows that Stheno is in San Francisco and that she knows me. She told Ursula about me."

"Do you have any idea who she means?"

"No clue."

I squeeze the phone. "Then how are we supposed to find her?"

"I honestly don't know."

This is a lot to take in. I'm usually pretty steady on my feet, but all this news has me a little shaken.

"And Gretchen," she says, her voice taking on a sympathetic tone. "She wanted me to tell you she misses you. Terribly."

I can't remember the last time I cried. Maybe the time Phil turned his violent anger against Barb and I pleaded with her to leave him. Maybe the night I ran away and found myself alone and scared in that empty warehouse. Maybe my first night in the loft, when I realised I would never be alone and scared again. But there is no mistaking the sting of salty tears in my eyes.

I quickly wipe them away.

"Thanks, Grace," I say, trying to sound fine. "I appreciate it."

What I can't tell her is that I'm relieved to have her on my side. Even if I am scared at the moment, terrified for Ursula and whatever is going on, I know I don't have to go through it alone.

"No problem," she says. "Do you need me to come over?"

"Nah," I say, not wanting her to think I'm as concerned as I am. "I'm out. I'm fine anyway."

"Okay." She doesn't sound convinced, but she lets it go. "I should probably get home."

"Be careful," I say, meaning it more than ever.

"Yes, boss."

My finger is shaking as I click off the call.

Why is everything going so wrong so quickly? Two weeks ago, I was totally settled. Ursula was here, I was a runaway with no family, and I hunted monsters – one at a time after dark – to protect the human world from real creatures straight out of Greek mythology. Now Ursula's imprisoned, I have two sisters and two great-many-times-over-aunts and the rules I used to know and love have gone to Hades.

And there's nothing I can do about any of it.

I give Moira's floor a solid kick, like that's going to solve anything. Exhausted – from the fights and the news and everything just adding up – I'm headed home, pulling out into traffic, when my phone rings again.

"Yeah, Grace," I say, thinking she must have forgotten to tell me something.

"Sorry," the male voice at the other end of the phone says. "Not Grace."

If it's not Grace, then who could have this number? "Who the hell is this?"

"It's Nick," he says with a laugh. "Glad to know your manners are just as endearing on the phone as they are in person."

I want to scream. I *do* scream. *"Aaargh!"*

Why won't he leave me alone? I've given him every possible stop sign I can without breaking any bones or major laws. So why does he keep trying?

I should hang up. I should block his number and change schools, but curiosity gets the best of me.

"How did you get this number?" I snap.

"I have my ways."

I can hear his cocky grin through the phone. Trust me, if I could reach through the airwaves and strangle him, I'd do it. Twenty to life would be worth it right now.

I should have let the skorpios hybrid get him.

"How?" I repeat. "It's unlisted."

"Nothing is *that* unlisted."

"My cell number is." I clench my hand around the steering wheel as I cut over to Market. "No one has this number."

"Someone must," he argues. "Otherwise what's the point in having a phone?"

"Where did you get my number?" I shout.

Normally I have a lot better hold on my emotions, but it's been a rough few days. Plus, this boy has an unparalleled talent for pushing all my buttons in the wrong order. For a moment, I consider flinging my phone out of the window. The only thing that stops me is that if Grace is in trouble or if – scratch that – *when* Ursula gets free, they'd have no way to reach me. I consider throwing my*self* out of the window. Or maybe driving into the Bay. An icy-cold dunk might be exactly what I need right now.

"Relax," he says, in a tone that makes me do anything but. "Look, I just have a question about Biology. You don't need to jump down my throat."

"Didn't you promise me you'd back off?"

"I did."

I grind my teeth in the brief silence.

"I lied," he admits. "Sorry."

Okay, enough. "Look. Haven't I made it crystal sparkling clear from the start that I want less than nothing to do with you?"

"You've tried."

"Don't I keep saying, over and over and over again, that you should back the hell off?"

"And over again," he echoes. "Yep, I remember something like that."

"Then why," I ask with a sigh of despair, taking a turn without signalling and ignoring the angry horn blast that follows, "do you keep trying?"

Seriously. What kind of psycho masochist keeps returning for more rejection? Is he trying to drive me insane? After all the craziness lately, it's not a long trip.

"Guess I never learned to take no for an answer."

I don't know what else I can say or do to get him to back off. Seeing me take down beasties on two occasions

– even if he couldn't see their true form – didn't scare him away. What kind of guy wants a girl who gets into fist fights on a regular basis?

Obviously, this kind.

I drive in silence, not knowing what else to say, but not wanting – for some unfathomable reason – to hang up yet. When I pull into the garage, I'm suddenly struck by how very empty the loft upstairs is going to feel. For the first time, I don't have even the tiniest hope that Ursula will be waiting inside. Without her it's like an empty shell of the place that used to feel like home.

What if Ursula never comes back? The question sneaks into my thoughts before I can block it. Bracing myself on the steering wheel, I take deep breaths. My hands are shaking as fear speeds through my bloodstream. I've never felt like this, not even when Phil was on a bender and his fists were swinging.

Until now, monster hunting was business. A duty, a responsibility I upheld as a part of my legacy, because it is my destiny. It was a straightforward job and I did it well. But I cared about as much as I cared about the colour of my non-existent nail polish.

Ursula in danger makes it personal, and I feel the fear like a tight fist around my heart.

She's the only real mother I've ever known. I don't buy for a second her insistence that she's safe. I can't just sit around and do nothing while she's in danger. I might feel helpless right now, but I'm not. I have to do *something*.

"Gretchen?" Nick prods.

"What?" I snap into the forgotten phone in my hand.

"I have a confession to make," he says, ignoring my anger, as usual. "I didn't call to ask about biology homework."

"Really," I say sarcastically. "Had me fooled."

"I'm tricky like that," he replies. "No, I've got tickets to a concert in Golden Gate Park tomorrow night. Actually, the concert is free, but I've got a blanket and picnic basket and I was wondering if you wanted to—"

I click the phone off before he can finish his question. I know exactly what he was going to ask, and there's no way I can say yes.

Slipping the phone into my pocket, I get out of the car and climb the creaking staircase up to the loft.

Girls like me can't date. Imagine, sitting down to a nice dinner and catching a whiff of rotten meat. It's not like I could say, 'Excuse me. Have to go take care of the Nemean lion that's prowling the streets. Be back in a jiff.'

My phone rings again and I ignore it. The situation isn't going to change. Girls like me have to be alone.

I toss my ringing phone onto the couch and head to the fridge. Maybe some dinner will help clear my mind. I yank open the freezer door. It's stocked with a month's supply of frozen dinners.

I grab a turkey-and-stuffing box, tear it open, and pop it into the microwave. While the microwave whirrs and my dinner spins hypnotically in circles, I can't help feeling more alone than I've ever felt. Not only because Ursula, my one and only true friend in this world, is being held prisoner. Not only because I've discovered I have two long-lost sisters, one of whom is safe at home with her loving family and the other who wants nothing to do with me. Not only because I can never, in any conceivable universe, let Nick or any other ordinary human boy close enough to discover the true me. Not only because I'm not even sure who the true me is any more.

No, I feel completely and utterly alone because, for the first time since the day I realised my adoptive parents were abusive trash and I was better off on the streets than with them, I don't *want* to be alone. For the first time, I *want* to let people in. I didn't want to hang up on Nick, I *had* to. Because, for the first time, I wanted to say yes.

And I can't imagine anything more dangerous. For me or for him.

The microwave beeps, and the jarring sound pulls me from self-pity into the real world. It's like I have an instantaneous moment of absolute clarity.

"I know how to find Stheno," I blurt out to the empty kitchen.

Without another thought for my dinner, I grab my phone, jacket and keys and dash back to Moira at full speed. My best chance of finding Ursula's sister is the same person who told me I was destined for greater things than what Phil and Barb had planned.

The oracle.

The storefront looks exactly as I remember. Plain, nondescript, with dark velvet curtains that might have been red at one time blocking any view inside. Hanging in the door is a small wooden sign that reads FORTUNES TOLD, with a line of ancient-looking letters below: μαντεον.

At twelve I thought they were magical symbols. Now I recognise the text as Ancient Greek: ORACLE.

Just as before, the place looks deserted from the outside. A thick layer of grime covers the windows, no light shines through even the tiniest crack in the curtains or door, and there is no sign indicating whether the place is open or even when it might be. But I know, in the same unnatural way I knew four years ago, that she's inside.

I walk up to the door, grab the tarnished brass knob and twist. The door glides open like it floats on air. Except for the street light streaming in the now-open door, the space inside is dark as night.

"You came back," a gravelly voice says from the void. "I knew you would."

She steps into the beam of light, looking the same as before. Long black robes swirling around her tiny frame.

Long black hair falling down her back in thick waves. Long beaked nose protruding out from a haggard and wrinkled face. She looks like an evil witch from a child's fairy tale.

"I know what you came for," she says, her voice crackling.

"I'm sure you do."

When I passed her door four years ago, taking the long way home from the grocery store to avoid going by Phil's favourite bar, I was desperate. Searching for any light at the end of the dark tunnel I saw my life becoming. The nameless fortune-teller greeted me, as she did now, with the promise of things I wanted to know.

She led me to a table in the back room, studied my palm and told me I was marked for a great destiny. Despite my protests, she insisted I had to run away, to get away from the people who kept me from greatness.

I thought it was all garbage until she said, "The creatures are your future."

No one but Phil and Barb knew I saw monsters, and they beat it into me that I was crazy to say so. But this woman knew, and she thought it was important.

That night I ran away.

Ursula found me a few weeks later. All of Olympus, she later explained, received reports when an oracle – a fortune-teller – read a prophecy to a lost descendant. My visit to this oracle four years ago sent immediate red flags up around the mythological world.

Because Ursula had been paying close attention, anticipating my appearance, she found me first.

Walking into this place again brings all those memories flooding back. It's amazing how much my life has changed since then, and all because of this woman's reading.

"Then tell me," I say, stepping inside and closing the door. "Tell me what I want to know."

Even though my eyes aren't adjusted to the dark, I sense her turning and walking to the back. I follow her into the same room where my path shifted four years ago.

"Sit, sit," she says, waving at the table as she lights the candles scattered around the room.

When there is a soft ambient glow illuminating the round table and the otherwise empty space, she takes the other chair and sits across from me.

"First," she says, a hint of an old-world accent rolling the word, "you wish to find the sister."

I don't ask how she knows. She just does.

"Yes, that's right."

From the folds of her robes she pulls out a piece of paper. As she smoothes it onto the table, I see that it's a map. While I'm studying it, identifying it as a map of San Francisco, she pulls another object out of her folds. A small, pointed crystal at the end of a gold chain.

"We must concentrate," she says, dangling the crystal over the map. "Focus your mind on the woman you seek."

I do my best, spending the next few minutes thinking

about Stheno and where she might be and what I'm going to do once I find her. But my mind keeps drifting to Ursula, to the news of her capture and her real identity.

"Psha!" the fortune-teller spits, jerking the crystal and stuffing it back into its hidden pocket. "You do not focus."

I don't bother denying it. I'm trying, but my mind is just too full, I guess.

"There is another way." She peers at me in the faint light. "Blood."

"Blood?" I echo. "Whose blood?"

"Yours."

I meet her unwavering gaze for a long moment. Then, knowing I don't really have another choice, I reach down and pull the dagger from my boot. In one swift movement, I slice a line down the centre of my palm – my right palm – drawing a fine trail of healing blood from my flesh.

"Here," I say, holding out my hand as I slip the dagger back into my boot. "Does this work?"

She nods. With craggy, gnarled fingers, she folds my hand into a fist and wraps her hands around mine. Holding it over the map, she squeezes tightly until a single drop of blood drips from the bottom of my fist.

Releasing my hand, she pushes the map at me. "There, it is revealed."

I wipe my palm on my trousers as I look at the map. The single drop of blood landed in the marina district, only a few blocks from my loft. With a shaking finger,

I smear the blood away and read the name of the building beneath.

Alpha Academy. Grace's school.

Well, at least now we know where to look. Stheno is someone at her school.

"Good?" the fortune-teller asks.

I nod, taking the map and folding it into one of my cargo pockets.

"The other question," she says. "The one you are afraid to ask."

I don't have to say it out loud to confirm she's talking about Ursula. There are a million questions I'd like to ask. Where is she? How do I find her? Is she safe? But I ask the one that answers them all. "Can I save her?"

"You can," she says, and I release a tight breath. Then she adds, "But it has yet to be written whether you will."

I take a shaky breath. I could be terrified by that prediction, by the fear that I might not save Ursula in the end. But I'm not. The bottom line is: I *can* save Ursula, and so I *will*. I won't allow myself to fail.

CHAPTER 20

Grace

When I showed up at Gretchen's on Saturday morning, the first thing she told me was what the oracle said. That the immortal gorgon Stheno is at my school.

Now, I don't know if that means she's a teacher or student or staff or administration or what, but I've spent all day Monday studying every single female at Alpha to see if anyone, I don't know, *clicks* with me. Someone who reminds me of Ursula maybe. So far, no such luck. If Stheno is here, she's doing a great job of disguising herself.

By the time Lulu and I walk out of Computer Science after the final bell, I'm starting to think the oracle was wrong. Gretchen is adamant, but maybe she just wants to believe her.

"Do you think Miss Mota is ever going to notice that Orson hid that perverted message in his web page?" Lulu asks, pulling a compact out of her giant tote bag and checking her fire-engine-red lipstick.

"She hasn't so far," I say, relieved to think about something other than searching out my immortal ancestor.

"Well she obviously adores you." Lulu drops her compact back into her bag. "You could create a page about cow manure and she'd still call us all over to admire it."

"Yeah," I agree. "She's kind of over the top."

Maybe she—

"Grace," I hear a woman call behind me. When I turn, I see Miss Mota running after me. "You forgot your handout." She's panting and a little out of breath, but with a huge grin on her face. "Can't do your homework without the style guide, can you?"

"Thanks," I say, taking the handout.

She has been kind of over-nice to me. I thought it was just because I'm a solid computer geek – aka her ideal student – but maybe it's something more. Could she be Stheno?

As she turns and walks back to her classroom, I start to analyse everything I know about her, to see if anything fits.

Before I can think back to the first day of Computer Science, I sense Miranda marching up behind me and Lulu. I catch sight of her a split second before she moves to Lulu's side and rushes forward, knocking into my friend, sending her stumbling forward and her bag flying.

I have an instant flashback of my first day at Alpha.

Only instead of acting like an entitled brat, Miranda spins round and says, "Omigosh, I am *so* sorry."

I help steady Lulu on her feet and we give each other

a confused look. Apologies are very un-Miranda-like behaviour.

"Yeah," Lulu says hesitantly. "It's fine."

My jaw drops as Miranda actually squats and helps gather Lulu's belongings back into her bag. Part of me hopes she's realised that being mean and nasty doesn't get her very far. But I'm not the same naive new girl who started here less than two weeks ago. So much can change in a short time. Miranda's up to something.

I bend down to help, snatching Lulu's bag back when Miranda tries to pick it up.

She gives me a hurt look. "I was trying to hand it back to her." She huffs out a breath that sends her bangs floating. "Jeez, sorry."

I hand Lulu her bag and watch as Miranda turns and stalks away. Okay, maybe I was wrong. I feel a little guilty about jumping to…

As Miranda rounds the corner into the next corridor, I see her pull something out of her back pocket.

Lulu's phone.

I have had more than enough of this girl.

"Here," I say, shoving Lulu's bag into her arms.

I chase after Miranda, ignoring Lulu as she asks, "What's wrong?" Her peep-toe pumps clack on the floor behind me as she hurries to keep up. "Where are you going?"

"Miranda," I call out as I catch up with her, dodging around a couple of jocks who are throwing a football back and forth. When she doesn't stop, I shout, "Miranda!"

She spins round so fast, I'm surprised she doesn't keep going full circle. She demands, "What?"

My hand is shaking as I hold it out, palm up. "Give it back."

She throws an incredulous look at my hand. "Give what back? What nonsense are you—"

"Cut the garbage," I interrupt, drawing on my inner Gretchen for the courage to carry out the confrontation. "I saw you with Lulu's phone. Return it now and I won't report the theft."

Next to me, Lulu digs through her bag. When she finds her phone missing, she says, "You're right. It's gone. I know I had it before Computer Science, because Jax asked me to look up the Kiss Me Kitties concert schedule."

Miranda looks like she wants to deny it again. I take a step closer, let my fangs drop a fraction, and say, "Now."

Her eyes roll halfway around the corridor, and her jaw clicks to the side, like she's going to gnaw on the inside of her cheek a little before telling me where to stick it.

My fangs drop a little more. "Miranda…"

She huffs out another breath. "Whatever." She pulls the phone out of her bag and slaps it into my palm. Then, spinning on her heel, she calls out over her shoulder, "Losers."

As soon as she's out of sight, my fangs suck back into place and I gasp in a shaky breath.

"You," Lulu says, grabbing the phone off my palm, "have backbone. Vail will be so proud."

Every limb is shaking with the after-effects of my confrontational adrenaline. I can't believe I stood up to Miranda like that. And *lived*.

"Holy goalie," I whisper.

Not only will Vail be proud, so will Gretchen. And, if I think about it, so am I. I never knew I had it in me. Maybe doormat Grace is finally stepping aside. Monster-hunting, Miranda-confronting Grace is welcome to take her place.

"Go long, dude!" one of the football jocks shouts.

The other one takes off at a run, racing down the corridor… and directly towards Ms West, who is heading this way.

"Watch out!" I call out.

But it's too late. The jock turns, sees Ms West, but can't stop his runaway forward momentum.

"Whoa there," she says, taking half a step to the side and reaching out her arm right as he passes by.

I wince at the certain disaster, but instead of jock boy taking Ms West down with him, she manages to bring him to a dead stop without even losing her footing.

"No running in the corridors, gentlemen," she says, catching the football that jock-boy was supposed to grab and handing it to him. "That includes chasing footballs."

"Yes, Ms West," the one who threw the ball says.

The other one blushes. "Sorry, Ms West."

"Just don't let it happen again." She grins at them, waves at me and then walks away.

It takes about ten seconds of me standing there, jaw dropped, to realise what just happened. Ms West should have been knocked to the ground, but she held him off like he was nothing. That was an amazing display of strength.

"Lulu, I have to run," I blurt as I take off after Ms West.

"Bye," Lulu calls after me. "See you at lunch tomorrow."

I rush round the corner and find myself staring down an empty corridor. Ms West is nowhere in sight. I check every classroom, every door, but she's vanished. Standing in the middle of the empty corridor, I can't help the massive grin that spreads across my face.

Ms West is Stheno.

Gretchen is going to be so excited.

Since it's such a lovely day, I decide to walk to Gretchen's loft. It's only a few blocks away, and after standing up to Miranda and uncovering Stheno's secret identity, I feel like bouncing the whole way there.

I'm just walking down the front steps at Alpha when my phone rings.

"Hi Thane," I say as I head down on to the sidewalk. "What's up?"

"I have to go away."

"What?" I pull to a stop. That sounded very ominous.

"What do you mean you have to go away?"

"Not for long," he says. "Maybe two or three days."

"But why? Where are you going?"

"I…" He hesitates and I get nervous. Thane doesn't normally hesitate. He either answers a question or he doesn't, no indecision involved. Finally he says, "I told Mom I'm staying with Milo. Because of our soccer training schedule."

He *told* Mom that, which means that's not where he's really going. "Thane, I don't like this."

"I know," he says, his voice gruff and unhappy. "I don't either."

"Why are you telling me?" I ask. "You lied to Mom, you could just as easily lie to me."

"Because you should know the truth," he answers. "Or at least part of it."

"Thane, just tell me—"

"And because you might talk to Milo in the meantime and then you'd find out anyway."

"This is ridiculous," I say, getting a very bad feeling about this. "Just tell me where you're going. I won't tell Mom, I swear."

"I know you wouldn't."

"But you're still not going to tell me."

"I can't," he insists. "Not now. I just… have to figure a few things out."

I've always known Thane had things going on he didn't

talk to me about. There's a look he gets that makes it seem like he's thousands of miles away in his mind, and that look has a touch of pain. He won't tell me what's wrong, but I know it's something big. And if wherever he's going will help him fix the thing that haunts him... well, then I can't exactly begrudge him the chance to try.

"Okay," I finally say. "I understand."

"Thank you, Grace-face," he says, using the nickname he hasn't used since we were kids.

"Call me?" I start walking again. "To let me know you're okay."

"I'll..." He huffs out an unhappy breath. "I'll try."

"Hey, I love—"

He's gone before I can finish. For the next few blocks, my mind wanders, trying to guess where Thane might be going and why. But since he's never let me into that part of his life, I have less than no clue.

I've found the missing part of me – my sisters and my legacy – and I can only hope that he finds the same kind of fulfilment on his quest as I'm finding on mine. He's my brother and he deserves at least that.

CHAPTER 21

Greer

After my unwelcome dip in the Bay, I'm ready to forget about recent events, forget about my sisters and mythological monsters and just focus on the life I've worked so hard to create. That's really hard when monsters keep showing up everywhere I go.

It's as if, when my sisters showed up on my doorstep and resurrected that memory of the centaur in my room, a switch flipped in my brain. All those costly hypnosis sessions – and that final one with a different therapist – unravelled, and now my mind is trying to make up for years of not seeing any monsters.

I see the first one on Saturday morning on my jog through Golden Gate Park. On my second loop around Stow Lake, I move aside for someone I sense running up behind me, and as they pass, realise it isn't a person but a gigantic, slobbering boar. And it's wearing running shorts and a headband.

Without finishing my run, I turn off at the Japanese Tea Garden and head inside for some head-clearing ginseng.

Later that afternoon, Kyle invites me to visit the

Exploratorium at the Palace of Fine Arts. I'm not a huge fan of the science museum, but I adore the neoclassical grace of the building and the peaceful pond out front. I agree to go and – after walking through the special exhibit about soap bubbles – convince him to sit on a bench with me and feed the birds. Splashing around among the gulls, ducks and swans is a bizarre creature with the upper body of a horse and the tail of a fish.

I close my eyes and count to ten. When I open them, the creature is still there, frolicking. Just playing in the water. I close my eyes and count to one hundred, alternating each number with a mantra.

One. *There is no monster.* Two. *There is no monster.*

By the time I reach a hundred and force my eyes back open, the beast is gone.

See, I am still in control of my life and my mind.

Mother wakes me up on Sunday morning to remind me that I promised to play hostess for her event at the de Young that afternoon. As much as I want to stay in bed with the covers over my head all day, I know can't back out on that commitment. Besides, it's the *de Young*. There is a special exhibit of Picasso from Paris that I've been dying to see. My primary job is to hand out name tags, making sure I give special attention to Mother's most generous and prestigious donors. I fail to recognise the ex-mayor's ex-wife because, it turns out, she is actually a woman with the body of a lioness.

This cannot be happening! I mentally scream. Why are there suddenly monsters everywhere? And from what I can tell, none of them are trying to attack or eat anyone, least of all me. The ex-mayor's ex-wife is on numerous committees with Mother; I've known her for years. Has she been a sphinx all this time?

I feel a complete mental breakdown coming on.

I'm sure Mother will be furious, but I hand over my name tag duties to the nearest server and leave without even having the chance to see any of the exhibit.

By the time I get to the end of the school day on Monday, I feel like every nerve in my body is stretched tight and I'm just one monster away from snapping.

"If no one has any other new business," I announce to the assembled Alumnae Tea Committee, "then I'll declare this meeting over."

A quick scan of the ten girls – the socio-economic elite of Immaculate Heart – seated around the antique mahogany conference table reveals not a monster in sight and one predictably raised hand. Veronica. She's been ignoring my order to forget the ice sculpture idea and has been petitioning the other committee members to support the proposal.

I inhale and immerse myself in the leadership role, to the exclusion of all other distractions.

"Very well," I say, ignoring her. "Let's adjourn and—"

"Excuse me," Veronica says, obviously annoyed.

She has no talent for disguising her true feelings. While that kind of open-book honesty might be refreshing, it won't serve her well in a society that operates on a smile-to-your-face-and-stab-you-in-the-back principle. Poor thing.

"I would like the committee to consider—"

I cut her off before it goes too far. "We have already discussed the ice sculpture." Ad nauseam. I can't let her turn this meeting into a circus, with an ice sculpture in the centre ring.

She stands, her chair legs squeaking across the hardwood floor. In her ragged graphic T-shirt and worn-and-torn jeans, she looks like a perfect thrift-store match for her starving-artist boyfriend. She does *not*, however, look like Immaculate Heart alumnae material. Nor does she sound like it.

"There should be a vote," she whines. "It's not official unless there is an accounted vote."

We have a brief stare-down across the conference table. After the weekend I've had, I'm in no mood for a debate. My patience metre is at zero. Time to end this patronise-the-arts campaign once and for all.

"Fine," I say, turning my attention to the rest of the committee. "Veronica proposes we have a hideous melting ice sculpture of a dragon—"

"Greer," she complains.

"On the buffet table. All in favour?"

If the other committee members know what's good for their social standing, they will read the correct answer in my piercing silver glare.

Only Veronica raises her hand.

"All opposed?"

Every hand in the room – except Veronica's – shoots up.

"The matter is decided."

"But—"

"This meeting is over." I gather my paperwork into the Alumnae Tea ring binder. "We will meet here again next Monday at the same time, for our final planning session before the tea on Saturday."

Veronica, I'm sure, is ready to explode. I could care. Actually, I couldn't. Let her explode, preferably somewhere brilliantly public and reputation damaging.

Sliding the ring binder into my grass-green Coach satchel, I turn and walk from the room before she starts begging or crying or some embarrassing combination of the two.

"Hey Greer," Annalise calls out, jogging to catch up with me. "Rory and I are going to drive down to Santa Cruz for the afternoon. Want to come?"

Normally, I would relish the chance to head down the coast and spend a few hours on the sand. Just me, my friends, a giant towel and generous amounts of high-SPF sunscreen. But today my mind is racing too much to relax.

I would be terrible company. I should really be alone.

"Not today," I say. "I have a ten-page report for Huffington due tomorrow."

It's not a fib. Only I left out the part where I've had the paper finished since last weekend. A little lie of omission is a small price to pay for the solo time I need at the moment.

"Okay," she says with a bright grin. "Next time."

"Definitely," I say, as she hurries down the corridor.

As I slowly make my way through the empty school to the main entrance, the only person I see is the janitor, quietly mopping scuffs and dirt off the tiled floor. Everyone else has vanished.

As I pass by, I turn to nod. Only I don't see Harold, our kindly school janitor. Instead, I see a giant spider, rubbing the mop back and forth across the tiles.

It takes the last little bits of my control to not freak out completely and run screaming from the building. What, did the spider eat Harold and take over his job, so no one will know? Harold's been at Immaculate Heart for decades. Everyone loves him. He's an integral part of the school. How dare that... *thing* eat Harold.

I will not just stand by and let the spider monster get away with this tragedy. I'm not certain what I can do, but I have to do something.

"Goodnight, Miss Greer," the spider says as I start marching in its direction. "You be careful of that wet tile there."

I jerk back.

Harold? The spider *is* Harold? Harold is the spider? What…? How…? I don't think my brain can handle this information. Insanity overload.

I mumble a quick goodbye and burst out into the open air.

What is happening to my carefully constructed world? A week ago, everything was perfect. Simple. Understandable. I was simply Greer Morgenthal, daughter of Elliot and Helen Morgenthal, most popular girl in the junior class, if not the entire school, and girlfriend of the most popular boy at St Stephen. Future CEO, Junior Leaguer, and – if my plans work out right – first female president. Now, suddenly, I'm adopted, I have triplet sisters and I see mythological monsters round *every* single corner!

I think my brain is imploding.

Without thinking about where I'm going, I walk right past the bus stop and head towards Fillmore, to the one place that always makes me feel in control of my world.

Before I know it, I'm pushing open the door and a tiny bell is tinkling to announce my presence. I collapse into one of the four hot-pink armchairs in the centre of the space. As my satchel hits the floor, Kelly Anne emerges from the back room, a beaming smile on her face.

"Greer," she squeals with delight. "Darling, it's been weeks."

"I know," I reply, welcoming her hug as she leans down to give me a quick squeeze. "I've been busy."

She laughs. "I was beginning to think you joined Shoe-aholics Anonymous."

"Never." I smile, a real and true smile.

At least some things remain the same.

"What can I show you today?" she asks, swinging her arm in a broad gesture at the walls of shoes lining either side of the shop.

"I need a new strappy date shoe," I explain. "One of my silver Jimmy Choos…" Well, I can't exactly tell her it got lost in the Bay when a giant serpent creature tried to drown me. Not unless I want a one-way ticket to the psychiatric ward. "It's beyond repair."

Kelly Anne gasps. Shoes are her life, and telling her that one is damaged is like telling someone you ran over their dog. Only with more tears.

Before she starts crying, I say, "I'm feeling colourful today."

She nods, swallowing her grief. "I have just the thing."

She slips into the back and I sink against the chair. With my eyes closed and new shoes on the way, I almost feel back to normal. What I need to do is will the monsters away. I'm a strong believer in mind over matter. Surely, if I focus my willpower on the issue, I can make the monsters disappear back into my subconscious.

I kick off my Ralph Lauren espadrilles, wiggling my

toes against the plush white rug, and harness my mental powers. Fall will begin officially in a few days and I'll have to put my warm-weather wardrobe away. But for now, I'm holding on to the last bit of summer. And my last bit of sanity.

Soon, schoolwork and extracurriculars and other responsibilities will overwhelm me on a daily basis. I'll have limited time for shoe shopping, let alone more important things. Like Kyle.

The other night, when I bailed on him, he bought the phoned-in "I got seafood sauce on my top" excuse and was totally understanding. Or uncaring, I can never really tell with Kyle. Still, he was a good sport. Now I owe him.

Pulling out my cell, I call Kyle's number. He answers on the fourth ring.

"Babe," he says with an exaggerated drawl. "What's up?"

I cringe, then release the tension. I don't need to allow any more stress right now. "Hello, Kyle," I say politely. "Would you like to come over tonight?"

"Abso-righteous-lutely." He laughs at his made-up slang. "What time?"

I ignore his display of idiocy.

"I'm doing a little shoe shopping right now, but I'll be home soon," I answer. "Come over anytime."

"Right on."

I'm about to hang up, to sink into the bliss of shoe

shopping and pretend surfer-boy isn't in prime form tonight.

"Greer," he says, dropping the overwrought-dude act. "You okay?"

"Yes," I answer, closing my eyes and leaning my head back against the chair. "It's been a stressful few days."

Saying that makes a little of the tension ease from my neck. Nothing can make it go away altogether, but every tiny bit helps.

"I'll bring my magic hands," Kyle says. "That stress will be history by the time I leave."

I grin. A massage would be—

"*If* I leave," he adds, with a suggestive undertone.

Did he have to ruin the moment? Well, I won't let him. I need him tonight. And maybe... Maybe...

"Kyle, honey," I say, in my sweetest tone. "Bring some strawberries."

I hang up before he says something that changes my mind. After all the ridiculous things that have happened in the last few days, taking the next, not-quite-all-the-way-but-pretty-close step in our relationship might be precisely the memory eraser I need.

"Here we go," Kelly Anne says, emerging through the curtain with a trio of shoe boxes in her hands.

She puts two of them down, opens the third and pulls out all the stuffing to reveal a high-heeled strappy sandal in a brilliant shade of dark lime green.

"It's beautiful." I take the shoe and run my fingertips over the satin straps.

"Try it on," she instructs. "It feels divine."

She holds out her own foot to show me that she's wearing the same shoe in bright purple.

The bell above the door tinkles. Kelly Anne goes to greet the new customer as I unbuckle the ankle strap and slide my foot into the shoe. She's right, it does feel divine. I quickly step into the other one.

"Let me go grab that for you," Kelly Anne tells the new customer. She rushes by me, asking, "Don't you love them?" as she goes.

"They're gorgeous," the new customer comments, with a weird click in her voice. "Are they comfortable?"

I glance up, ready to say, "Yes, quite." But I freeze when, instead of a fellow shoe-shopping woman, I see a woman's body with the head of a raven.

She twists her feathered head to the side, studying me. *There is not a bird-woman in the shop*, I tell myself. *There is* not *a—*

"Here you go," Kelly Anne says, bringing a pair of boxes to the woman who – no matter how hard I try to convince myself otherwise – has the head of a big black bird. Her inky black feathers gleam yellow in the fluorescent light.

I can't take it any more.

Standing, I grab my satchel and head for the door.

"Is something wrong, Greer?" Kelly Anne asks,

rightfully concerned about her favourite client – me –
walking out of the shop.

"No," I squeak. "Fine. I love these. Put them on my tab."

"No problem."

I push open the door, desperate to get away.

"Greer, wait!"

I ignore whatever Kelly Anne is trying to say. She has
more important things to worry about, like finding the
perfect shoes for the bird-woman. Probably something in
a black patent pump.

Sweet mercy, not even Kelly Anne's boutique is safe
any more.

As I hurry down the sidewalk, I hear her call out, "You
forgot your espadrilles."

A small price to pay to escape the presence of yet another
monster. Why? Why is this happening to me? I've been
a good girl, for the most part, all my life. I try to meet
and exceed everyone's expectations. I don't lie unless it's
absolutely necessary. I'm loyal to my friends, I get stellar
grades, I make my bed every day. I don't drink, do drugs,
sneak out or break any laws. What did I do to deserve this
kind of fate? I'm going insane as I'm surrounded by ever-
increasing numbers of freaky monsters.

Seriously, a woman with a raven's head?

I jerk to a stop in the middle of a pedestrian crossing.
There is only one person – well, two people, actually –
who can answer my questions. Who can tell me why

this is happening and how to make it stop. Because it has to stop. The same two people whose presence in my life seems to have been the harbinger of my descent into madness.

My – I swallow tightly – sisters.

A blaring horn bursts my thoughts and reminds me I'm standing in the middle of the street. But now I know where I need to go. Only I don't know *where* to go. It's not like I collected business cards when they showed up on my doorstep. Or when Grace and I were fighting the crazy sea snake.

I don't even have a phone number for them.

Something in my gut compels me to head downhill to the marina. It's such a strong feeling, I don't stop to think. I jog across the street – Kelly Anne was right about these heels, they *are* ultra-comfortable – just in time to catch the bus. Seven minutes later I jump off at Marina Boulevard.

Not sure why, I turn and head east towards the nearest pier, towards the big warehouse-like building jutting out over the water. It's like I'm on autopilot.

Before I know it, I'm banging on a big metal door. An echo thunders around me and through the building beyond the door. It sounds empty.

After a couple of minutes I'm starting to think my insanity must be expanding to new and different levels. Why would I come here, of all places?

But when I'm about to turn and walk away, the door swings open with a painful screech.

"What do you want?" Gretchen asks, her seemingly ever-present scowl in place.

Oh, thank goodness.

"I'm seeing monsters," I explain. "Everywhere."

She shrugs, as if to say, *What should I do about it?*

"They're in the park and at my school and just… everywhere! I need to know what exactly is going on," I explain. "I need to make it stop." Because clearly my force of will isn't going to be enough.

"Greer!"

I turn and see Grace hurrying across the driveway. When she gets to the door, panting, she says, "I'm so glad you're here."

"And how exactly did you get *here*?" Gretchen asks with a snarl.

I look from Grace to Gretchen and answer honestly, "I don't know."

Grace gasps. "Did you autoport?"

"Did I what?"

"Autoport," she repeats. "You know, did you just zap here?"

"No." I am so confused. "I took a bus."

"Oh." Her face falls. Then, after a beat, she beams. "*Oh!* You must have Medusa's gift. Second sight."

"Look, can we…" I struggle to retain my trademark

calm. "Can we go somewhere and talk?"

Gretchen doesn't speak, but she steps out and pulls the door shut behind her. As she walks past us, I share a look with Grace. She shrugs and heads off after our sister. Not having anywhere else to turn, I do the same.

CHAPTER 22

Grace

I can't believe I'm sitting at a table in a sushi restaurant with my two sisters. My sisters! I don't think I've been this happy since we adopted Thane – who is hopefully busy working on his own bid for happiness – and this is happy on a whole different their-blood-is-my-blood level.

Gretchen and Greer don't seem to share my excitement.

To my left, Gretchen's arms are crossed and leaning on the table, a stormy look on her face. There's a line between her eyebrows where she's squeezed them together. Her eyes are a darker shade of grey than I've ever seen in my mirror. I wonder if that's what I look like when I'm angry.

Or am I more like Greer, sitting stiff-spined in her chair, exuding haughty annoyance and looking like she might fracture into a million pieces at any second?

Either way, the tension at the table is practically killing me. I'm not just going to let things go and pretend like everything is okay, though, because big things are going on and we need to talk about them. Sitting up straight in my chair, I look at Gretchen.

"I know who Stheno is."

Immediately her demeanour changes. "Who?"

"My counsellor, Ms West," I say, so proud to have figured it out. "I didn't get a chance to talk to her about it because, well, she disappeared."

"Not like you?" Gretchen clarifies. "Not autoporting?"

"No, she just walked out of the building—"

"I'm sorry," Greer interrupts. "But, Stheno? As in the immortal gorgon Stheno?"

"The same," I say with a grin. "After you and I fought the serpent-lady at the wharf—"

"Sea dracaena," Gretchen mutters.

"Right." I flash a scowl at her. As if that's helping right now. "Anyway, after you left, then Gretchen's mentor, Ursula, visited me. Only she's not just Ursula, she's really the other immortal gorgon, Euryale."

"An immortal gorgon visited you on the wharf?"

"Yes." Am I being unclear? I don't think so. "She autoported to me, thinking I was Gretchen, because she's been imprisoned somewhere and I guess her autoporting wires got crossed—"

"Grace," Gretchen interrupts with a snarl. "Can we get back to the part where you discovered your counsellor is Stheno?"

"Oh, right." I guess it's better to stay on track. "Anyway, she got away before I could ask her, and I thought maybe, if you want, we could go talk to her together. I could make an appointment for after school or something."

Gretchen nods and I sigh with relief. We've found Ursula's sister and now maybe we can figure out what's going on and why things are changing. That's one thing checked off the list of unanswered questions today.

"Great," Greer says, not sounding thrilled. "Can we get back to my problem here?"

Gretchen scowls. "Of course," she sneers. "Because this is all about you."

"Now, Gretchen," I say, wanting to diffuse the sudden tension.

"No," Greer says before I can finish. "That's fair."

Gretchen seems stunned that Greer would make that kind of concession. I guess I'm actually a little surprised too. They look at each other – okay, *glare* – and I feel caught in the middle.

Thankfully, the waitress arrives, breaking the unsister-like tension.

"You girls ready to order?" she drawls, looking from Greer to me to Gretchen. "Well, aren't you three adorable? Triplets, huh?"

I smile. "Yes, we—"

"I'll have salmon nigiri and a bowl of miso soup," Greer says, cutting off my answer.

"The tempura platter," Gretchen says. "With extra shrimp."

The waitress quickly scribbles down their orders and then looks at me.

"Can I just get an avocado roll?" I ask. When the waitress nods and adds it to the order, I say, "Thank you."

The waitress grabs our menus and leaves, probably eager to escape the tension-filled table. If only I could go with her. No. I'm not going to run away. I'm going to face this and find a way to make them see reason.

"We're here to talk," Gretchen says. "Let's talk. Ask your questions."

Her gaze doesn't waver from Greer, who's been practising the silent treatment since we left the loft. I don't have to know her like a sister to literally feel the anger pouring off her in frosty waves.

While they have a little stare-down, I drum my fingers on the underside of my chair, feeling powerless. With two such strong personalities, how can I ever make them see how lucky we are to have found each other? We need to find an element of common ground, beyond our shared DNA and monster-hunting destiny, something to show my sisters that we aren't as different as we seem.

Looking around the table, though, I can't help but worry that maybe we are. One is a gruff, tough commando chick, who dresses all in black and drab and prefers to fight alone. Another is a pretty, preppy, popular girl, who wears the finest fashions and prefers to keep her social calendar intact.

And then there's me. What type am I exactly? The eco-conscious computer geek who'd rather be comfortable than fashionable and who is still learning how to stand up for herself. On the surface we don't have much to bond about.

"Listen," I begin, "I really think we should—"

"Tell me about the monsters," Greer says. "Where do they come from?"

"Another realm," Gretchen replies. "Sealed off from ours."

Greer asks, "Then how do they get here?"

"Well, there's this—"

"The seal is cracked," Gretchen explains.

Speaking of the seal… "You know, I read in that Medusa book that we're supposed to—"

"What do they do here?" Greer continues, as if I hadn't spoken.

Gretchen shrugs. "Feed on humans. Drain their life force and then either kill or control them."

"Kill or…" I stutter. Did Gretchen just say *control* humans? "You never said anything about—"

"But there are others, right?" Greer asks, interrupting me *again*. "Ones that don't… *feed* on humans."

I'm thrilled that they're talking, but do they really have to keep cutting me off? Letting me finish a sentence would be nice. Now is not the time for that battle, though, so I bite my tongue and listen.

"I don't know," Gretchen says with a sigh.

"Really?" I gape.

"Maybe that's one of the things that's changing."

She rubs her neck. "There might be beasties coming through that aren't pure evil."

That's news to me. From the start, Gretchen has been very clear. Monsters are bad, end of discussion. Something must have made her question the truth of that conviction.

"Why are we the only ones who see them?"

"It's our legacy as descendants of Medusa. We are the huntresses who keep the monsters in their realm and out of ours."

Greer leans forward across the table. "No, *you're* a huntress," she says, looking only at Gretchen. "Grace and I are obviously sweet, normal girls."

I want to take offence, but I'm thrilled that she's found something to connect us. "But we took down that serpent crea—" I glance at Gretchen. "That sea dracaena the other night. We *are* huntresses."

Greer glares at me.

Gretchen gives me a tight smile. "You're working on it."

"When we fought that sea whatever," Greer says, gesturing at me, "it disappeared. One moment it was there, the next it was gone. What happened?"

"I bit it," I explain, jumping at the chance to explain something. Glancing quickly around to make sure no one is watching, I focus on my teeth and slide my fangs down into view. I've been practising. "We have *fangs*," I whisper. "They inject a sweet venom that sends the monsters back to their realm."

Greer looks like I said we cut off their heads and fry them up for breakfast. Her lips move, and I know she's licking her tongue along her front teeth to make sure she didn't suddenly sprout fangs.

"They're instinctive," I explain. "They'll come out when you need them."

"The venom is a one-way ticket back to their realm," Gretchen says. "Some kind of supernatural express train."

"That," Greer says with a sneer, "is one of the most disgusting things I have ever heard."

"It's not that bad," I say, though who am I to say? I've only bitten one beastie. I'd been so full of fear and adrenaline, it could have tasted like burned garbage and I wouldn't have noticed.

Gretchen adds, "You learn to deal."

From the look on Greer's face, she doesn't want to learn to deal. She wants to wake up from this terrible nightmare and pretend none of this is true. Totally understandable. It's not as if this news is easy to digest.

"How many are there?" she asks.

"What? Monsters?" Gretchen shrugs again. "Who knows? Hundreds. Thousands. Hundreds of thousands. Your guess is as good as mine."

"Hundreds of thousands?" Greer echoes. "Here in the city?"

"Oh no," I hurry to say. Gretchen may be keen on scaring Greer away, but I'd like to keep her from bolting.

"Not all at once. They used to get out only one at a time."
I glance at Gretchen. "But that's changing too."

"Everything is changing," Gretchen says. "None of the old rules seem to apply any more."

"Why?" Greer asks.

"Because we're reunited," I say. "I moved to the city and now things are weird."

Gretchen may not have said it out loud, but I'm sure she thinks that too. And after what Ursula told me, I must be right.

"But some of them live here?" Greer asks. "In this… realm. Right?"

"No," Gretchen replies. "They can only be here temporarily."

"But what about Harold?"

"Who's Harold?" I ask.

"The janitor at my school," Greer explains. "He used to be normal, or at least I used to *see* him as normal. Today, when I looked, he was a giant spider. And I think he always has been, and I just couldn't see it before."

"That makes no sense," Gretchen says. "Haven't you always been able to see monsters?"

Greer's face shutters, like she's blocking something out. "I… Just once," she says, shaking her head. "When I was a child. But then not again until you two knocked on my door. Now it's like non-stop monstervision."

"That's weird," I say. I get the feeling she's not telling

us something. "Maybe some of them have been released. If they can get out permanently as a reward for bringing us in, then maybe they can get granted release for other things too."

Gretchen shakes her head. "I just can't believe I haven't seen any of those long-term visitors before this week."

"Maybe they stayed away from you," I suggest, giving her a sympathetic smile. "You do have a killer reputation for monster hunting."

The look on Gretchen's face makes it clear she thinks the idea is ridiculous. Hey, it could happen.

"Why doesn't anyone else see them?" Greer asks.

"We're special that way," Gretchen retorts.

"Monsters create a false appearance, an illusion when they're in this realm," I explain, throwing Gretchen a you're-not-helping look. "Ordinary humans see them as human."

Greer scowls. "And we're *not* human?"

Right then the waitress returns with a tray of food. As she puts down plates and bowls, we sit there in silence. When we've assured her that everything looks great, she leaves and I let out a huge breath. I'm as eager to hear this answer as Greer is, I think.

"We are human," Gretchen explains, stabbing a piece of broccoli tempura with her fork. "We're just not *ordinary*."

"We are descendants of Medusa and her human husband," I add, repeating the information from the book that led me to finding Greer. "They had three half-human daughters. They in turn had three daughters, and so on until now."

"So, there are more of us?" Greer asks.

I can sense her eagerness, can practically see her hope that maybe she doesn't have to feel so responsible for this if there are others to take up the fight. I'm almost sad to burst her bubble. Almost.

"No," I say. "There are only three in every generation." I look at Gretchen, then back at Greer. "There's only us."

I don't have an answer to the unspoken questions, though. Not yet. What about our mother? What about our aunts? Grandmothers and great-aunts? Cousins? Are they alive? If so, where are they and what are they doing?

We all fall silent in our own thoughts. Gretchen shoves a full forkload of tempura vegetables into her mouth. She doesn't seem happy or excited or even hopeful about our sisterly reunion. I can't help but be all three. This is what is supposed to happen.

As I stir my wasabi into a dish of soy sauce, I watch Greer take an elegant sip of soup. Her fingers hold the spoon perfectly, and she doesn't spill or drip a single drop. Her face doesn't betray any of the thoughts and questions I'm sure are racing through her mind.

Finally, she puts down her spoon next to the bowl, taking a moment to compose herself before asking, "What's the point?"

"I don't get the question," Gretchen replies, then stuffs a big bite of shrimp into her mouth.

"The monsters come out," Greer says. "One of… Somebody bites them. They go back. That's it?"

"That's pretty much it." Gretchen takes a gulp of her water.

"And this goes on for, like, what? Forever? For the rest of our – your life?"

Gretchen looks thoughtful as she puts down her glass and considers Greer's question. It's a valid question. I mean, Gretchen's been doing this for years, since we were twelve. Maybe she's never thought about where it's all going. Maybe she's always been willing to devote her entire life to stalking monsters in the night. Or, as it's been lately, in the day and dusk and dawn and any other time. Maybe she's never asked herself the question, *Then what?*

"I…" Gretchen stammers. She looks uncertain for the first time since we met. Then, as if realising her display of weakness, she clenches her jaw and flattens her palms on the table. "I don't know."

"I do," I say.

Both girls look at me.

"Well, I know part of it," I add. "It was in that Medusa book that told me about Greer, about the three sisters in every generation. It says that the monsters are sealed in the other realm until the Key Generation is born."

"The Key Generation?" Greer echoes.

Gretchen asks, "What's that?"

"It's a set of triplets." My heart races as I tell them everything I know. "Triplets that had to be separated at birth for their protection, and who are reunited when the time is right to break the seal."

"Break the seal?" Gretchen barks. "That's the only thing keeping the beasts from overrunning our realm. Why on earth would we break it?"

"The book didn't say," I answer quietly.

"Well, the book is wrong," she snaps, pushing back from the table and lurching to her feet.

I wish that were true, if only to stop the pain I see in her eyes. She's been dealt a lot of jarring and emotional blows in the past couple of weeks. It's no wonder she's having a bad reaction to the latest news.

"The book is wrong, the rules are wrong." She closes her eyes. "This whole situation is wrong. I'm out of here."

I stand too, needing to be on equal ground. "Gretchen, don't—"

"No." She grabs her jacket off the back of her chair. "I've had enough."

"You don't mean that," I say, desperate. She can't walk away.

"I do," she says, shrugging into her jacket. "Things were better before."

My stomach plummets. "Before?"

Her silver eyes look directly into mine as she says, "Before we met."

A thousand things run through my head, everything that's happened in the past few days. The fact that she kidnapped me that first night. That we're blood. That things are changing and she can't do it alone any more. That she agrees I need training, for my own protection.

I focus on the last one.

"What about my training?" I demand. I won't let her toss me aside. Or Greer, either. I've been missing something all my life, and now that I know what it is – my sisters, my destiny – I can't just let it slip away. "Greer needs training too."

"You don't need training," she says, flicking a sneering glace at Greer.

"But—"

"You need to keep your heads down." She shrugs into her leather jacket. "If you see a monster, look the other way."

This can't be happening. "But—"

"No," she says. "Don't. Don't look the other way. Don't react at all. As long as they don't know you see them, they won't know what you are."

What I am. Who I am. Being a huntress is my heritage, my destiny. I won't pretend that I don't know. I won't go back to being ordinary. I choose to embrace this life, this fate. I'm done being a cowering doormat.

I want to stand up and be powerful.

"You're not thinking this through," I say, trying to reason with her. "What about the bounty? And talking with Stheno? Or what if you get outnumbered because more monsters are getting out? What if they trap you or corner you in a—"

"I can take care of myself," she says with absolute finality. She doesn't look me in the eyes. "You do the same."

She reaches into her pocket, pulls out a few crumpled bills and throws them on the table. Then, without a glance at either me or Greer, she stomps out of the restaurant.

"Is she always so difficult?" Greer asks.

I sigh. "She's had a tough week."

"Tell me about it," Greer says with a laugh. "And that's not even taking into account the madness you two brought to my door."

I study her, the image of poised perfection. Perfect hair, perfect clothes, perfect make-up. I wonder if the rest of her life is this perfect, or if it's just the image.

"What are your parents like?" I ask. It's a question I can't ask Gretchen – I don't need to ask – but I want to know more about Greer too.

"Wonderful," she replies automatically. Almost like a robot. Then she blinks a few times and admits, "They're gone a lot. Doing very important jobs and supporting very worthy causes, of course."

"Of course," I agree. But I definitely get the subtext.

"They… I… " She breathes in and out purposefully. "I had no idea I was adopted."

My mouth pulls into a silent *Oh*. "No wonder you were so shocked to find us on your front step," I say. "I've always known, and it just never entered my mind that you might not."

"Yes, well." She straightens her spine and smiles. "What about your parents? Are they… nice?"

I can't help but beam. "Oh, they're great. They're very loving and supportive and I can't imagine better parents. And I have a brother named Thane."

"What kind of name is Thane?" she asks, and I can't tell if she's intrigued or appalled.

"The kind he came with," I say, kind of defensively. "He's great too."

"I'm sure."

This time I can tell she's mocking me. She has no idea. Maybe she's okay with parents who are off running businesses and saving the world, with no time left for her, but she shouldn't make assumptions about anyone else's parents.

We fall into a kind of awkward silence until, suddenly, she pushes back from the table and stands.

"You know what?" she says, pulling out her wallet and throwing a fifty dollar bill on the table. "Gretchen had the right idea."

"What do you mean?" I ask.

"I have a busy life," she says, slipping her bag on to her shoulder, "and a bright future. I have an alumnae tea to organise and class president duties and a very busy social calendar. Monsters don't fit into the plan."

"What about sisters?" I ask, my voice small, afraid I won't like the answer.

She looks down at me, her silver eyes cold and empty, and says, "Sisters don't fit either."

Then she turns on her very high heels and strides away. I watch, helpless, as she disappears out the front door. She can't mean that. She can't walk away, *they* can't walk away from this. I mean, we're *sisters*. That has to count for something. That has to count for *everything*.

I drop back into my seat, completely deflated. How could this all go so wrong so fast? How could my sisters – my *sisters*! – not see how wonderful it is that we've found each other after all these years? How can they not see how important it is for us to stick together in this crazy monster-hunting business, especially now that so much is changing? Our lives, and the lives of countless humans, depend on us.

"Your sisters leave?" the waitress asks, eyeing their empty seats.

"Yeah," I say with a sigh. "They're gone."

I shove my barely-touched avocado roll away. My appetite isn't about to return now. The waitress clears away our plates and I'm left feeling completely alone at a table for three. This isn't right.

I'm not sure how long I sit there, staring blankly at nothing in particular. Hours maybe. But all of a sudden, after processing the swirl of sadness, depression and helplessness, I come to a decision. I'm done watching things happen around me. I'm going to take action.

"I can't let them walk away."

I push to my feet, leaving my money on the table with Greer's and Gretchen's – that'll be one very happy waitress when she counts her tips – and head out on to the sidewalk with a sense of purpose. They may think they can go back to the way things always were, to pretend that we never met, but everything has changed. And I'm going to make them see that.

I don't know how, for sure, but I will not sit by and let my long-lost sisters vanish back into oblivion.

CHAPTER 23

Grace

By the time I get to my apartment building, I have the rudimentary basics of a plan. Tomorrow after school I will go to Gretchen's as usual, like I've been doing for a week. I will convince her that I still need to be trained, just in case I slip up or a monster recognises me. She feels responsible for my safety, so that shouldn't be impossible. Then, once I've got her back on board, I'll convince her we need to train Greer for the same reason. It's perfect.

In fact, I'm feeling so optimistic that I decide to be proactive about one more thing in my life. Sitting down on one of the white concrete benches in the courtyard, I pull out my phone and search for Milo's number – which I might have accidentally kinda saved when I overheard him giving it to Thane.

I pause to take a deep breath before punching the call button.

If I'm going to be brave in some areas of my life, I might as well be brave in all of them.

It rings twice before he answers. "Hello?"

I almost hang up.

"Um, hi, Milo." I bite my lip and then blurt, "It's Grace, Thane's sister."

"Oh, hey Grace," he says, like he's happy to hear from me. "What's up?"

My insides kind of melt. Even though I'm pretty sure I'm going to puke on the perfectly manicured grass, I say, "I wanted to ask you something."

"What's that?"

"Have you heard from Thane?" Okay, so it's going to take me a minute to build up the courage.

"Oh, uh, sure," Milo says, sounding uncomfortable. "He ran out to, um, get new laces. For his—"

"I know he's not there, Milo," I say to relieve his stress. "I was just wondering if you knew where he'd gone."

"No," he says, his voice back to normal. "No clue. Just asked me to promise to cover for him if it came up."

"You're a good friend."

"Thanks," he says, and I can picture his grin. "But I'm an epic failure at lying."

I laugh. "Me too."

Something we have in common. That makes me feel a little more at ease with Milo. And a little more ready to ask the real question I called to pose.

"Would you…" Oh no, I was wrong. *I can't do it. I can't, I can't, I—* "Do you want to go out sometime?"

I smack my hand over my mouth after the blurted

question, as if I can take it back. In the moments of silence afterwards, my hopes sink lower and lower.

Finally, he sighs.

I drop my head into my hand. Great, Grace. Just great. That's what you get for being bold, for taking the initiative and not sitting around waiting for things to happen. A giant slap in the face, that's what.

"I wanted to ask you out first."

I jerk upright. "What?"

"I was getting up the guts," he says. "But you beat me to it."

"Really?" I practically sob. Relief courses through every last inch of my bloodstream. "*Really* really?"

"Yes, really." He laughs, and I can't help but laugh too. "How about tomorrow?"

"Tomorrow is—" I remember my plan to talk to Gretchen. I don't want to put that off any longer than I have to. "I have an, um, appointment right after school," I say. "But maybe after that?"

"Perfect," he says. "How about I stop by your place after soccer practice?"

No, bad idea. Then Mom will wonder why Thane isn't with him, and we'll have to either lie or tell her what we know.

"How about we meet at the dim sum place?" I suggest, hoping there's no repeat of the minotaur sighting. Knowing that even if there is, I can handle it. "At six o'clock?"

"It's a date." I can hear the smile in his voice.

I'm sure Mom will forgive me missing another dinner for a date – a *date!* – with Milo. We say goodnight, and I head inside. I'm positively bouncing as I push through the apartment door.

"You missed dinner," Mom says.

She is clearing the dining table.

I drop my backpack by the door and then take the stack of dishes from her hands. "Oh, sorry, the study session ran late," I say, the now-familiar lie slipping easily off my tongue. "We ordered sushi."

"Next time let me know, please," she says. She's trying to sound like a cool mom who doesn't make her kid call home every two seconds, but I hear the undertone of concern. I'm not sure which would be worse: the truth of where I've been or the worst-case scenario of what she might imagine I've been doing. Hopefully she'll never find out.

"I promise." I can't stop grinning. It takes all my self-control not to tell her about my date with Milo. But I can't risk her asking about Thane.

As I help her do the dishes, mindlessly drying every piece she hands me, I think more about my plan to bring my sisters and me back together. I start reciting phrases in my head, trying them out so they're perfect when I use them on Gretchen tomorrow. This feels like the most important thing I've ever done, and I don't want to leave anything to chance.

And then I'll have my date with Milo.

"Everything okay?" she asks, handing me a wet glass.

For a heartbeat I want to say no. I want to tell her what's been going on, about my sisters and the monsters and how I'm a descendant of a mighty guardian. She's my mom and, no matter how clichéd it sounds, my best friend. All my life I've told her everything, from crushes to betrayals to worrying to failures. And she's always listened with a patient and non-judgemental ear. Even when I told her about my disastrous first kiss in the back of the bus on my freshman end-of-the-year field trip.

But I can't tell her this. I can't tell her *any* of this.

Just the part about finding my sisters could break her heart, to know that I've found some of my blood family. I know she'd be happy for me, but she and Dad try so hard to be more than enough. I love and care about her too much to do that to her.

"Yeah," I finally say. "Everything's fine."

It's better this way.

"Your father's working late again," she says, and I can hear the disappointment in her voice. He's been working so much at the new job that we barely see him. Of course, she barely sees me any more, either. And now Thane won't even be around to keep her from feeling lonely. I hope he comes home soon.

She asks, "Would you mind taking out the trash?"

Hanging my wet towel on the oven door, I say, "No problem."

I'm gone so much lately; the least I can do is help out with chores when I'm here. I head for the trash can but then turn back. Walking up behind Mom, I wrap my arms around her waist. "I love you."

She turns around in my arms, wrapping her own around my shoulders. "I love you too, Grace."

I pull away when I feel tears tingle in my eyes. Don't want her thinking I'm upset when I'm really not. Could a girl get any luckier? I have two parents and a brother who love me as much as humanly possible. I've been – whether they like it or not – reunited with my two long-lost sisters. And I'm a bit of a mythological superhero who keeps the world safe from monsters.

Even dragging a big bag of garbage to the huge bins behind our apartment building can't sink my mood or my determination to make everything work out okay with my sisters. And I have a date with Milo! If I weren't below a whole bank of bedroom windows, I'd shout that news into the night.

I'm so caught up in my mental cheering that I don't hear a sound in the alley. The smell radiating from the garbage overpowers any other odours in the air. It's not until I sense a shadow passing over me, blocking the glow from the street light above, that I know I'm not alone.

I spin around just as the enormous bear rears up,

its huge, meaty paws swiping down through the air towards my neck. I feel the scrape of claw against skin. A scream catches in my throat.

CHAPTER 24

Greer

Good riddance to would-be sisters, I think as I unbuckle the ankle straps on my new shoes. I had
a voicemail from Kelly Anne letting me know she charged
my account and that I can come by anytime to pick up my
espadrilles. These really are the most comfortable heels
ever. I skipped the bus home from the sushi bar, opting to
walk off my frustration instead. Between getting myself
to Gretchen's loft and back home, I must have walked
three miles in them, and my feet feel as fresh as ever.

I'm glad to be done with those freak girls. I don't want
sisters, I don't need sisters. And I definitely don't need to
hunt monsters for the rest of my life.

"As if I have time for that."

How ridiculously depressing to look forward to that
never-ending future. I really feel sorry for them.

Opening my closet, I slide the new strappy sandals
into the spot vacated by my Bay-sunk Jimmy Choos.

I smile wryly at the memory of my unexpected swim
in the Bay. If I'm being truly honest with myself –
and I try very hard to be – I have to admit it was a bit of

a thrill. Holding on to that serpent tail for dear life, I felt… invincible. Like I could take on any mythological creature that gets thrown my way.

Most of my life is barely a challenge. Having to actually fight for something felt, well, it made me feel like I'd actually accomplished something. I'd never felt that way before.

I've replayed the battle in my head a hundred times, and every time I change the course of events a little bit. Sometimes Grace is the one getting splashed into the Bay. Sometimes I'm the one who bites the creature in the neck. Every time we're victorious.

And every time I'm energised by our success.

This time, in the mental replay, the fight concludes with a group hug shared by me and my sisters.

"My sisters," I whisper.

I picture Gretchen, looking all gruff and tough in her leather and cargos. She's had a tough life, I can tell, and I don't even know anything about her. Maybe I misjudged her at first. When they first showed up here, I had no idea what kind of craziness she has to face on a daily basis. She's basically giving up a chance at a normal life to keep the unsuspecting populace safe from monsters they can't even see.

I can't help but admire that kind of sacrifice.

And then there's Grace. Cute, sweet, good-girl Grace. She's the girl-next-door type, the kind who gets to be friends with cute boys and is always a teacher's favourite. She might not be the most bold or confident or aggressive type, but she's just as willing as Gretchen to dive headlong into this world of monster hunting. I'm sure she's scared, but she doesn't show it. Much.

And they're my *sisters*. My identical flesh and blood. I've never had anyone but Mother and Dad, and, to be honest, they are barely around enough to feel like family. What would it be like to have Gretchen and Grace in my life? To feel like I truly belong, without having to be the best or the prettiest or the smartest girl in the room to win their approval? We share a genetic code and a mythological legacy. I belong just… because.

A tight feeling fills my chest, and my stomach sinks. As much as I try to keep emotion out of my life, I'm not completely immune. I know what this feeling means.

"Sugar," I mutter.

I thought I could just walk away, but my heart has other ideas. My heart knows that I belong side by side with my sisters. I have a duty, a responsibility I can't deny. Although I'd like to think my walking away from that table, following Gretchen out of the door and leaving Grace sitting alone, is the end of the story, I know my conscience won't let that happen.

I've always planned to become a successful professional, blaze a trail into government office and have the kind of life everyone dreams of. But this other thing, with my sisters and my legacy, it's bigger than a plan.

Clearly the pair of them could use a leader, someone to keep them from doing imprudent things, like showing up on someone's doorstep and blurting out that they're mythological monster hunters.

And my second sight, that power to just… know things, well I must have that for a reason. Maybe it has something to do with the Key Generation thing Grace mentioned. Maybe they need me and my power to make it work.

Helping them is the right thing to do. And I always do the right thing.

I repeat, "Sugar."

I hate grovelling.

The doorbell rings. I take a deep breath.

That'll be Kyle. Time to make up for bailing on him at the Wharf the other night. I'll figure out how to apologise to my sisters tomorrow. Just because I'm choosing to embrace my destiny doesn't mean I'm abandoning the rest of my life. The two will just have to coexist.

I bound down the stairs, thankful that it's Natasha's night off. My parents are at a cancer research fundraiser. The house is empty, and I want to greet Kyle with a welcome that shows him precisely how sorry I am about the other night. He'll definitely be getting more than a goodnight kiss this time.

As I reach the door, I pause to catch my breath and check myself in the foyer mirror. Perfect, if a little flushed. All that walking did wonders for my complexion. I'm practically glowing.

With a huge grin, I pull open the door, ready to throw myself at Kyle.

"Hey baby, I'm—"

My scream pierces the night.

The hulking, six-armed giant standing on my doorstep lumbers towards me and laughs. At least I think it's a laugh. "Hello, huntress."

I slam the door as hard as I can in its face and turn to race through the house. Self-preservation instinct takes over. My only thought is escape. If I can just make it down the back steps to the garage.

As I dash down the stairs three at a time, I hear the monster pounding across the kitchen floor above. It must have smashed down the door. I snatch my keys from the rack, fly to my car, yank open the door, stab the key into the ignition and punch the garage-door-opener button. My honey purrs to life, and I'm waiting for the door to clear my roof height when the monster bursts into the garage. It slams all six meaty paws on my hood, leaving three matching pairs of dents.

Screw the garage door.

I pound the clutch, shift into reverse and release the clutch as I floor the accelerator. I only hope there are no cars coming as I squeal out on to the street.

CHAPTER 25

Gretchen

"The book." Punch. "Is." Punch. "Wrong." Punch, punch, punch.

The training dummy shudders at my assault. It hasn't done anything to deserve my fury, but I have to let it go somewhere. Otherwise, next time I see Nick, I might punch him in the face for no particular reason. Not that that's such a horrible idea.

I swipe a hand over my head, slicking my bangs back with sweat. Too bad I can't wipe my thoughts away that easily.

I don't even know why I'm so upset. I'm happy with how things have worked out. I don't need anyone new in my life anyway, so it should be a relief that my sisters are out of the picture now. That I pushed them out of the picture. I'm just annoyed that everything got so mixed up in the meantime. That's all.

"Then why." Punch. "Am I." Punch, roundhouse, side kick. "So freakin' mad?" Uppercut, jab, swing punch, back kick, flying roundhouse.

I throw so much of myself and my anger into the flying

345

roundhouse that I knock the training dummy back two feet and my momentum carries me the rest of the way round, spinning me off-balance and sending me crashing to the floor. "Son of a centaur."

For a few seconds I allow myself the embarrassment of lying facedown on the floor. I've got to pull myself together. My focus is all over the place. If a beastie hit the streets right now, I'd probably end up in the hospital. An "*evil* beastie, I guess I should say, since apparently there are other kinds.

Pushing up to my hands and feet, I force myself to stand and walk to the door, where my water bottle is sitting on the floor.

Why am I so distracted? It's not like me to be so scatter-brained.

I spin the cap off and throw back a long gulp. Cool, crisp water pours into my stomach. As I wipe the extra drops from my lips, the answer clicks into place.

"They're my sisters," I say, knowing that means everything. "It's my duty to train them. It's my duty to protect them."

And, by walking away, by pushing them away, I let them down. I let myself down. I let the whole lineage of descendants of Medusa down.

"*Aaargh.*" I roll my head back and wince. I'm going to have to apologise.

I set the open water bottle back on the floor and take

off at a full run towards the dummy. I'm soaring through the air, a perfect flying side kick aimed right at the dummy's left temple, when the odour of mouldy cabbage overtakes the room. The scent isn't familiar, but I know the reek of monster when I smell it. Even if it's a new one.

And this one is close. Like, in-my-loft close.

My attention distracted, I miss the dummy and end up flying right past his shoulder. Thankfully, I twist myself in mid-air quickly enough to land on my feet, falling into a crouch and scanning the room for the beastie du jour.

Before I can even make a three sixty, a massive weight knocks me to my stomach, pressing me into the floor. I can barely breathe.

"This is the end, huntress," the monster says, slobbering against my ear. "Your sisters are no more. And you're next."

No! I struggle against the crushing weight, only managing to twist around to my back because the creature allows me to. I stare blankly into the eyes of the manticore. Grace and Greer can't be dead. They can't, not when we've just met. Not when I finally realised we need to stick together. Not when I haven't had the chance to apologise.

A wave of super strength washes over me, and I shove against the beast's stonelike lion chest with all my might. It moves enough for me to roll to the left, out from under its mass, and bounce to my feet. At twice my height and

347

quadruple my weight, the monster is too big for me to beat in hand-to-hand combat. The thing is so much stronger than me, my only chance is to reach the wall of weapons. I don't have to use them often, but this is exactly the worst-case-scenario I've trained for. And once that massive spiked tail starts swinging, I'm going to need something that can take out this monster from a distance.

I'm only a few feet from the collection of battleaxes when I feel fur-covered arms wrap around my legs, knocking me to the floor.

"You like the chase," the manticore says.

Keeping my legs secured, it climbs along my body, closing its massive paws over my wrists when I try to claw myself away. With all my limbs pinned spreadeagle, I can't move an inch. I buck my torso, trying to dislodge the manticore without success.

This is it, I think. *I'm going to die. Just like my sisters. And they will never know I wanted us to be together.*

I lay my head down on the rough carpet, strangely calm in the face of my demise. It could be worse, I suppose. I could have been forced to watch them die first.

I feel the creature's face loom closer. Then it stops.

At first I'm not sure why – I'm easy prey at this point – but then I hear it. Pounding. On my door.

And shouting.

"Gretchen!" Grace screams. "Let us in!"

Greer shouts, "We were both attacked! We don't know if we've been followed!"

They're alive!

"No!" I shout back. They can't be here. "Get away! Run!"

The beast slams my face against the floor. "Silence."

The pounding and shouting and rattling of the door handle continue. With the loft's ultra-high-tech security system, they'll never get inside. The best thing they can do – the only thing they can do – is save themselves.

I suck in as much breath as I can and then shout, at full volume, "RUN!"

The pounding stops. I release a relieved sigh. Good, they listened. They'll get away and they'll be safe. They'll live. I relax against the carpet, thinking that almost makes this okay.

Then, just as I'm accepting my fate and ready for the creature to finish this, it starts wailing and flailing around. Suddenly free, I jump to my feet, shocked to see Greer wrapped around the monster's body and Grace holding on for dear life to its tail.

Needing to slow the beast down, I turn and grab a broadsword from the wall. It takes me three running strides to reach the creature, and one thrust to send the battle sword deep into its chest. It barely flinches. After a second, a dark-orange liquid starts trickling out of the wound. That won't kill it or send it home, but it will sure as hell hurt. And hopefully give one of us a chance to get a bite in.

With its wild movements, I can't get close enough to finish the job.

"Be careful, Grace!" I shout. "The tip of the tail is deadly."

"Kinda figured that." She has both arms and legs clamped around the tail, which is swinging wildly back and forth.

Maybe if I move around to its back, I can get close enough to—

Grace and the tail come swinging in my direction. She loses her grip, flies through the air and tackles me to the ground.

"It's so strong," she gasps, pushing off me and to her feet.

As she pulls me up after her, I say, "Tell me about it."

"Hang on, Greer!" Grace shouts.

"We need to stop the tail," I say. "It's too dangerous."

Grace nods at the wall of weapons. "What about one of those?" she suggests. "Maybe we can pin it down."

"Great idea." I grab a pair of spears and hand her one. "I'll go around the other side. You move from this side. Whoever gets first stab…"

"Goes for it," she finishes. "Got it."

As I circle around, I see the manticore trying to snap at Greer with its rows of sharp teeth. When that doesn't work, it lifts its spiked tail, ready to strike.

"Grace!" I shout, because she's closer.

But she's already seen the movement and dives onto the tail, throwing the creature's aim off just enough to miss Greer. I close the distance to the tail and, as it rebounds to the ground, tossing Grace off to the side on the first bounce, I lift the spear above my head and slam it down as hard as I can into the scaly flesh.

My shoulder feels like it's on fire.

The beast yowls in pain. Though its tail still wriggles, the creature is pinned into place.

I race around to the front, holding my right shoulder with my left hand, searching for a spot to get close enough to get a bite in. But between the flailing claws and the snapping jaws, there's no opening that won't get me a seriously painful injury. Even if I could, I'm not much better than a monster chew toy with my shoulder out of joint.

"Greer, you have to bite it!" I shout.

"Me? I…" She looks at me, helpless. "I can't. I don't know how."

"You have to. Close your eyes and do it," I insist. "Instinct will take care of the rest."

Grace shouts up from the floor, "We believe in you!"

Greer's eyes widen in terror and then narrow in determination. *Come on.* Squeezing her lids shut, she opens her mouth and sinks her teeth into the creature's shoulder.

I didn't see her fangs descend. But when the monster disappears beneath them three beats later, sending Greer into a heap on top of Grace, I know she did it.

Gasping with exertion and adrenaline and recovered breath, I grab Greer with my good arm and roll her off Grace before collapsing onto the floor next to them.

For a long time we lie there, side by side and panting, trying to absorb what just happened. If they hadn't shown up, I'd be monster meal right now, some beastie's one-way ticket out of the abyss.

Grace was right. Things are changing and I can't do this alone any more. Without Ursula – I mean Euryale – around to help me figure things out, I need my sisters even more. And I need to tell them that. My near-death moment has made me realise that I'd better say what I have to say before I lose the opportunity.

"I was going to call you two," I say, swallowing my pride. "Tomorrow, I was going to call and apologise and say we should train together. We're sisters and it's my duty to make sure you're safe. Training you to protect yourselves is the best way to assure that."

"Really?" Grace squeals, pushing herself up to a sitting position. "I was going to come tell you the same thing," she says. "Tomorrow."

"Looks like the monsters moved up our timetable," I reply with a laugh.

We both turn to look at Greer, who hasn't responded.

She is lying there with her eyes closed and a completely disgusted look on her face, but otherwise looking like her normal icy self. Maybe she'll need some convincing after this. A manticore would horrify anyone who saw it on the street. Let alone having to fight it.

"All right," she finally says. "I'm in."

I release a relieved breath and sense that Grace does the same. Neither of us wants her to walk away.

"On one condition," Greer adds.

"What's that?" Grace asks.

"This monster fighting gig can*not*," she says, "interfere with my social schedule."

She hasn't moved, hasn't altered her expression. She's lying there in bare feet and what are probably designer clothes. She's just sent some hideous unknown monster back into the abyss. And she's worried about her *social schedule*?

I'm on the verge of telling her to stuff it when she cracks a smile.

Grace and I burst out laughing.

Thank goodness.

"I'm joking." Greer sits up. "Mostly. But I'm also kind of serious. I have a lot of responsibilities that don't involve," she makes a vague gesture that kind of encompasses the whole room, "any of this. I can't cast them aside."

My laughter dies.

She's right. This world might have been my whole

existence for the last four years, but Greer and Grace have been living real lives. They have people who care about them and others who depend on them. They're not alone, like me. It's not fair to ask them to give up all that for something they didn't choose.

"Fine," I say reasonably. "We'll work around all the other stuff whenever we can."

"Excellent." Greer pushes up to her feet. "Now, do you have any mouthwash around here? That monster tasted nasty."

I point her to the bathroom, and she disappears to wipe out the taste of beastie. I don't blame her – monsters taste like rotten garbage, and the sweet taste of our venom is never quite enough to counteract it. You learn to deal, but you never get used to it. Not really. Monster is not an acquirable taste.

"Were you really going to call us tomorrow?" Grace asks quietly.

"I was."

She's silent for a few seconds before asking, "Why?"

I'm ready to shrug off the question, as if it's nothing major. But when I look in her eyes, I can tell it's a very big deal.

"Because we belong together," I answer honestly. "Whatever kept us apart all these years, I think we belong together in the end. Things are changing, and although that scares me a little, it's obviously part of something bigger than all of us. We have a destiny to fulfil, and I don't want to fulfil it alone. I don't think I can."

Oh, she mouths.

Then, before I can react, she lurches forward and throws her arms around my neck in a tight hug.

"Ow, ow, ow, ow, ow!" I scream.

"What?" she gasps.

"My shoulder," I explain, my eyes clenched against the sharp pain. "It popped out of the socket when I skewered the beastie's tail."

"Oh, what can I do?"

I give her a quick lesson and then, before I can take a fortifying breath, she shoves everything back into place. I gasp at the shock, but can tell that she did a fine job.

"Okay?" she asks.

I nod.

"Can I hug you now?" When I nod again, she wraps her arms gingerly around my shoulders. "I'm so glad you realised we belong together."

"I can tell."

I shrug it off with sarcasm, but inside I feel a strange sensation of warmth. Compelled by some unknown reason, I lift my own arms and hug her back.

"I'm glad we got here in time," Grace says, squeezing tight. "If we hadn't…"

She lets her words trail off. She doesn't need to finish the sentence. I was there, I'd accepted my fate. And then they'd— "Hey," I say, pulling back as I remember the moment. "How did you guys get inside anyway? The loft's security is military grade."

"Oh." She beams. "I guess my autoporting kicks in when I really need it."

That solves the mystery of how the girls got inside, but not how the manticore snuck past the system. I'll have to do a full inspection. There must be a hole somewhere, and I need to keep other monsters from showing up unexpectedly.

"Am I missing a group hug?" Greer asks.

"Come on." Grace removes one arm and waves her close. "Gentle with Gretchen's shoulder though."

Greer kneels down next to us, and Grace and I each wrap an arm around her back while she does the same. I'll worry about securing the perimeter later. Right now, I'm enjoying the moment. For once.

"Triplets," Greer says, shaking her head.

"Who'd have thought?" I ask.

"Reunited," Grace adds. "I can't imagine a more perfect ending.

Strangely enough, neither can I.

CHAPTER 26

Gretchen

After I let the girls wash off their sweat and slime first, there is barely enough hot water left for me to grab a quick shower. But it's enough. And with clean clothes on, I feel completely refreshed and revived. Even my shoulder feels practically normal.

Rubbing my hair dry with the towel, I head out into the loft to find them. They're sitting at the dining table, hunched over one of the monster ring binders and giggling. With the balcony doors open wide, a fresh breeze blows in off the Bay. It feels like everything is fresh and new.

"Look at his feet," Grace exclaims, pointing to an anatomical drawing of a nulus.

Greer makes a face. "Gross."

"You should see the panotii," Grace says. "They have ears the size of their bodies."

"Have you memorised all the ring binders?" Greer asks.

"No." Grace blushes. "I've digitised most of them, though, and the funnier images stand out."

I'm impressed. That's a lot of work she got done in not a lot of time. I bet she has the entire library scanned and catalogued in less than a month.

I keep back, not wanting to disturb their moment. It feels weird to have people, other than Ursula, making themselves at home in the loft. Before I brought Grace back here, no one else had ever been in the loft.

Still, as weird as it feels, it also feels completely right. Meant to be. Like the pieces of a puzzle I didn't even know I had to solve have finally fallen into place.

Now, if only Ursula were safely back home—

Greer stands, knocking her chair back behind her.

I step into the room.

"What's wrong?" Grace asks, a note of panic in her voice.

"I..." Greer holds her hands out as if to steady herself. "I don't know. It's just, all of a sudden, I got this really awful feeling."

Grace looks at me, her face creased with concern.

"What kind of feeling?" I ask.

Greer turns to face me, drained of colour. "Like something bad is about to happen."

As if on command, my phone rings.

I dash into the kitchen, snatching my phone off the charger. I can't help the tiny spark of hope that it's my mentor on the other end of the line.

"Hello," I gasp into the receiver. "Ursula, is that—?"

"Get out!" a male voice shouts.

"What?"

"Get out of the loft," he screams. "Get out now!"

Something about the absolute terror in his voice stabs me right in the chest. Without stopping to think, I move, grabbing each of my sisters by the arm, and shout, "Run!"

Dragging them behind me, I race for the open door. At a dead run, we fly out onto the balcony. I launch my sisters over the railing and then follow them down into the Bay below.

Before we hit the water, the air above us explodes in a burst of heat and light, slamming us hard against the ice-cold waves. I lose track of my sisters as I'm propelled into the inky depths, short of breath and trying to orient myself to find my way back to the surface. Following my air bubbles, I break through into the night, gasping and choking.

I scan the area, relieved to see Grace and Greer treading water nearby. They seem whole and unhurt. They both have their eyes glued to the spot above me, to the loft. I can see flickering yellow-and-orange flames reflected in their glassy eyes. I think Grace might be crying.

Afraid of what I'll see, I force myself to turn and look up.

I suck in a gasp.

The entire upper level is blown out, and the building is engulfed in flames. Smoke billows out of my home, glowing in the light of the fire inside. My face burns with the heat of the raging inferno. My mind is reeling, and the only coherent thought I can grasp is how very close we came to getting blown up with the loft.

"This is bad," Greer says.

"Somebody tried to kill us," Grace says, unnecessarily.

I look at her. "You think?"

She ignores my sarcasm, shaking her head. "All those books," she says. "Thank goodness I got most of the ring binders done, but all those resources…"

I can't think about that right now. I can't think about the library or the weapons collection or the handful of mementos I've gathered in my lifetime. None of that matters more than the safety of Grace and Greer. We are lucky to be alive tonight.

That was two close calls in a row. First the synchronised monster attack, and then this. If it hadn't been for that perfectly timed phone call, then I wouldn't be here having these thoughts. And neither would my sisters.

Somebody clearly wants us dead.

And somebody else clearly wants us to live.

If I have to hunt them to the ends of the earth and beyond, I'm going to find out who.

ABOUT THE AUTHOR

Photograph by Amy K. Smith

Tera Lynn Childs is the award-winning author of many books for teens, including the mermaid romances *Forgive My Fins* and *Fins are Forever*, published by Templar. She spends her time writing and blogging wherever she can find a comfy chair and a steady stream of caffeinated beverages.

Although Tera always dreamed of discovering a secret twin (or triplet), she's sad to report she's still an only child.

For more about Tera and her books, visit www.teralynnchilds.com

OUT NOW...

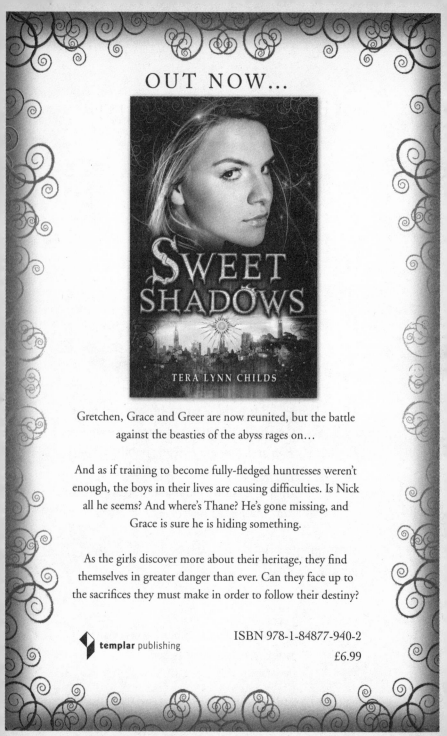

SWEET SHADOWS

TERA LYNN CHILDS

Gretchen, Grace and Greer are now reunited, but the battle against the beasties of the abyss rages on...

And as if training to become fully-fledged huntresses weren't enough, the boys in their lives are causing difficulties. Is Nick all he seems? And where's Thane? He's gone missing, and Grace is sure he is hiding something.

As the girls discover more about their heritage, they find themselves in greater danger than ever. Can they face up to the sacrifices they must make in order to follow their destiny?

templar publishing

ISBN 978-1-84877-940-2

£6.99